W9-BZE-690

Séances Are
for Suckers

Séances Are
for Suckers

Tamara
Berry

JOHNSTON PUBLIC LIBRARY
6700 MERLE HAY RD
JOHNSTON IA 50131-1269

KENSINGTON BOOKS
http://www.kensingtonbooks.com

WITHDRAWN

KENSINGTON BOOKS are published by

Kensington Publishing Corp.
119 West 40th Street
New York, NY 10018

Copyright © 2018 by Tamara Berry

All rights reserved. No part of this book may be reproduced in any form or by any means without the prior written consent of the Publisher, excepting brief quotes used in reviews.

All Kensington titles, imprints, and distributed lines are available at special quantity discounts for bulk purchases for sales promotion, premiums, fund-raising, educational, or institutional use.

Special book excerpts or customized printings can also be created to fit specific needs. For details, write or phone the office of the Kensington Special Sales Manager: Attn. Special Sales Department. Kensington Publishing Corp, 119 West 40th Street, New York, NY 10018. Phone: 1-800-221-2647.

Kensington and the K logo Reg. U.S. Pat. & TM Off.

Library of Congress Card Catalogue Number: 2018944166

ISBN-13: 978-1-4967-1962-1
ISBN-10: 1-4967-1962-X
First Kensington Hardcover Edition: November 2018

eISBN-13: 978-1-4967-1965-2
eISBN-10: 1-4967-1965-4
First Kensington Electronic Edition: November 2018

10 9 8 7 6 5 4 3 2 1

Printed in the United States of America

Séances Are
for Suckers

Chapter 1

"Hand me the maiden's sacrifice."

The woman standing beside me frowns through the haze of burned sage, the air a perfumed whirl that cloaks the senses and confuses the eye. The whole room is dark save for the flickering candles from the mantelpiece, which cast fluid shadows on the blood-splattered walls. It feels as if we're all standing at the gates of hell.

"Maiden's sacrifice?" she echoes.

"Yes, please. And with all due expedience. Her spirit is retreating."

I extend my hand, my bracelets filling the air with the clack of protective obsidian, and wait. Then I wait a little more, because no one is putting anything in it.

"The sacrifice, if you please," I demand again. "She's aware of our intentions. I don't know how much time we have."

"She means the wine," a voice hisses from the depths of the darkness. I don't turn my head for fear of losing concentration, but there's no need to identify the owner of the voice. I felt the young man's aura enter the room about five minutes ago. He's only a half-believer, which is why I'm having such a hard time holding on to Mary as it is. She senses his disdain and is recoiling from it much more strongly than I'd anticipated.

"Do you think she wants merlot, or is cabernet okay?"

I bite back a sigh. "You'll find that it's actually a 1945 Beaujolais—the year of Mary's death. It's by the door."

The three people in the room release an exhalation of understanding, which continues until one of them finally places the bottle in my hand. The cork has been pre-loosened, so all it takes to open it is a tug and a loud pop that's swallowed by the choking silence settling over the room.

The silence grows as everyone collectively stops breathing to see what happens next. It would have been nice to spend a few more minutes with Mary in hopes of communicating with her directly, but I don't choose the time.

The time chooses me.

A preternatural howl fills the air, starting at the ceiling and working its way downward. The smoke and candlelight move with it, flickering out and filling our lungs as the entire room is plunged into blackness and a bone-deep cold. The wine bottle flies from my fingers before I have a chance to recite a prayer of goodwill. It crashes to the ground with a thump and the muted shatter of glass on carpet.

"What's happened?"

"Is she still here?"

"That's my foot—ouch! You're stepping on my foot."

The lights come on so suddenly that we're plunged into painful, blinking awareness of our surroundings. My vision, accustomed to the playfulness of spirits and their quick changes of light, clears right away, so I wait patiently for the other three to catch up. Mrs. Levitt is the first to cross the line. The prematurely white-haired matron emits a scream that's half horror, half delight.

"She was here! She was actually here!"

Since the furniture that's been thrown around the room and the blood-spattered walls have already proven that beyond a reasonable doubt, I wait for one of the other two—Mrs. Levitt's next-door-neighbor, a pretty young woman by the name of Becky, or her son, the latecomer to our little session—to elaborate.

"Is that . . ." The son, whose flat, black hair matches the dullness of his aura, takes a step forward, careful not to land where the wine has left an imprint on the white carpet. "It can't be. It's impossible."

"Nothing is impossible," I say, but I doubt he hears me. I've been present at enough cleansings to know that I've suddenly become the least important person in the room. Never mind that I was the one to break through to Mary, to see beyond the mischief of her spirit to discover the troubled and restless soul underneath. Of even less importance is the fact that I'm the only person she treated with a modicum of respect—enough respect to actually listen when I urged her to move out of this house and into the next realm. As is always the case, only the bloody, gory, macabre details matter.

People love the bloody, the gory, the macabre.

"I can see the outline of her body!" Becky gasps and reaches for Mrs. Levitt's son. Their auras mingle with a spark of electricity. I sense a match in the future, despite the inauspicious conditions of their meeting. "Her feet are right here, and her arms are spread out on either side, and her head . . ."

Her voice grows thick as it trails away, not stopping until Mrs. Levitt's son offers a willing shoulder for her sob.

"Her head, as you've noticed, is twisted off to one side. I believe we finally have the answers we've been seeking." I reach for a knitted afghan draped over the back of a couch and lay it gently over the outline of the figure, formed from the spilled wine. The dark red liquid has seeped into the carpet around what appears to be the shape of the fallen woman's body. I don't have to look up to the balcony to set the rest of the scene.

My audience's imaginations are more than capable of filling in the details of her final plunge.

The chill in the room is less apparent now that Mary has gone, but my body has grown tired of the exertions put on it over the past forty-eight hours. I wrap my arms around myself for warmth. Mrs. Levitt, the only person in the room not preoccupied with comforting embraces and sobbing shoulders, sees me and offers a seat on the aforementioned couch.

"No." I shake my head. "I don't want to linger. My prolonged presence can sometimes act as a conduit for the spirit to find its way back."

Mrs. Levitt's mouth opens and closes again. "Really? That can happen?"

"It's not common, but it's not unheard of. Now that Mary's claim on the house has been cut off, I'm the only remaining tie she has to this realm. The negative energy in your home should clear in the next few weeks, but enough of it lingers to act as a lure. It's best for me to get as far from here as possible to avoid a recurrence."

And to immerse myself in as many positive energies as I can find, but I don't say that part out loud. For some reason, my clients like to imagine that I go from dark possession to dark possession, never resting my earthly feet anywhere there might be sunshine or light. But after a cleansing like this one, sunshine and light are essential.

This time of year, I'm thinking Mexico. *Definitely Mexico.*

"Of course." Mrs. Levitt's son is the one to act this time, and he nods as if he hasn't spent the past forty-eight hours doing everything in his power to prevent me from finishing the job. He even seems to forget the part where he threatened to call in the police. "You'll want to get on your way. I'll see you out."

"I need to gather my things first," I say.

His eyes narrow in suspicion. "What sort of things?"

"My overnight bag, my toothbrush, the talismans I placed in your mother's energy vortexes . . ."

He blinks at me. The average human being's ability to understand the nuances of my profession is slim, to say the least.

"It shouldn't take me more than ten minutes," I say as calmly as I can. In addition to flagging energy, my patience has a way of wearing off rather quickly after an event like this one. "No, no—it'll be faster if I do it on my own. And this will give you a chance to come up with the other half of the payment."

"The other half?" His expected outrage comes out in full, though I suspect he's attempting to hold some of it at bay for Becky's sake. "But we already paid you two thousand dollars!"

"Yes, and I understand that kind of money isn't easy to come up with on such short notice. But I wasn't kidding about that being a 1945 Beaujolais—the wine alone means I'll barely be breaking even on this exorcism."

"You couldn't have used a bottle of the table wine we have in the kitchen?"

I smile sadly at him. Some people will never appreciate the finesse that goes into what I do. "Not unless your ghost happened to be the murdered remnants of a 2016 vintage. Sorry. You should be grateful your haunting was restricted to the twentieth century. You wouldn't believe the going rate for medieval ghosts. It's almost impossible to find anything corked in the middle ages."

On that parting shot, I leave him to figure out the details with his mother. I don't think they'll give me any trouble regarding my fees, but I can always threaten to park myself in their living room until they manage to come up with the cash. Now that they know keeping me around means Mary might make a return appearance, I get the feeling they'll do anything they can to see the last of me.

It takes the full ten minutes to gather my supplies, which have been carefully placed throughout the house for maximum efficacy. The Levitt home dates to the early nineteen-twenties, which means there are dozens of hidden nooks and crannies where evil spirits can dwell. I concentrated most of my efforts in the attic, so that's where I head now. Hoping they're too busy arguing over my payment to notice the telltale creak of the attic stairs being lowered, I slip up into the wooden rafters to grab the most important tools of the trade—a bottle of super-hydrophobic spray and a portable air conditioner I placed near the home's HVAC vents.

The spray, one of my favorite tricks, is a prime example of the latest nuances of nanotechnology and its domestic applications. Some day in the near future, people will coat their homes in the stuff. It acts as a barrier for moisture of all kinds. Neither water nor bleach nor, as my activities downstairs have proven, red wine are able to pass through it to the fabric below. I used the spray to paint the shape of the dead woman on the carpet late last night, when Mrs. Levitt was huddled in bed, ignoring the thumps of her haunting.

The thumps, by the way, were a family of rats in the attic. I relocated them to the field out behind the house.

The portable air conditioner is just as easily explained. Cold drafts have long been associated with ghosts, and I needed a quick and easy way to snuff the candles at the moment of crisis. A perfectly timed gust of air-conditioning will do the trick— and because my system is set to last only a few minutes, no one thinks to question the ventilation system afterward.

It sounds bad, I know. And it *looks* even worse, especially once you figure in the work this family's going to have to do to set their house to rights after I broke all that furniture and smeared chicken guts on the wall. But the reality is that I haven't done anything Mrs. Levitt didn't ask for. When I got the phone call last week, she was tearful, frantic, desperate for someone to rid her home of the phantasmagoric plague that had cursed it ever since she found it listed on an online ghost registry.

You see, the real crooks in this world aren't the people like me, who eliminate ghosts when people have nowhere else to turn—it's those who invent them in the first place. The owners and operators of www.HowHauntedIsMyHouse.com are the ones who truly deserve our censure.

And to be fair, I did exactly what I promised. I got rid of the cause of trouble (those disgusting rats in the attic), and even more to the point, I purged Mrs. Levitt of the *belief* of said trouble. There's an important lesson in there. When I first became a ghost hunter, called to the profession nobly and with the most earnest of intentions, I didn't pay as much attention to the theatrical side of things, and my customers were almost always dissatisfied.

What do you mean, it's only termites?

Don't be absurd—there are no geomagnetic fields under my house.

My son would never switch the pictures on the wall in the middle of the night just to mess with me.

That lack of appreciation for my hard work hurt, to be honest. People don't want termites and obnoxious sons. They want dead bodies, and they'll go to alarming lengths to get them. Better a fake ghost today than one of them taking up murder as a hobby tomorrow—that's my motto.

As if to prove my point, the three members of my audience stand huddled around the body's outline when I return to the living room. They gasp and drop the blanket as if caught peeking up a lady's skirt. I smile to show them I understand the fallibility of mere mortal beings such as themselves.

"I left the protective amulet above your headboard," I tell Mrs. Levitt. "I don't think you'll need it any longer, but it's always nice to have that extra layer of insurance in place. Especially for a single woman living alone."

"Oh, thank you! Yes. How lovely." She rushes forward and presses a piece of paper into my hand. *A check.* "Jimmy is furious with me, but I added a little something extra to your fee. I can't tell you how grateful I am to have helped Mary's spirit find its eternal rest."

I do my best not to show my disappointment. Cashing checks is always a tricky business in my line of work. Naming my company Eleanor's Cleansing Service proved somewhat beneficial, since it sounds as if I carry rolls of paper towels instead of rolls of ectoplasm in the back of my hearse, but I never like having the watchful eye of Uncle Sam coming too close.

Uncle Sam is a judgmental old bastard.

"Thank you, Mrs. Levitt. I'm the one who should be grateful to you." I give her hand—and the check—a squeeze. "Putting restless spirits at ease is fatiguing but so rewarding. Not everyone has an opportunity to help people on both sides of the ether. I wouldn't change professions for this world. Or, you know, the next one."

And with that, I hoist the vintage medical bag containing all my tricks of the trade over my shoulder. To show you what a good person I am, I pause before making my escape, leaning forward as if to brush a light kiss on Becky's cheek.

"You two will be very happy together," I murmur. "You'll live a long, fruitful life free of spirits—restless or otherwise. I see three children. All girls."

Her blush and gasp of delight is all I need to know that I've done everything I can here. Pulling my gloves on tightly and making for the door, I notch one more happy customer on my figurative belt.

Now. Who said something about Mexico?

Chapter 2

"I don't want your dirty margarita."

As if to prove how much he means it, my brother pushes his beverage across the table, sloshing tequila and lime all over the salsa verde. The frown he's been wearing ever since he walked through the door disappears as he smiles up at the waiter, a large, mustachioed man who happens to be his type. "I'll have a glass of water, thanks. And if she orders me anything else, you can go ahead and cancel it in advance."

"Good. That means there's more for me." I also smile up at the waiter. I've never been fond of facial hair, since there's something so scruffy about it, but largeness is a trait that appeals to me on a much baser level. "You'll have to forgive my brother. He's on a diet."

My brother, William, an elementary school gym teacher who works off about a billion calories a day, puts his frown back on. "I am not. I'm opposed to beverages bought with immoral money, that's all."

"My money is *not* immoral."

"Oh, really? Why don't you tell"—he breaks off to read our

waiter's nametag—"Kevin here what it is you do for a living, and we'll let him be the judge. Go on. I'm sure he's dying to hear all about it."

To his credit, Kevin does appear to be interested in my story, but I imagine that's mostly because he assumes I earn my keep on a pole.

"I'll drink the second margarita for him," I say primly. As soon as we watch Kevin's large, retreating form disappear around the corner, I hiss, "Thanks for that, Liam. Now he's going to tell the entire kitchen staff about the exotic dancer at table twelve."

Liam snorts. "No one here thinks you're an exotic dancer, Ellie. I promise you that much."

If my brother's words seem harsh, I should probably note that I haven't yet changed out of the costume I wear when ghost hunting. In the ordinary way of things, I like to think I'm attractive enough. Though a little on the pale side, I have extremely dark hair and eyebrows, which I've been told have a striking effect on men when they first meet me. If *some* people say that's only because I look like an angsty high school student who's finally reached the legal age of consent, I would counter by saying that he's jealous his own youthful good looks don't lend themselves to impressing other men at the gym.

To make myself appear older and wiser than I really am, I've found it necessary to adopt the vocabulary of a Victorian schoolmarm, a task helped along by the numerous gothic novels I devoured in my teens. I also have to build up my appearance in layers. *Ethereal* layers, to be precise, the kind that float as I move through graveyards and down haunted hallways. My flapper-style shift dress is tied at the waist with a trailing wisp of gauze, and another scarf wrapped around my neck wards off the chills from all those extra air conditioners. My hair, which is so long it reaches almost to my waist, is pulled back in a series of coils that take a full hour to pin up in the morning—complemented, of course, by yet another scarf woven into the braid. Smoky eyes, deep red lips and fingernails, and a pair of T-strap heels I found at a vintage shop complete the overall aesthetics of my trade.

"Well, he thinks I'm an exotic *something*," I counter and apply myself to the first of my two margaritas. It's sour and strong, two of my favorite qualities in a drink. "I take this to mean you won't be coming with me on my all-expenses-paid trip to the Yucatán?"

"What? You're going to Mexico?"

"*Sí.*" I wave my hand at the walls around us, my obsidian bracelets now incongruous to the setting. "What did you think all this was for? I bought us both tickets. We leave tomorrow evening."

"How dare you?" Liam slumps in his chair. "You know how much I love the beaches this time of year."

"And it's nonrefundable, so if you don't go, I'm going to have to ask someone else . . ." I look off in the direction Kevin wandered, but Liam's too clever to fall for it. He knows I never sleep with strange men. I like them to be perfectly normal as compensation for my own oddities.

"You know I can't leave work on such short notice. I'm still trying to get the kids to understand the nuances of pickleball."

"Quit," I say around a mouthful of salsa.

"Ha-ha. Very funny. I'll never be able to quit. I owe my soul to the student loan company."

I keep crunching my way through the bowl of chips. For some reason, I'm always ravenous after I've cleansed a house of its spirits. Liam thinks it's psychosomatic on the basis that a *real* medium would be weak with hunger and fatigue afterward. I think he's only partially wrong—fake mediums have to work hard to get results, too. Catching those rats wasn't easy.

"Stop it, Ellie."

"What? I'm hungry."

"I mean it—you know how I feel about this."

"About tortilla chips? They aren't *that* bad for you. They're technically a vegetable."

"You always do this, you know that?" He pounds the table for effect, but all it does is make me spill more of my margarita. "If you had any self-respect, you'd quit your job instead of encouraging me to quit mine. It isn't right, what you do to those people. They *trust* you."

"Okay, fine." I sit back in the booth and cross my arms. This isn't the first time we've had this conversation, and I doubt it will be the last. "Since it bothers you so much, I'll pack it all up and turn to something more respectable. Of course, it'll take me a few months to find a new job, especially given my lack of professional references, and even then, I doubt I'll be able to find one that pays me as much. But that won't be a problem, will it?"

Liam's face slumps in an unhappy frown, and I'm hit with a sudden pang of conscience. I *do* have one, all evidence to the contrary, and when it makes its rare appearance, it tends to hit hard.

With a profession like mine, however, there's not much else I can do. I can't have money *and* morality. There isn't room in my life for both.

"I should be able to cover a few more months at the sanctuary, but we'll need to come up with an alternate arrangement by the year's end. I hear they might have a few openings at the state hospital. They've been working really hard to improve services lately. Only half the patients are abused now."

"Stop."

"Or we could care for her ourselves. Remember how well that worked before? She only almost died those three times."

"Ellie. Stop."

I don't. I *should*, I know, because by this point, I'm not convincing him so much as I am convincing myself . . . and I'm a tough woman to sway. I have to be bludgeoned over the head sometimes.

"But it'll be fine, because at least you won't feel guilty any-more—and that's the most important thing, right? Making sure you're comfortable with the life I'm forced to lead?"

It's too much for him to take. I knew it when I got started on my tirade, and I know it now as I watch him spring out of the booth and reach for his coat. He shoves his arms through the sleeves before extracting a few bills from his wallet and throwing them on the table.

I immediately move to return them to him, but he stops me with a sigh. "Let me have this much dignity, okay? I can at least pay for your celebratory dinner."

"I'm *not* celebrating. There's no need to make me out to be worse than I am."

"No? Expensive drinks, whirlwind trips to Mexico, laughing in the face of other people's misery . . . What part of that isn't a celebration, again?"

I shouldn't fall for it. It's always wrong to rise to my brother's provocation, even worse to say her name out loud. But despite my costume and my profession, I'm still just a weak, fallible human being. I don't have the answer to this world or the next.

"The part where I have to leave Winnie in that stinking, ster-ile place," I say. I think I might be yelling, but I'm not sure. "The part where we get to go on living while she slowly wastes away."

"Hello, Eleanor. So pleased you're back."

"Ellie! You haven't been here in ages. I swear, you look younger every time I see you. I don't know how you do it."

"No boyfriend in tow? One of these days, I expect to see you waltzing through those doors with a husband on your arm. You're too pretty to stay alone for long."

"She's out on the observation deck, love."

This last one is said by my favorite of all the nurses at the Happy Acres Sanctuary. She's an efficient, bustling woman in her fifties named Peggy. These places tend to have a fairly high turnover—it's depressing, taking care of people who either cannot or will not acknowledge your presence—but Peggy's been here for the entire four years that Winnie has. "It's a bit chilly this morning, but she seems to prefer the sunshine, so I wheeled her out first chance I got. You can take her an extra blanket, if you want. Grab one for yourself while you're at it. That way you two can settle in and have a comfortable visit."

"I'll do that, thanks," I say, and stop at the linen cabinet on my way to the wide veranda set out behind the facility.

It's a nice veranda and even nicer facility, which says a lot from someone who dislikes institutionalized atmospheres as much as I do. All of them—from schools to the DMV—set my pulse racing and force me into a cold sweat, which is why I have only a high school diploma and drive without a license. When Liam told me he'd chosen teaching as his one true calling, I spent the entire first year he was at college believing it to be some kind of elaborate hoax.

But Happy Acres isn't so bad, despite the banality of its name. It *is* situated on a nice expanse of acreage in upstate New York, though whether or not anyone is truly happy here is a subject that's open for debate. I doubt it's seen many joyful moments. In its early years, it served as a home for rich consumptives, which means the views are nice and the rooms spacious, but you can't change the fact that hundreds of people shuffled off their mortal coil within its walls.

It gives me the creeps, to be honest. And yes, as a ghost hunter, I'm aware of the irony.

"Hey, Winnie," I say as I step through the French doors to the white marble terrazzo. I keep the blankets pressed against my chest for comfort. As is usually the case, my sister is the only resident out getting some air this early in the day. Her catatonic state means she's not likely to wander off, so she gets some pretty nice perks out of the deal. "Peggy wanted me to bring you some blankets, but the sun is so bright here, I doubt you need them."

I take her soft hand in mine to make sure I'm right. Her fingers feel warm to the touch, and I relax. I wish I could say I relax only because I don't have to worry about her being too cold, but the reality is that I need that touch, those ninety-eight-point-six degrees, to reassure myself she's still alive.

Well, mostly alive. I often wonder if there's anyone really living behind those blank, beautiful eyes of hers.

"You always were the good-looking one of the bunch," I grumble as I pull one of the Adirondack chairs closer to hers and settle myself in it. "Liam's the smart one, you're the pretty one, and I'm the one no one quite trusts after dark. I'd hate you if I didn't think I got the best deal out of it. You have no idea what a relief it is not to have to live up to anyone's expectations."

When we were younger, I wasn't quite so blasé about my position as the last triplet—in birth order and in terms of importance—but twenty-eight years have settled us into our roles fairly well. William, the responsible older brother. Winifred, the peace-loving middle sister. And me, Eleanor, the baby of sorts, usually up to some kind of trouble.

"Liam is sorry he couldn't make it," I lie. Since the outburst at the restaurant last night, my conscience has once again resumed its natural, static state, so I don't feel too bad about the falsehood. "He sends his love, but he's been really busy at school lately. He's also mad at me, so if you need someone to blame for his absence, I volunteer for the role. I said some pretty mean things to him, poor guy. I sometimes forget how much harder this is for him."

I sigh and settle more comfortably in my chair. The sun really *is* nice out here. In the summer, it's unbearable, beating on these white tiles and baking the terra-cotta walls, but in the late fall air, it's refreshing.

"I wish I could have your patience with him. You know how much he hates that he can't do anything to fix you. Part of him still thinks you could just snap out of it, if only you'd apply yourself."

I release a soft snort of laughter at that. I'm no expert on traumatic brain injuries, but I've learned enough over the years to realize that Winnie's unresponsive wakefulness isn't a personal choice. She's been stuck in a place between life and death for over a decade, and no amount of medical or spiritual intervention can reach her.

Believe me—I've *tried.* A hack of a psychic medium I might be, but at least I came by my expertise honestly.

"But then, that's the burden of being the smart one, I suppose," I add with a sigh. "He can't help himself. Give me a wilting intellect and bitter sense of self any day."

"The bitter sense of self I might be able to accept, but I hope the wilting intellect part isn't true." A voice, deep and male, arises from behind me. "Please forgive the intrusion, but you *are* Eleanor Wilde, are you not?"

Although I'm startled by the interruption, I don't turn to glance at who's accosting me. There's no need. The way my name trips easily over the man's tongue, his clipped British accent rattling off the syllables with no fuss, gives me a good idea who he is.

The answer? Yet another specialist, come all the way across the pond for a chance at greatness.

It's no real surprise. Winnie's case is unique enough that she's visited every few months by a medical researcher hoping to make a name for himself. I used to let them, assuming any progress was good progress, but not so much anymore. After the first few failed attempts, I couldn't. Optimism isn't a renewable resource—at least, it's not for me. I ran out of the stuff years ago.

"That sounded suspiciously like a compliment," I say and twist to peer at him.

I'm not sure what to make of what I see. If the man is indeed a doctor, he's unlike any I've seen before. He bears the height and wide shoulders of a man who spends more time hefting heavy objects than staring through a microscope, but those features are offset by a perfectly sculpted swoop of brown hair and an air of languid grace. He also carries deep lines of dissipation on either side of his mouth, which means he either spends a large amount of time laughing or frowning. Based on his dark suit, which is as somber as my ghost-hunting attire, I'm guessing it's the latter.

Not that it's an *unattractive* face. Harsh gray eyes and a forceful chin aren't traits everyone can pull off, but this man seems to make it work to his advantage.

"That's because it was a compliment." He steps forward but doesn't make a motion to sit. I know, without quite understanding why, that he'll wait until he's invited. "I'm buttering you up because I want something from you."

Of course he does. He wants access to medical records, a few pints of blood, maybe a CT scan or two. I should start charging for them. I could make a fortune.

"Then by all means, don't let me stop you." I motion at the chair on the other side of me. "And sit down. You're making Winnie nervous hovering around like that."

"How can you tell she's nervous?" He folds himself into the chair. It can't be easy for such a tall, loose-limbed man to lower himself into a low-seated Adirondack, but he manages to accomplish it with grace. "She looks fine to me."

For some reason, I find the easy confidence with which he addresses me and my catatonic sister unnerving. Most people—

most doctors, even—tiptoe and speak in hushed, reverent tones when confronted with the devastation of our tragedy.

"I can sense it," I lie. I place a tentative hand to my temple and feign solemnity. "Due to her condition halfway between this world and the next, her emotions come through the ether perfectly. It's as if our souls are connected by an invisible umbilical cord. Right now, she's upset at having our visit interrupted by a stranger."

Instead of finding my declaration odd, the man unfolds himself from the chair again. "How terribly rude of me," he murmurs.

I watch in some surprise as he presents himself at Winnie's feet, going so far as to bend at the waist in what I swear is a formal bow.

"I'm Nicholas Hartford III," he says, still in that smooth voice. "It's a pleasure to meet you, and I sincerely apologize for barging in on your privacy like this."

He says privacy with an emphasis on the *priv*, as in privy.

"I'll only take up a few minutes of your friend's time, if that's not too much to ask." He turns to me with a slight upturn of his lips. I can't decide if it's a smile or a sneer. "What's her response? Does she approve?"

I close my eyes and lean back in my chair, pretending to be able to read the emotional umbilicus of my sister's catatonic state.

"She reserves the right to withhold judgment. She's only just met you." My eyes snap open again as his words penetrate. A medical researcher come to seek my signature on a release form wouldn't call me Winnie's *friend*. "And she's not my friend. She's my sister. Her name is Winifred."

I can tell, from the way his dark eyebrows lift, that he wasn't previously aware of the relationship between us. It's not a revelation I find comforting. *If he's not here for Winnie, then what does he want?*

He recovers quickly. "She's lovely."

"I know." I shrug. "People in comas never seem to age. Some girls have all the luck."

Nicholas hesitates, as if unsure how to respond in a way that will remain true to his chivalrous leanings, so I give him an out. "That was a joke, by the way."

"Ah." He nods. "You're not very good at those. I expect you don't get much practice in your line of work."

I blink, wondering if I could have possibly heard him correctly, when he nods once again—this time in Winnie's direction.

"I can return in a few hours if you'd prefer some time with your sister first," he says. "I wouldn't have come at all, but I didn't know how else to find you. This is the only listed business address for Eleanor's Cleansing Service."

Yes, because I don't *have* a real business address. It's not good for a woman of my profession to stay too rooted. I'm a nomad, airy and drifting and, more importantly, untraceable by the FBI. Most of the time, I either sleep in the back of my converted hearse or on Liam's couch. Happy Acres is the closest thing to permanence—*to a home*—that I have.

Of course, that doesn't mean I invite all the ghost-seekers of the world to find me here. If anything, I actively discourage it.

"My clients know they have to call to set up a consultation," I explain, somewhat icily. "They also know I work by referral only."

He doesn't seem to notice the shift in my tone. "I apologize for the break of protocol, but I find myself in urgent need of your services. I'm in something of a bind."

"Aren't we all? Unfortunately, you caught me at a bad time. My services aren't currently available. I've got a hearse full of suitcases and a flight to Mexico to catch."

"Fleeing the country?" he asks with a lift of one brow.

I choke. "Fleeing adult responsibility." And then, because

I'm starting to get the impression I'm not going to shake this guy easily, I add, "Would you please sit down? I'm getting a headache from squinting up at you. You're directly in the sun's path."

He apologizes with apparent sincerity and once again settles in next to me. I perform a quick check to make sure Winnie is tucked in and comfortable—she hasn't moved except for the gentle rise and fall of her chest—before I resume my interaction with Nicholas Hartford III, potential client and man of mystery. I haven't yet figured him out, but I suspect he leans more toward foe than friend. He *claims* to want my services, but the sudden appearance, the questions, the dark suit . . . if those things don't scream suspicious authority figure, I don't know what does.

They're also why I don't make an attempt to speak right away. It's amazing how much insight you can glean from people with a little awkwardly prolonged silence. In this fast-paced, constantly-plugged-in world of ours, few people know how to deal with quiet. They push it, close it, fill it—anything to avoid the company of their own thoughts.

And often, in the process, tell me everything I need to know about the *real* things that haunt them.

"So, Ms. Wilde," he says, "how long do you plan on remaining in Mexico?"

It's not the burst of human insight I was hoping for, but the man's easy air of conversation does tell me a few things—namely, that he has social polish and he's not afraid to use it. Those facts don't fill me with ease. Practiced liars are the worst kind.

"Two weeks of rest and relaxation," I reply. "In my line of work, I find that caring for the body is just as important as caring for the soul."

"That's unfortunate," he says. "I don't have a few weeks."

"Why? Are you dying?"

My question is meant to shock him into revealing something

of himself, but he turns the question on me with an appreciative glint in his hard, gray eyes. "Not that I'm aware of. Do you foresee that sort of thing, too?"

"I can foresee anything if the money is right. I'm quite good, you know. You won't be able to afford me."

"Oh, dear." He feigns a worried look. "Are you very expensive?"

With that, I realize this man definitely falls under the foe category. It's his delivery that does it—to look at him, you'd think he's engaging in a perfectly serious conversation. To hear him, however, leaves little room for doubt. That rich, polished voice is mocking me. It's *testing* me. My heart thumps heavily.

"Yes," I reply, matching my voice to his so as to give nothing away. "Especially when you plan to offer me a job in an attempt to out me as an imposter and a charlatan."

He doesn't miss a beat. "Is that what you are?"

"You're not the first to try it, you know," I say. "I've seen and done it all before. *You'll* beg me to eliminate a ghost. *I'll* politely decline due to continued scheduling conflicts."

"One can hardly vacation in Mexico forever," he points out.

I ignore him. "At which point you'll double your offering price. No, you'll triple it—quadruple it. Anything to get your life back in order. My fees are already high, so I'll naturally become suspicious at your generous offer. That's when you'll put other incentives on the table. Maybe you have a famous friend you can refer me to, or you'll promise me a bonus once the ghost is gone. Either way, I'll find a way to keep increasing my fees until even you have to balk at the cost."

"I hate to criticize a woman I've just met, but that seems like a highly unethical way to run a business."

"Yes, well." I press my lips together in a tight line. "It's the only way I'll get you to realize I have no intention of falling for your trap. You don't believe in ghosts any more than I believe my sister will someday awaken from the coma that's been her entire life and livelihood since the day we turned eighteen. I appreciate you coming all this way to find me, but I'll not be made a fool of. Not for any price."

He doesn't speak right away, but I don't feel any triumph at winning this particular battle. It's never fun to pull back the veil and expose myself as a snake oil charmer, but it has to be done sometimes. I've spent far too many years in this business not to recognize a skeptic when I meet one. The best thing for me to do is get rid of him—and quickly.

"Does believing in ghosts *have* to be a prerequisite for your services?" he eventually asks.

"Absolutely," I say. "I'm afraid the spirits can sense a disbeliever from miles away. You'll taint the process."

"What if I promise not to be present at the, uh, exorcism?"

"I prefer to call it a cleansing. And it won't make a difference. Your aura is quite powerful."

"Thank you."

At his easy reply, a surge that's equal parts annoyance and laughter fills me. I suspect that getting the better of this man requires a more lengthy campaign than I'm willing to wage right now. I still have a plane to catch, after all.

"Can I be frank with you, Nick?" I ask, falling into saucy familiarity with his name.

He sighs. "*Would* you? I can't tell you what a relief that will be."

"I like you," I say as neutrally as possible. "More than you deserve, and more than is probably good for me. In fact, I'm tempted to perform your cleansing for free if only to discover what you've got up your sleeve. But as you can see for yourself, I have more than just myself to think of. This facility doesn't come cheap, and my sister is young."

"Are those two things related?"

"They are to the woman responsible for paying for her lifetime of care." I splay my hands. "As enlightening as I'm sure it would be to help you, I can't afford to have you diminish my reputation. Literally."

The movement he makes as he shifts in his chair to face me is so slight as to almost not count as movement at all, but I can feel the full weight of his regard.

"May I be frank in return?" he asks.

"By all means. Let's get it out in the open."

"I've done my research on you, or as much as I *can* do, given your lack of an online presence." There's a slight note of criticism in his voice.

"The spiritual world and the virtual world are natural enemies. I don't need the Internet when I can just plug in to the entire universe."

"Yes, well, not all of us remembered to upgrade to that package," he says. "You have a positive reputation, all things considered. Not everyone sings your praises, of course, but most of the time, you leave behind a family that's satisfied and at peace in their residence. Now, I don't believe in ghosts, not by any stretch of the imagination, but I do believe that in each case, you exorcised *something*—whether that be marital strife, memories of the past, or"—he gently clears his throat—"rats in the attic."

"Nasty things, rats," I say, my head tilted. "Do you happen to know someone named Mrs. Levitt?"

"I may have talked with her son this morning."

Aha. That explains how this man tracked me down. And after I smoothed Jimmy's romantic path for him and everything.

Nicholas clears his throat. "You're good at what you do, Eleanor Wilde. Even more to the point, you're capable of making other people believe you're good at what you do. *That's* what I want to hire you for."

Intrigue pricks at my spine, almost against my will. I can't help it any more than I can help breathing. Pretending to be a medium is a financial necessity, yes, but I'd be lying if I didn't also say I enjoy the work. It's the *mystery* of it all—figuring out what's behind each haunting, learning enough about a family to make them believe it when I finally get rid of the ghost.

"Why do I get the feeling you're buttering me up again?"

"Because I am. Again." He draws a deep breath and continues before I have an opportunity to voice my protest. "If it's not too much trouble, I'd like you to come to my ancestral estate and purge my mother of her mistaken belief that she shares the space with a ghost."

Ancestral estate? That sounds old. And promising. I'd love an opportunity to break out my 1830s Châteauneuf du Pape. I've been saving it for a rainy day—I piped Carlo Rossi into the vintage flea market bottle last year in anticipation of just such an event.

Still. It won't do to show too much eagerness.

"No offense, but why don't you just purge your own mother?" I ask. "You strike me as a man who doesn't balk at getting his hands dirty."

"Ah, yes." He studies his fingernails as if inspecting them for metaphorical dirt. "Well, I'm afraid my mother thinks I lack imagination."

"No kidding. You?"

"My sentiments exactly. Her words were, and I quote, 'Of course you don't notice the ghost. You can't see a bloody thing without your ego getting in the way.'"

That almost seals the deal right there. "She sounds delightful."

"She is." He coughs. "Or she would be, if she could get beyond this possession. I'm afraid it's taken over her ability to make sound judgments. The sooner you can, ah, lay this particular ghost to rest, the better it will be for all of us."

"You know, this is starting to sound an awful lot like you want to hire me to con your own mother."

"It does, doesn't it?" He sighs. "And I tried so hard to frame it as something else."

I can't stop a burst of outright laughter from escaping my lips. "I don't con people. What I do is provide a necessary service."

"I know," he says. "And I'm *trying* to hire you to do it."

With remarks like that, he's almost accomplished his goal, too.

"Getting someone to believe in an exorcism is all well and fine, but what's really causing the haunting?" I ask.

"Not what. *Who*." For the first time in this whole conversation, there's a glimmer of actual human emotion in his voice. It doesn't make him softer or more approachable, but it does strike whatever empathetic cords I have left. "And I don't know. That's the problem. I was hoping you'd be able to tell me."

I pause. I don't doubt that, given enough time and incentive, I'm capable of exactly what he's asking. No one can hide a haunting forever, especially if I'm there watching every move. But ghosts caused by people rather than circumstance are tricky, because at least one other person in the house *always* knows I'm a fraud.

As if hearing my doubts aloud, he lowers his voice and adds, "Please, Ms. Wilde. Just come to England and meet the ghost for yourself, that's all I'm asking. If you decide you can't take the job after that, I'll fly you to Mexico on my personal jet. Word of a Hartford."

I narrow my eyes at him. "What do you mean, your personal jet?"

"Oh, did I forget to tell you that part?" As if out of nowhere, he grins, cementing the heavy lines of his face. "I'm afraid I'm terribly wealthy. I can afford you no matter what outlandish price you set."

I look over at Winnie in alarm. As expected, she's impassive and still, her beautiful face as serene today as it was the day I brought her here. She was serene at the last place, too, which was state-run and in deplorable condition, but I vowed that I would never make her go back while it was within my power to prevent it. I could *feel* how unhappy she was there, how lonely.

Don't ask me how, but I did. One might even call it a gift.

And that decides it. There's nothing I wouldn't do for my sister, including the sale of my soul to the devil. If my illustrious career as a ghost-hunting psychic-cum-medium has proven anything, it's that I've done exactly that.

"Well, Nick. I guess that means we're in business." I extend my hand, unsurprised when he takes it and gives it a perfunctory shake. "And for the record? Next time, I suggest you lead with the cash."

Chapter 3

Although my line of work takes me to private residences of all shapes and sizes, my opportunities to cleanse a castle—a *real* castle, complete with crumbling stones and gargoyles—are disappointingly rare. Ghosts these days have an annoying tendency to hang around in newly established areas where the houses are stamped from cookie-cutter patterns and prefab from the eighties.

I blame the rising crime rate in the suburbs for it. Well, that and the fact that people who live in rambling old homes in the middle of nowhere are used to the squeaks and bumps of centuries-old architecture and the occasional rodent in the walls. Their first suspicion isn't a haunting; it's the plumbing. And they're usually correct.

Which is why, when the taxi drives up the circular drive of the ancestral Hartford home, I'm not prepared for the glorious vision that awaits me. Large, ungainly, seeping with moisture—the whole house appears to have been pulled out of a Poe story, with windows for eyes and a sinking tarn out back. I can't help but wish I'd been able to time my arrival for later in the day, when rain would batter against the window and my skin would glow eerily pale in the moonlit mist, but Nicholas insisted I book the first flight out.

I don't love being ordered around like that, but I take comfort in the box of "vintage" wine I brought. I think Old Nick will find that several bottles need to be shattered before this ghost is laid to rest. We may even have to drink a few of them.

"Well, this is it," the taxi driver informs me with something approaching glee. I can tell that he, too, is delighted by the spectral spectacle before him. He spent the better part of the hour-long drive from London to Sussex outlining the various ways in which young, unaccompanied American women are likely to meet their untimely end this far south. High on his list are rich, psychopathic landowners. "You sure you want me to leave you all alone? Seems an awful lot of places to hide bodies out here . . ."

I laugh. He's right. There are dozens of great body-hiding spaces, not excepting the moss-covered cemetery we passed on the way in, which featured several huddled dirt lumps of questionable origin. As if any of that's supposed to make me *less* likely to take on the job. This place is the perfect setting for a haunting—fake or otherwise. Ghostly fingers walk up and down my spine just thinking about it.

Those ghostly fingers kick up in earnest as I pay the driver. He unloads my suitcases and boxes of supplies while I lift my vintage medical bag and head for the door. This time, it's not the dark gloom causing my delight so much as the cherry-red Porsche I find parked on the crunching gravel walkway. The car is as unsuitable to this estate as it is tacky. I hope it belongs to the man of the castle. Few things would make me happier than to find that Nicholas Hartford III is as susceptible to flashy overcompensation as the next eccentric British millionaire.

I wave the driver off with a cheerful smile and a promise that

I will have someone collect my things. I'd carry them myself, but it's better to make an entrance without looking like an unwanted relative struggling under the weight of mundane things like toothpaste and underwear.

Besides—I'm too distracted by the front door. It's as gothic as the rest of the place, the heavy wooden portal rising to a point in the center arch as though transported from a medieval cathedral. There isn't a doorbell in sight, so I lift the heavy cast-iron ring on the knocker and let it fall instead. Even from outside the huge slab of a door, I can hear the hollow echo of the sound moving through the house, can almost feel the shaking of plaster and stone as my presence makes itself known.

Silly Ellie. The house isn't shaking. It's shivering in anticipation.

I blink, unsure where the voice came from and unwilling to indulge it further. It's one thing to enjoy gloom and despair for ambience's sake; it's another to fall prey to it. That's a fake medium's first rule of business: Never buy your own lies.

The door creaks open to reveal a young woman dressed in flannel pajamas with a winter parka thrown over the top. I *think* she's pretty—her cheeks appear round and flush, her violet eyes vibrant—but it's difficult to tell through the blanket she has wrapped around her head like a scarf.

"Hullo," she says. She's not unkind, but she's not welcoming, either. "Who are you?"

I take a moment to extract a business card from my medical bag and extend it in her direction. She takes it carefully, her hands wrapped in fingerless gloves, and examines the print. "Eleanor's Cleansing Service. Are you a maid, then?"

"Clean*sing*, with an *s*." I point out the letter. "As in purging."

"How is that different?"

She hasn't made any effort to welcome me into the house yet, so I shift from one foot to the other, trying to peer around her to see inside. "Well, Miss . . . I'm sorry. What did you say your name was?"

"Hartford. Rachel Hartford."

Hmm. A daughter, perhaps? Maybe a younger sister? Nicholas had been reluctant to tell me anything about his family or the manifestations his ghost prefers to take, so I don't know what to expect on the other side of this door. *I want you to see the ghost through virgin eyes* had been his excuse. *Untainted by any suspicions I might already harbor about its origins.*

Which, to be honest, is the way I prefer to work. Mysterious. Powerful. *Alone.*

"Well, Miss Hartford, a cleaner would show up on your doorstep with bleach and scouring pads," I say. "I've shown up with electromagnetic analytical equipment and talismans used by the druids to forge bonds with the ancient gods. I'm here to *cleanse.*"

"Oh, you're the ghost lady. Got it." She finally pulls open the door. "I heard you'd be arriving today. Come on in. And if you brought a coat, you should probably put it on. It's always freezing in here when Xavier comes calling."

Actually, I suspect it's always freezing because the walls are made of damp stone and there don't appear to be any modern heating appliances installed, but I keep my mouth shut. Clearing out the chimneys will fix that in a trice.

"Thank you, but I'm quite comfortable." I gesture to the shawl I have draped around my shoulders. It's dark purple and paisley—the perfect accompaniment to the rest of my attire, which rests on the slightly shady side of bohemian chic. "I anticipated the chill. One thing you'll find about spirits like Xavier is that they lack imagination. They have the capability to make a house blazingly hot instead of ice cold, but they almost never do it."

"Is that so?" Rachel asks. I can't tell from her tone whether she's interested or mocking me. Considering she's a relative of Nicholas's, I want to say she's mocking me, but she *is* layered up like she's expecting an attack on Winterfell, so who knows? "If I ever become a ghost, I'm going to turn the house into a perfect summer day. Well, this is it. Do you need a tour, or do you plug in to some kind of spiritual map?"

A spiritual map? What am I, a mystical GPS?

"I'll have Mr. Hartford show me around later," I say. "Is he here?"

"Uncle Nicholas?" Through Rachel's muffled layers, I see one of her brows raise. "I didn't think he was coming back. Before he left, he said he'd rather slit his own throat than hear one more word out of Xavier."

Interesting. "Xavier talks to him?"

"Oh, no. Not directly." She shakes her head. "He doesn't talk to me, either. Most of his information passes through Grandmother."

Ah, yes. That makes sense. Latching onto the most gullible party is common in cases like these.

"I find it interesting that Xavier is able to communicate at all, given the violent nature of his death," I muse, and purposefully turn my back and examine the room around me.

I soon find that the term *room* is pushing things a little. A room has four walls and a ceiling, contains finite space and definable boundaries. What I'm in right now is a portal to a different world. It's a foyer of sorts, which opens to the second floor via a winding staircase that looks dangerous enough to cause several more ghosts to be created. There's very little furniture to alleviate the vast openness of it—just a few pieces I imagine date back to William the Conqueror and are worth enough to pay for all the care Winnie will need for the rest of her life. There's also a pair of heavy axes hanging above the fireplace, confirming my belief that many a murder has taken place inside these hallowed walls.

It's not the slightest bit warm or welcoming. I love it.

"What did you mean by that, you're surprised Xavier can talk?" Rachel asks from behind me.

I turn with cool disinterest. "Oftentimes, spirits exhibit limited abilities based on the cause of their death. A spirit who drowned may be hesitant to enter a bathroom or kitchen. One who hurt his legs may be unable to move or walk without a thumping limp. Since Xavier had his voice box cut when he was killed, it's odd that he'd retain the capabilities of human speech."

Rachel gives a slight gasp.

"Odd, but not unheard of," I reassure her. "I promise it's not in any way extraordinary."

"But how did you know his cause of death? Did Uncle Nicholas tell you?"

"Your uncle said nothing except that he finds this whole thing a nonsensical farce," I say with perfect honesty. "I got the impression he's not very open-minded about these sorts of things."

A round of slow applause sounds from the doorway to the house. I'm unsurprised to find the prodigal uncle standing on the threshold with all the looming lankness I remember from Happy Acres. Although I half expected him to show up in a tuxedo—or, now that I've seen this place, a suit of armor—he looks surprisingly casual in a wine-colored sweater paired with gray wool slacks.

Warm clothes, I note with some amusement. He came prepared.

"No, no, don't stop on my account," he says in that soft, yet powerful voice of his. "I'm merely showing my appreciation for a performance well done. I didn't intend to bring it to a close. Tell us, Ms. Wilde—how *did* you know the cause of Xavier's death?"

The true version of events would be that Rachel herself told me as soon as we walked into this room. She noted that her uncle had claimed to want to slit his *own* throat rather than hear from Xavier, which implied that Xavier had met a similar fate. People often let small pieces of their personal history fall that way.

But although I have the feeling that the cynical Nicholas Hartford III might appreciate hearing that story, divulging my secrets so soon would ruin my reputation with his niece.

"Xavier's imprint is all over this place," I say with a prim smile. "His misfortunes are woven into its primeval energy."

Rachel gives a shiver of delight at my words, but Nicholas only chuckles and moves further into the foyer, bringing the door to a heavy close behind him. Sealing that wooden portal is like closing off all the light and air, and the house plunges a good five degrees as a result.

Rachel squeaks. "He's here. Is he here?"

No. It's just the magic of drafts at work, but I incline my head and close my eyes, breathing deep. "Not in full," I say after a long pause. "He's testing his boundaries, toying with me. He's shy."

"Uh oh," Nicholas says with a heavy tsk. "There's your first error. Xavier isn't the least bit shy—according to my mother, he's gregarious and outgoing in all things. Personable, too. She likes him."

I smile tightly. "Yes, but he's never before encountered someone who specializes in eliminating his kind. Naturally, he'd react differently to me than he would to family."

Rachel nods as if this makes perfect sense. Which, if ghosts were real, it absolutely would.

"I assume your things are out front?" Nicholas turns to Rachel, the heavy lines of his face deepening into a genuine smile. I'm starting to realize it's not a smile he shares all that willingly—or that often. "Brat, will you please have Thomas load up her belongings and take them to the yellow bedchamber?"

"The yellow?" She pushes back her head blanket, revealing herself to be younger than I realized—no more than a teenager, really—and remarkably pretty. The soft roundness of youth has yet to flee her face, and her hair is a beautiful wave of tawny straw that makes me feel like a wizened crone in comparison. "But that's the room—"

"Exactly."

"Where Xavier manifests most often?" I guess. From Rachel's widened eyes, I know I'm right. "Lovely. It'll give the two of us a chance to get to know one another."

"You're braver than I could ever be," she says, but I notice that one curt movement of her uncle's head has her complying with his request and loping off to find Thomas. The help, I'm assuming. I hope he's wise and elderly and full of local folklore.

As soon as she's out of earshot, I level Nicholas with my best glare. It's bad enough that he knows me for the fraud I am; he doesn't need to broadcast it to all and sundry before my work has even begun. "Enjoying yourself?"

"Immensely." His grin—that genuine, devastating one—deepens. "You're even better at this than I expected. You're worth every penny of your—ah, what did we decide your fee would be, again?"

We didn't decide on one, as he's well aware. He paid me a deposit of five thousand dollars to cover the initial expenses, and I have every intention of racking up the final price based on how difficult he makes this. So far, things aren't looking good for him.

"You could take it a little bit easy, you know," I say. "Belittling me in front of your niece isn't going to help."

He offers me his arm in a gesture so smooth and gallant, I'm taken aback enough to accept it. I'm even more flustered when I realize how firm it feels under my own. There's no hesitation in this man, no uncertainty. How wonderful it must be to live like that every day of your life.

"On the contrary, belittling you is the only thing I *can* do," he says. "If she or anyone else in this household suspects me of having warm feelings toward you, they'll know it's a trap to catch the perpetrator. Come along. I'll introduce you to Mother."

"Are you even *capable* of warm feelings?" I wonder as he leads me toward the staircase.

"In this house?" he asks. Yet another cold draught descends upon us. "I wouldn't dare."

My premonition that I would enjoy the company of Nicholas's mother is proven one hundred percent accurate.

"And I know how it looks, a woman of my age talking to ghosts, but it's not senility. I know what senility looks like. It's muttering to yourself and forgetting where you put your spectacles even though they're perched on top of your head." Vivian Hartford, the family matriarch, smiles at me with the kind of warmth my own mom had always been far too preoccupied to bestow. With triplets and a full-time job waiting tables, one could hardly blame her. "I'm not like that. My elocution is always precise, and I have no need for corrective lenses. My eyes are as good as an eagle's."

"Is that the medical description of senility?" Nicholas murmurs. "And here I thought it was a series of complex symptoms of decreasing mental acuity."

"If you can't contribute to the conversation in a meaningful way, then I suggest you go make yourself useful" is her tart reply. *Tart* is the only way to describe this woman, and I mean that in the most literal sense of the word. She appears to be in her mid-seventies, with the same lean build and erect bearing as her son. But while Nick is all languid indolence, she's clearly cut from a different cloth. Lycra, from the looks of it. Hot pink Lycra. "A cup of tea would be nice."

"Yes, it would, wouldn't it?" he asks, and then sits more comfortably in his chair by the fire. Whatever can be said for the temperature of the rest of the house, Vivian's fireplace seems to be in full working order.

I sit on the other side of the fire with my pen poised over a pad of paper. "So you wouldn't call Xavier an evil spirit, then?"

"Not at all. He can be quite annoying at times, but he's not malicious."

Nicholas coughs but doesn't look up from the newspaper spread out in front of him. "It wasn't malicious when that tray almost hit Rachel in the face last week?"

"Of course not, darling. I thought it was rather cruel of him at the time, but you convinced me it was nothing more than Thomas being clumsy with the dishes."

He coughs again. "Oh? And what about the time he tried to push me out that open window?"

"But that wasn't Xavier, either," she protests. "Don't you remember? You decided you tripped on the curtain."

I bite on the end of the pen to avoid laughing out loud. I didn't think it was possible, but I almost feel sorry for poor Old Nick. His mother isn't the type to meekly knuckle under. No wonder he had to come to me for help.

"Would it make the pair of you feel any better if I told you that it's not uncommon for a family to be divided in this way?" I ask. "Spirits will often only manifest themselves to those who have a—shall we say—sensitivity to these sorts of things."

"How convenient for them," Nicholas says.

"It's not *convenient* for any of us," Vivian says. "Least of all me. Did Nicholas tell you what he's going to do if I don't admit that Xavier is nothing more than a figment of my imagination? He's going to have me declared legally insane."

At that, Nicholas finally glances up from his paper, one corner folded down. "I beg your pardon."

"Well, you wanted to move me to the group home in Crawley, which is essentially the same thing." She gives an airy wave and leans toward me, an impressively firm set of breasts pushing up over her athletic top. I don't know what kind of genes this family has, but I want some of them. "Do you know what they do for fun there? Whist. Whist and television game shows."

"That sounds . . . terrible?" I offer.

"Yes, I know. I may be old, but I'm not dead." She laughs and casts a furtive look around. "Poor Xavier. I shouldn't say things like that. It might hurt his feelings."

"I doubt it," I reply.

Nicholas tsks gently. "Are you saying the dead don't have feelings? How callous of you."

"Not at all," I reply. "I'm saying he probably doesn't even realize he *is* dead. Spirits who linger rarely do."

"And you'll really be able to communicate with him?" Vivian asks with the eagerness of a child. When I nod, she breaks out into a wide smile. "Excellent. Then I'm so glad you're here. I don't mind Xavier living with me, but it would be so nice if you could convince him to tone down his antics while I have houseguests. He upsets them."

I set down my pen and paper so I can focus my attention more fully on Vivian. Already, it seems, we're getting to the meat of the problem. "Are you saying that his behavior worsens when you have company?"

"Oh, yes."

I cast a sideways look at Nicholas. "Any company in particular?"

She tilts her head, considering. "Well, he especially seems to dislike Nicholas. I'm sorry, darling, but it's true—it's no use looking at me like that. He's always at his worst when you're here."

Once again, I find it a struggle to keep my laughter down. *Darling* Nicholas hasn't changed his expression in the slightest, but it's clear his mother can read his moods anyway. Despite our short acquaintance, I'm pretty good at reading them, too. It's time for Madame Eleanor Wilde to earn her fee. No matter how much Vivian might like her ghost, she can't be allowed to keep him.

I place a hand to my temple and draw a deep breath. "Restless ghosts like Xavier only grow worse with time," I warn. "It sounds like a cliché, but I can promise you that until we help his spirit find peace in this world, he'll never be able to move on to the next one."

"You're absolutely right," Nicholas murmurs. I look at him, surprised, until he adds, "That does sound like a cliché."

"Well, I'm off to my spin class, so you're free to roam around looking for Xavier on your own." Mrs. Hartford leaps out of her chair with the sprightliness of a woman half her age. "We don't dress for dinner, but we do meet for sherry in the parlor beforehand. You'll like that."

"Sherry? I don't think I've had it before, but I'm sure it's fine."

"That's not why I think you'll like it," she says enigmatically, and bounces out of the room.

I wait until the vibrant pink of her top is well out of sight before turning to Nicholas with interest. "Why am I going to like sherry in the parlor? Is she expecting me to start smashing wine bottles already? I usually save that for the climax."

"I have no idea what she's cooking up." He returns his attention to his paper. "But if you want to prove yourself worth your exorbitant rates, I suggest you make an effort to find out. For all we know, she's planning to hold a séance. You'll want to put magnets in the table and set up fog machines."

"I don't use magnets and fog machines," I say with a huff. And then, because it only seems fair, "I've always been more of a wind power and tricks of the light sort of girl."

Chapter 4

As it turns out, I do like meeting for sherry before dinner.

"So I said to him, 'If you want the cemetery attached to the vicarage that bad, I'll go ahead and include it in the purchase price. But don't come crying to me when the dead start walking at night.'" The man in the middle of the story, a crass fellow American by the name of Cal Whitkin, slaps one massive hand on an even more massive knee. "Guess how long it took to settle the negotiations after that?"

"One hour, four minutes, and fifteen seconds," Nicholas says with perfect solemnity.

Cal slaps his leg again. It's the tenth time he's done it since I walked into the parlor, each blow a little harder than the last. I can only assume his nether limbs are crafted of iron. "Not even close! The papers were signed in ten minutes flat."

Nicholas is careful not to meet anyone's eye. "Fascinating. As a general rule, do you time all your real estate transactions, or is it only the difficult ones that get the honor?"

Instead of taking offense, Cal hooks a thumb at me. "Did you ever meet anyone like this guy back home? I can't get enough of him. Quick—tell her what you said when I asked if you liked my new haircut."

"I don't need to hear—" I begin, but it's too late.

"He told me he once saw something similar on a baboon's backside," Cal says. He follows it up with a crack of laughter. "Get it? Because my hair's so red."

"Actually, that wasn't the resemblance I was referring to," Nicholas corrects him, but he needn't have bothered. Cal has fallen into another knee-abusive fit of the giggles, delighted to find himself the recipient of such distinguished scorn.

I'd feel bad for the man, suffering at the hands of the dubious wit of Nicholas Hartford III, but he seems impervious to insult. To be perfectly honest, he seems impervious to everything. It's not just the *size* of him—though that's substantial enough—so much as the way he commands the attention of everyone in the room. His curly thatch of red hair threatens to take over his whole head, his voice booms so loudly it actually causes a damp patch to shake off some plaster over by the fireplace, and he's dressed in a beige linen jacket that's better suited for a 1980s buddy-cop show than a stately drawing room.

"Was the graveyard really haunted?" I ask, if only to keep Cal at center stage as long as possible. I don't know how long pre-dinner sherry is supposed to last, but by the way everyone is settling in their chairs, I imagine it's long enough for me to start digging for clues. No one has yet mentioned *why* this man is staying at the castle, but I have no doubt all will be revealed to me soon enough.

The truth almost always is.

"Well, I don't know," says Cal. He considers the question with the rub of his finger along one side of his nose. "I don't go in for that sort of nonsense, no offense, but I suppose it could have been. I never visited the vicarage at night."

"It's a common misconception—*almost a cliché*—that ghosts are more active at night." I glance pointedly at Nicholas as I say this, but other than a slight twitch of the lips, he doesn't acknowledge my hit. "In reality, spirits don't operate on any kind of schedule—at least, not schedules as we know them. They're often stuck reenacting a loop of their own past events irrespective of time or place."

"What do you mean, irrespective of time or place?" Rachel asks. She's once again wrapped in layers of blankets and shawls, the pale jut of her nose all that's visible of her face.

I turn to her, eager to have such an interested audience. "We have to remember that our realm isn't their realm, even though we share a physical space. Most people see their ghosts over and over again in the same location, right? Say, in the garage window or walking through a wall at the end of the hallway. There's a reason for repeat appearances. It's usually because that's a significant moment in their own life story—the moment of their death or of severe emotional trauma."

Across the room, Nicholas sighs. "I suppose that means I'm doomed to this dinner party for all eternity, doesn't it?"

Everyone in the room ignores him.

"We tend to think of flitting across windows and through walls as an eerie spectacle designed to frighten us, but the reality is almost always that the house has been modified in the years since the spirit was alive," I explain. "*We* see them walking through that wall—but to them, it's just a regular hallway that used to exist in their lifetime. The same thing is true of time. Ghosts don't come out at night to scare us; they come out whenever their own past disturbances occurred."

"But my Xavier is always more active at night," Vivian puts in. She's dressed, inexplicably, in a white track suit that rustles like plastic bags every time she moves. "I'm sure you'll see what I mean later. I understand you requested the yellow chamber in order to be closer to him. Very well done of you, my dear."

Nicholas lifts his glass of sherry at me in a one-sided toast.

"But that's just it," I say, doing my best to block him out.

"Of course I'll think he's more active at night—I'll be inside the room for eight hours in a row. I'm not there *now*, nor have I been there for much of the day except to unpack my things and get settled in. And if we did hear anything from that direction, it would be easily explained away by our conversation or the dinner preparations. We're more attuned to the sounds and sighs of the household at night, when we're left to lie alone in the dark with only our own thoughts for company."

"Bravo." Nicholas claps his hands politely. "I couldn't have put it better myself."

"Speak for yourself, young lady," Cal intervenes. "*You* might be lying there without anyone but your own thoughts for company, but when I stay overnight at Castle Hartford, I'm not alone. I'm far too busy enjoying—"

Rachel shrieks and claps her hands over her ears. I think for a moment that Xavier has made an appearance that I somehow missed, but Cal dissolves into hearty laughter, and Nicholas's face takes on such a martyred expression that it doesn't take me long to come to a conclusion.

"Mrs. Hartford?" I ask before I can stop myself. I didn't realize the old girl had it in her. "I had no idea. Have you and Mr. Whitkin been seeing each other long?"

"Lord, bless you. He's not *my* beau." She cackles and tops off her sherry for the third time. A few more glasses of this wine down her hundred-pound frame, and I'm pretty sure I'll have found the source of our ghost. "Cal is Fern's gentleman friend."

"Fern?"

"My sister, Rachel's mother," Nicholas explains. "Don't worry—she'll be down about ten minutes after dinner starts. She likes to make as theatrical an entrance as possible. You'll like that. You can share tips."

I bite my tongue to keep my sharp retort in place, but it's difficult. And not just because I'd love to get the better of that man for once. Some of it is caused by shame. In my preemptory reconnaissance of the castle, accomplished when I'd claimed to be unpacking my things, I hadn't come across *anything* that indicated Rachel's mother is currently in residence.

That such a person exists is, of course, perfectly natural. However, when I peeked inside Rachel's room, everything about the space made it appear that she's a permanent resident with her grandmother. Not only were her clothes and electronics scattered about the room as though she shed them like a skin, but she also had several drawings tacked up to cover the delicate pink flowered wallpaper of her room. They were beautiful drawings, all done in black ink, full of tortuous, elongated figures and morose landscapes.

They were the exact type of drawings a troubled, angst-ridden teen who may or may not get her kicks from pretending to be a ghost might draw. They were also clear signs that her grandmother was raising her, with the occasional not-so-helpful aside from good ol' Uncle Nick. A mother never figured in the conclusions I drew.

Oh, dear. It's not good for a medium to overlook an entire person living in a house. I hope I'm not losing my touch.

"If you ask me, Fern's entrances are worth the wait," Cal says, his words leveled as if daring us to disagree. "It's just that you're all so used to them, you don't know how to appreciate her the way I do."

"I'm sure you appreciate her more than enough for everyone," I say with a smile that invites him to open up. And then, on a hunch, "Xavier doesn't like her much, does he?"

Cal releases a huff, his whole body heaving with indignation. "No, he doesn't, and if you ask me, it just goes to show how the living and the dead should never share the same house." His booming voice fills the corners of the room. "Fern has more of a right to be here than he does, and if Xavier doesn't like it, then that's his problem. He can take his business somewhere else."

Business? That sounds promising, and I'd like to follow up, but there isn't an opportunity. Without any kind of warning, the door to the parlor swings open with enough force to cause a cold blast of wind to move through, flickering the flames of the fireplace and dropping the room at least ten degrees. The doorknob also slams against the wall, shaking a nearby painting until it's askew and dangling, a leafy frond in one corner shivering long after the intrusion has been made.

I half expect a ghostly apparition to appear in the doorway, but all that happens is a well-built young man in a flannel shirt and work boots apologizes for the noise.

"It's my own fault," he says to Nicholas. "I greased the hinges on all the doors this morning, like you asked."

"Yes, I noted as much. I'm sure Ms. Wilde appreciates your efforts, as this will allow her to move more stealthily through the house and around our private rooms. To, ah, investigate the ghost," Nicholas adds when I open my mouth to protest.

As he speaks, Nicholas also rises to his feet. It's the first real movement he's made in fifteen minutes, so I assume that means the flannel-clad man is Thomas, the butler-slash-manservant come to inform us that it's time to head into our meal. With his stocky build and full head of golden hair, Thomas couldn't be further from the wizened old folklorist I'd imagined. Especially when he winks at me, his playful blue eyes daring me to mention the indiscretion to my hosts.

I'd put the man at around my own age, give or take a few years. He's also much nearer to my own class—a thing that's evident in both his boots and his bearing. It's enough to reinforce that he and I are the hired help, the toiling drudges, the two bastions of sanity under a roof that probably doesn't see much of it. Even though I make it a point never to get too friendly with anyone on a job, I flash him a knowing grin. It's nice to know there's someone under this roof who finds these people as bizarre as I do.

"Welcome to Castle Hartford," Thomas says with a mock bow as he holds open the door.

We file out of the room with much less pomp than expected. I'd assumed we'd pair off in twos like animals boarding the ark, a gentleman's arm to support each lady, but it's more of an ennui-fueled shuffle. Nicholas does have the decency to motion for me to precede him, but Cal's hand prevents me from making good my escape.

"Wha—" I begin, but he shakes his head in such a fierce way that I drop silent at once.

Cal's hand stays on my arm until everyone else has moved out of earshot, causing my interest to pick up. When I come to a troubled house such as this one, it's not uncommon for my role as ghost hunter to transform into that of impromptu therapist. See, all families have their dramas and problems, and to get an unbiased outside opinion—especially from someone who's *sensitive* to these sorts of things—is like winning the lottery. You'd be surprised how many people confess their deepest, darkest secrets within hours of meeting me.

"Yes?" I ask as gently as I can. "Is there something you need to tell me?"

"Yeah. Take these." He shoves one of his fists at me.

I'm so startled that I don't stop him as he opens his fingers to drop a handful of cookies into my palm. I recognize them as the ones from the biscuit tin over by the sherry table.

I stare at the chocolate-covered treats as if examining them for clues. "O-kay. What do I need them *for*? Does Xavier like biscuits?"

He shakes his head and opens his jacket to flash me the interior breast pocket. It bulges with more cookies, a candy bar, and what I suspect might be a can of tuna.

"You're a tiny scrap of a thing already," he says. "I just wouldn't want you to starve, that's all."

And on that bizarre pronouncement, he adopts the role of gentleman and offers me his arm. There's not much else for me to do, so after tucking the biscuits into one of the folds of my scarf, I take it.

The reason for the biscuits becomes apparent about five seconds into dinner. I wasn't sure what kind of meal to expect from a bona fide English castle, but I had visions of whole roasted pigs, rich sauces poured over fifteen kinds of fish, and towering desserts that wobbled when brought in.

What I get is a thin, watery soup with chunks of what might be potatoes but are more likely turnips, and a roll of bread so hard I suspect it might be part of the home's original stonework.

"We don't bother with multiple courses here, so eat up," Mrs. Hartford informs me around a mouthful of potaturnip. "We go all out on special occasions, but most days we prefer to keep things cozy. I hope you don't mind that we consider you one of us already."

"Oh, how lovely," I manage before I catch Cal's eye across the table. He pats his breast pocket knowingly.

As I make an attempt at softening the bread by soaking it in the soup, I sneak a covert glance around the table to see how England's elite fares over fare like this. They must be used to the food—or at least have a direct pipeline to the kitchen later—because both Rachel and Nicholas calmly spoon in their meals.

I'm wondering how best to clandestinely smuggle a few biscuits from my scarf to my mouth when a distraction in the form of Fern Hartford appears. The double doors are thrown open, and yet another breeze gusts through, robbing our soup of the wisp of steam that was the only enticing thing about it.

The discomfort is soon revealed to be worth it. I'm not sure what I expected Nicholas's sister to look like—maybe a cross between Rachel's fresh-faced beauty and his urbane calm—but what I get is a vision of one of the most glamorous women I've ever seen.

She's severely underdressed for the weather inside the castle, her dress a silky, cream-colored sheath that looks fantastic on her long, lean form. I have no idea what kind of undergarments have to be worn to show no lines or creases like that, but she's perfect from head to toe. A voluminous fall of blond hair is swept off to one side, and her only concession to the cold is a muff she carries in one hand. I suspect she's using it to hide a few snacks of her own and make a note to come up with something similar. If my stay here is going to be an extended one, food-smuggling tricks are going to have to be added to my lineup.

She's a few years older than me, but still young enough that I have to do some mental arithmetic before I'm able to figure out how Rachel can be her daughter. My best guess is that Fern is in her mid-thirties. That would have given her enough time to enjoy a teenage pregnancy before investing in some great beauty products to keep people on their toes.

"You couldn't have waited ten more minutes to serve dinner?" she asks as she moves the rest of the way into the room. Slinks, really, moving like a fox or a minx or some other animal that makes liberal use of the end of the alphabet. She drops a kiss on Cal's forehead, leaving behind a bright red mark before seating herself next to him, "Really, Mother. I don't think it's asking too much to be able to partake in the family rituals."

"We have a guest staying with us," Vivian says without looking up from her soup. "It would've been rude to ask her to starve because you can't be bothered to invest in a watch."

"She's going to starve no matter what," Cal mutters under his breath. Only I hear him, which means only I'm forced to choke on my laugh.

"Good evening, Nicholas. Rachel, darling." She nods at each person as she speaks, finally landing on me. "You must be the guest in danger of starvation. I'm so sorry to have kept you waiting. I'm Ms. Fernley Patrice Hartford. You may call me Fern."

She reaches across the table to offer me her hand, which she does not in the gesture of a handshake, but limply, with the palm faced down, almost as though I'm expected to bestow a gallant kiss. Since I'm not accustomed to kissing rings—papal, noble, or otherwise—I merely take her limp fingers in my own and give them a wiggle.

"Madame Eleanor Wilde," I say in tones to rival her own. "You may call me Madame."

Across the table, Nicholas looks up from his meal with a glint in his eye. I note, with some satisfaction, that although he seems to be bringing his spoon to his mouth in regular intervals, the level of liquid in the bowl hasn't gone down in the slightest. Either he's good at discreetly refilling it, or he, too, has a candy bar hidden in his lap.

"Oh, are you French?" Fern counters with a pert air. "Où avez-vous étudié?"

"Not French," I reply just as pertly. "I commune with the dead."

"I can't decide if that's better or worse," Cal says with a loud chortle. "Can't stand the French, but then, I don't much care for dead people either. What say you, Nick, old boy?"

"I make it a general rule not to disparage an entire nation in one glib comment," Nicholas replies without blinking. "Besides—it's not possible to commune with the dead based on the simple fact that they're *dead*."

"Oh, nice," I'm goaded into saying. "You won't disparage a nation without cause, but you have no problems disparaging my profession."

He glances at me over the top of his empty wineglass. The wine is of a much higher quality than the food, which would account for so much of it being drained from our glasses already. "Show me actual *proof* of Xavier's existence, and I'll amend my words. Until then, I retain the right to consider him nothing more than a figment of my mother's overactive imagination."

"Xavier! All we ever talk about is that stupid ghost," Fern scoffs. I can't say that I'm surprised at her outrage. This is clearly a woman who doesn't enjoy being upstaged. "If you want my opinion, Madame Eleanor, he's nothing but a whiny, spoiled brat who didn't get enough attention in his own lifetime, so he's trying to make up for it now."

"Interesting," I say. "But you do believe he's real?"

"He'd better be," she says icily. "He ripped up four of my favorite gowns."

Ripped gowns, eh? I don't know for sure which family member is responsible for that sort of juvenile acting out, but I make a mental note to add it to my notebook later. So far, Xavier's manipulations extend to making a cold, draughty castle even colder, whispering to Vivian through walls, and destroying the wardrobe of a woman who I'm sure has plenty of dresses to spare.

In other words, no real manipulations at all. The lack of any major monetary damage or personal harm indicates that the culprit is most likely a member of the family. Someone is going to extreme measures to send a message, but not so extreme that the losses will be irreversible. That's an inside job if I've ever seen one.

A ping of disappointment fills me at such an easy answer to the Hartford ghost. When Nicholas swooped in with his promises of intrigue and ancestral estates and private jets, I thought for sure there would be something extraordinary afoot. But his family is much the same as every other one I've dealt with so far: a little delusional, a lot dysfunctional. Fifty bucks says Xavier turns out to be nothing more than Rachel acting out against her mother's crass beau. A broken bottle of wine and a stern talking-to, and all will be at peace again.

Alas. This is what I get for being optimistic. I, of all people, should have known better.

"Is everything alright?" Nicholas asks.

"Do you sense something?" Rachel adds.

"I hope it's not the soup," Vivian says. "This is one of my fa-vorite recipes."

Since I've already let my disappointment show on my face—an amateur move, if there ever was one—I place a hand to my head and feign intense concentration. "Xavier isn't happy that I'm here," I say, casting my own emotions onto the family's ghost. "He's pushing me away, I can feel it."

Nicholas's voice is sharper than I expect. "Does this mean you're not going to stay?" he asks.

"You can't go!" Rachel cries with every appearance of real dis-tress. "You knew all those things about Xavier's death and how spirits act and stuff. You're like a ghost genius. We need you."

Cal adds his entreaty to Rachel's. "It does seem a shame to come all this way before you've even met the guy. Er, ghost, I mean."

When I look up at Nicholas, he appears to have recovered whatever caused his outburst, but he's watching me with a close-ness bordering on the uncomfortable. "The decision whether to stay or go is, of course, yours," he says, his tone level. "But I do hope you'll stay."

I have no intention of leaving before this job is through—and not just because of the potential to hike up the costs. Strange as it may seem, I like this family. Liam is a great brother, and Winnie can hardly be blamed for her lack of sparkling conversation, but it's been a long time since I felt so comfortable anywhere.

Spiritual medium or not, I can *feel* that this family—that this house—welcomes me.

"I only meant that it wouldn't be surprising if Xavier's activ-ities start to increase or decrease at an accelerated rate," I ex-plain. "A medium's presence is often perceived as a threat, which means he may adjust his usual activities."

"Oh, right," Rachel says knowingly. "Because he knows you're out to get him."

Well, yes. That and the fact that whoever is behind Xavier's tricks will either amp things up in an attempt to get rid of me before I find him out, or he'll run into hiding out of fear of discovery. Naturally, I don't say that part aloud. One of a ghost hunter's most valuable tools is restraint.

"So you're not leaving?" Nicholas asks, still watching me.

I shake my head.

I can tell he'd like to add something more, his lips hovering open, but Fern interrupts her brother with an irritated sigh. "No one seems to care whether or not *I* stay put," she says, sounding more like her teenaged daughter than a grown woman.

"I care," Cal says loyally, just as Vivian harrumphs and points at her with her spoon.

"Oh, please," she says. "I've been trying to get rid of you since you came of age. If I thought something as simple as a ghost would finally dislodge you, I'd have invented one years ago."

Chapter 5

⤝⤞

Bedtime at Castle Hartford is disappointingly early.

Although I'd harbored hopes of after-dinner drinks, or, more importantly, after-dinner *snacks*, Vivian announces her intention to call it an early night soon after we finish our soup.

"We rise early in the country" is all the explanation she offers. While her declaration makes sense to me on one level—the level of farmers, for example—I doubt any of this lot rise with the dawn to toil in the fields out back.

I look to my other hosts in supplication, but no one bothers to meet my eye. Fern and Cal I can excuse on account of the fact that Cal's hand has been on Fern's leg under the table the entire meal. Rachel, too, I let off the hook, since the last thing any teenager wants is to entertain strange psychics while her mom canoodles with a man in a linen jacket. But *Nicholas*—my employer, my host, my savior. What a louse he turns out to be.

"I'm also going to call it an early night," he says, pushing back from the table. "I need to apply myself to some kind of work if I'm going to be making a lengthy stay in this godforsaken place."

Why he's so keen to oust the unrestful undead from a *god-*

forsaken place he dislikes so much, I have no idea. Nor do I have an opportunity to ask him about his work, because he languidly exits the dining room without a backward glance. One by one, the entire family trails away behind him, leaving me all alone with six bowls of uneaten soup.

"Don't take it too hard," a male voice says at my back. "They're like this with everyone."

There's a slight lilt to the man's accent, pleasing to the ear. I turn to find Thomas leaning against the door frame, a large tray tucked under one arm. He's still in flannel and work boots, a look incongruous with the setting but somehow suited to his gilded ruggedness.

"Everyone?" I echo.

"Oh, yeah. Last month, they had a baron come to stay. They served him butter sandwiches and made him bring his own linen. You must be important—you have sheets on your bed and everything."

I laugh. Thomas's friendly, lopsided grin allows for nothing else.

"Don't hold it against them," he adds and moves confidently into the dining room. Since he whisks out the tray and begins loading it with the not-so-used dishes, I assume he performs this routine on the regular. "These old families have to be odd—it's all they have left. The money's gone, and the houses are falling down around them. Eccentricity is all that remains."

"I take it you're from around here?" I ask. I grab my own bowl and cup and place them on the tray. Thomas makes a move to stop me, but I ignore him and continue helping.

I've only cleansed one other house that had permanent on-site staff, and it wasn't as awkward as I was afraid it would be. The family in question had a live-in nanny who refused to keep working unless they got rid of the spirit that stared in the window outside the baby's room and turned on the electric toy piano in the night. They promptly hauled me in to allay her fears—and allay them I did. The piano ended up being a manu-facturer defect, and the spirit in the window was the ghostly face of the neighbor's bichon frise escaping his kennel.

"Born and raised," he says, thus confirming my suspicions. "My family has lived in the gatekeeper's cottage between here and the village for five generations."

"Wow. That's some staying power. It must be a nice cottage."

He shrugs. "It's no Castle Hartford, but I get by." He pauses in a way that I know and recognize. "So you're a medium, huh? What's that like?"

Ah, yes. The inevitable question, wholly inadequate yet some-how the only thing anyone ever asks me. There are lots of profes-sions out there that define a person—teacher, doctor, politician, whore—but none of them, with the possible exception of that last one, take over an entire personality quite so effectively as *medium*. As soon as someone hears what I do for a living, it's impossible for them to separate my job from who I am as a per-son. Any and all conversations from that point forward revolve around the spiritual world.

I try not to take it to heart. After all, the alternative would be for them not to talk to me at all.

"Every day is full of dark, mysterious wonder," I say.

He laughs, showing a slightly crooked hitch to his two front teeth that only serves to increase his attractiveness. This is no cold, mocking lord of the manor. He's a man, pure and simple. "I suppose I deserved that. Rather a stupid question, isn't it?"

Very. But I appreciate his willingness to admit it, so I reply with one of my own. "What's it like being a . . ." I struggle for the right word only to settle on "servant?"

"Every day is full of dark, mysterious wonder," he replies easily. "But I prefer to be called a man-of-all-work. Yard work, household repairs, carting around luggage, serving the meals— if a task requires two legs, two arms, and a strong back, I'm the one to get it done."

I eye him askance, my stomach rumbling. "Are you also the cook?"

This time, his laughter fills the room. It brings a kind of light to the space, a simple joy lacking in the earlier company. "You think I'd admit to it even if I was?" He shakes his head. "No, that's one job I'm not asked to perform. Mrs. Hartford does all the cooking around here. She insists."

"How generous of her," I say and leave it at that. It's not good to insult one's employer-slash-hostess *too* much on the first day.

By this time, we've managed to get most of the plates loaded up. Thomas lifts the tray to his shoulder, unburdened by the fifty or so pounds of porcelain he's carrying. Man-of-all-work, it seems, is a title he's worthy of.

"I can take it from here." He winks as he heads for a door near the back of the dining room. "Thanks for the help."

"Wait—" I call after him. I'm not a hundred percent sure what I want him to wait for, but I suspect it's mostly a desire not to be left to my own sorry company for the rest of the night. I decide to make use of the moment to pump him for information about Xavier. "The ghost—have you encountered him?"

His eyebrows lift a fraction. "Recently?"

"Ever," I say. When I notice his brows go even higher, I rush, "I only ask because manifestations of his sort react differently to non-family members—act out more violently or refuse to show themselves altogether. They're oddly loyal, these spirits."

"Oh, I've seen him," Thomas says, and with such quick solemnity, I believe him. Maybe not that he's seen an actual ghost—because, *come on*—but that whoever is causing Xavier's antics has done it within his range of vision. "He's not a bad sort, when all is said and done. A few flickering lights, a laugh down a dark corridor. He saved me from falling down a stair-well once."

"Really?"

Thomas shrugs, his good-natured smile back in place. "One

of the boards was loose. I was carrying a stack of old lumber to burn in the kitchen, so I couldn't see it. He flitted right past me—all wispy and white—and scared me so bad I dropped every last piece of wood."

"That doesn't sound very helpful," I say.

He laughs. "No, and so I thought, too, at the time. But later, when I was cleaning up the mess I'd made, I noticed a pried-up board about halfway down. If I'd gone two steps farther with that heavy load, my foot would have snagged on the board and sent *me* flying instead. I figure I owe Xavier, if not for saving my life, at least for keeping me from a few broken limbs."

I'm intrigued enough to continue questioning Thomas about his experience, but he gives no indication of wanting to linger. Since that tray has to be growing heavy by now, I send him off with a smile.

I also make a plan to track Thomas down later to further our acquaintance. Ghostly fogs aren't impossible to fabricate, and I don't doubt that he could have easily dropped that wood and come up with a Xavier-related explanation later, but there may be more to his story than he's letting on.

And until I get to the bottom of this haunting and walk out the door with cash in hand, everyone's story is one I'm interested in hearing.

Since it appears I'll be on my own for the duration of the evening, I decide to make a thorough investigation, starting with—what else?—the yellow bedchamber. As the locus of supernatural activity, it makes the most sense for me to start my search there.

To aid in my efforts, I shed the top two layers of my costume, setting aside the wispy sheaths and scarves in favor of efficient floral leggings and a camisole. I also remove my shoes, since I don't want anyone to overhear my movements and realize just how detailed my investigation is about to become.

Without further ado, I begin my search.

The yellow bedchamber is appropriately named, although someone with more romantic leanings could have gotten away with calling it the golden room. The wallpaper is a lovely faded yellow that I know, from peering behind the hanging pictures, was once a glaring, horrible orange. The paintings, all of landscapes at sunset, are in gilded frames that hang so heavily they're starting to pull at the plaster of the wall. Although the floor is traditional wood, it's covered with a warm russet carpet that owes much of its luster to regular wear and tear. The whole effect begs for antique furniture and porcelain fixtures, but for some reason, most of the furniture in the room appears to have come from IKEA.

And I mean that literally. With the exception of my bed—a huge, ornate four-poster pushed up against the wall it shares with Rachel's room—everything else appears to have been brought in on the cheap. The minimalist chrome chair set up against the floating plastic desk even has the price tag attached.

"Okay, so if I were an ancient being trying to scare a fierce old lady and her wealthy offspring, where would I be?" I mutter. Pulling the chrome desk chair to one corner, I climb on top and start poking.

Poking is the official term I like to use in situations like these. Although I do a lot more than poke—I push and prod and twist and knock—the idea is the same. I'm testing the visible boundaries of the house to discover what kinds of secrets lay beyond. Hidden panels, attic access points, vents, rotted wood, rats' holes, birds' nests . . . you name it, I've seen it. Old homes are riddled with defects and areas where anything can get in.

And a castle like this one? I can't decide whether I'm more excited or overwhelmed at the prospect of what I'll find.

After a few hours of searching, however, I'm ready to call the yellow bedchamber a bust. Although there are more than a few damp, bulging patches, the walls are largely intact. The fireplace—inside which a fake, flickering electric heater buzzes—is completely closed off, and there isn't even a secret passageway to the room next door.

It's incredibly disappointing. It's also disconcerting, as I'm not sure what this will mean for the rest of my stay. If this room is where Xavier spends the most time, it must be because someone is sneaking in at night and making that appear to be the case. My staying in the room will most likely preclude any more nocturnal wanderings, as it will be difficult for the ghost to slip in without my noticing.

I guess I'll have to pretend that I scared Xavier off and request a new bedchamber. It makes me look unprofessional to fail to make a connection in the most haunted room in the house, but there's not much else I can do about it.

By the time I finish, it's closing in on eleven o'clock. Early for a medium's bedtime, but between the jet lag from my flight and the lack of food in my stomach, I'm starting to feel the hours weighing heavily on my shoulders. I decide to make a night of it.

I slip between the sheets with an extra heap of blankets and my phone—the former because the yellow room is much brighter than it is warm, the latter because I like to wind down with a few games of mahjong before I sleep. Before I can open the app, however, a flashing red light indicates I missed a call.

I don't have to look to know it's from Liam. My brother always worries about me when I'm in a new house, which is equal parts sweet and condescending. He finds people who believe in ghosts to be highly suspicious, and I'm pretty sure he thinks I'll end up kidnapped or murdered one of these days.

That's why I always give him the address in advance, with specific details about my employers. I also remind him that if I *do* disappear, he's obligated to show up and claim that my angry, disrupted spirit has taken up residence in the home and nothing short of confessing to the murder will cause me to leave again.

He doesn't find this plan nearly as amusing as I do.

It's still early in the day where he is, but I'd rather not get into a lengthy argument over the phone, so I text him instead.

alive, well, starving

My messages tend to be short and to the point. Like I said—the virtual world and the spiritual world don't always get along. Up until last year, I used a flip phone.

I watch the dots on my screen flashing as Liam painstakingly types out a novel in response. **How can you be well and starving at the same time? Don't they have food? Maybe you could take one of the mounted deer heads from the wall and eat that.**

It's not the worst idea he's ever had, and if I saw any mounted deer heads, I might take him up on the offer. But although there are tapestries and paintings and even antique dueling pistols hanging in various locations, I have yet to see anything with eyes.

already tried, exhausted now, going to bed

His response this time is much slower in coming. I'm afraid he's taken it upon himself to provide a play-by-play breakdown of his scintillating plans for the school gymnasium, but all that eventually comes through is **Sleep tight and call me tomorrow, okay? I don't like you being so far away.**

I want to remind him that I would have been equally far away, at least in terms of mileage, if I'd gone to Mexico, but there's no point. I know what he means. He doesn't like me *working* so far away. His overprotective brother impulses kick in hardest when he knows he can't come to my immediate aid.

I like to think he'd have been that way no matter what, that his genetic code predestined him for a lifetime of fraternal worry, but there's no denying when—and how—the anxiety first began.

The poor guy. He'd been out of town on our eighteenth birthday, out visiting college campuses and planning his future. Not in the twisted wreckage of the car with me and Winnie and Mom. Not at the bleak hospital in the hours that followed, our only parent dead, our sister nearly so. All the horror of that day was mine alone to bear, and he's never quite gotten over it.

Welcome to adulthood, kids.

stop worrying so much I text back and don't wait for a response. Why bother? Nothing I say matters. Liam will still worry and I'll still be here, and there's nothing either one of us can do to change those facts. Unlike the ghost world, the land of the living has rules, and we have to follow them.

With a sigh, I tuck the phone under my pillow and switch off the bedside lamp. It's a space-age-looking thing, a metallic ball that sends light splaying in every direction, but I don't mind the incongruity. The details, the feelings, the mysteries—none of them matter. All I need is a decent night's sleep, and I'll be able to face this job with all the attention it requires.

And a decent night's sleep is exactly what I intend to get, even in the most haunted room in the house. I guess that's the one great thing about being a ghost hunter who doesn't believe in ghosts.

Chapter 6

BANG! THUMP! MOOOOOOOAAAAAN.
BANG! THUMP! SIIIIIIIIGGGGGGGGGH.
BANG! THUMP!

"Oh, my God. I get it already!" I sit up in bed, my hands clapped over my ears. "Screeeeeech."

I say the word screech instead of actually make a screeching sound, but only because that's what Xavier is doing. The banging and thumping are actual sound effects, but for reasons that aren't clear to my muddled, wee-hours-of-the-morning brain, he prefers to say *moan* and *sigh* rather than perform those actions.

The sounds stop as suddenly as they'd started, but a bright flash fills the room, temporarily blinding me and my poorly adjusted pupils. It's the kind of brilliance I know from experience is caused by flash paper, and it's the kind of brilliance I know, from similar tactics of my own, will keep my eyes from adjusting long enough for any kind of evidence to be swept away in the meantime.

I close my eyes and leap out of bed, hands out as I grope

around and try to land on the body responsible for the scare. Most people assume that when their victim is confronted with unearthly sounds and a blinding flash of light, they'll hide under the covers—or, at the very least, run for help. Few expect a direct attack, which is why I'm so surprised when I hit nothing but freezing cold air.

No fire. Dark castle. That's why it's cold.

Large bedroom. Lots of hiding places. That's why I can't find anyone.

I spin on my heel and lunge in the opposite direction, hoping to catch my intruder off guard. At first, I hit nothing but more cold air and the weightlessness of gravity taking over. I make an attempt to cover my head as I fall, but when I land, it's into a wall of heat.

A wall of heat with arms, it appears. Arms that wrap around my waist and hoist me to a vertical position with a surprising amount of strength.

"Now I've got you!" I cry and squint to try to make out the features of my captor.

"On the contrary, it would seem I'm the one who has you," an unperturbable voice drawls in return.

"Oh, geez." I stomp my foot on top of Nicholas's, but since I'm not wearing any shoes and I'm still halfway suspended in the air, it does little more than glance off the top of his slipper. "I should have known it was you. Only someone with zero imagination would say the word *moan* instead of actually moan."

"Agreed."

"So why don't you moan next time?"

"I'd be happy to, but you'll have to give me more cause than this." His words are spoken close to my ear, his breath warm where it whispers over the sensitive skin of my neck. "Not much, mind you, but something."

I can't decide whether to be more outraged at his speech or

at the fact that he's making it in the same flat monotone he uses when describing the weather, so I stomp on his foot again. This time, I land squarely on one of the bones, and he releases me with a grunt.

A *real* grunt instead of a verbalization of it, in case you're wondering.

I fumble to switch on the lamp, but Nicholas beats me to it and flips the overhead light on. The fixture isn't from IKEA, but it's also not of recent origin, and the flickering bulb gives the room an eerie quality that isn't helped by the disarray caused by my flight from bed. The blankets have been cast on the floor, and almost all the contents of the bedside table are scattered in an arc after I toppled it. My clothes, which I didn't hang up after I took them off to begin my late-night examination of the room, only add to the disheveled look.

Nicholas bends at the waist to pick up one of my scarves— my favorite, actually, a ragged cream-colored silk that was a gift from Winnie on that fateful eighteenth birthday. "Our ghostly apparition, perhaps?"

"Give me that," I mutter, and yank it from his hand. "You know very well there was no ghostly apparition. Just that bright—Um. Oops. Fern. Hello."

"Oh, dear. Did you get a visit from Xavier already?" She crosses the threshold to my room in a silk purple robe that flutters around her legs like a pair of wings. Despite it being the middle of the night, every hair on her head is perfectly in place, and her face bears the immaculate sheen of someone whose skin hasn't touched a pillow.

In other words, she looks like someone who knew she'd have an audience tonight. *Noted.*

Vivian is close at her heels, much less put-together in a tattered robe with the bottom panel so frayed it's almost detached from the rest of the fabric. She doesn't have curlers in her hair to match—I doubt she's ever used them in her life—but her gray-streaked hair stands up on end in a way that signals she was deep at rest before the noises awoke her.

She laughs as soon as she takes stock of my room. "I guess he was in one of his moods. I haven't seen this much disarray since last month when we tried the Ouija board. I probably should have warned you, Eleanor—I hope you don't have one of those in your bag. He doesn't care for them. He finds them pedantic."

"That is the first sensible thing I've heard from Xavier," Nicholas says as we stand surveying the mess. "But you're mistaken if you think this was caused by our friendly spirit. This, I'm afraid, is nothing more than our medium's attempt at getting out of bed."

I glare at him through narrowed eyes. "Not all of it." I rush to pick up my personal effects and, in so doing, notice that the chair I left in the corner has been upturned. Although my arms are full, I manage to point with my foot. "I didn't push that over getting out of bed. It's too far away. Xavier must have done it."

"You didn't see him do it?"

"I didn't see anything. There was a flash of light so bright it blinded me. All I could see were stars. Playful, isn't he?"

"Oh, very," Vivian says, ignoring Fern's snort of derision. "I told you—he's not dangerous at all. These are just the types of games he plays. To get attention, you know. He's like a child that way."

I nod knowingly. "Ghosts are, at their cores, primitive beings—they don't retain all the memories and intellectual capabilities they had as adults, but they know they once had them, which means they often revert back to childhood. That's why they make such messes of things. It's like a baby acting out because he can't communicate his needs."

"That's quite the philosophical reasoning for a figment of our collective imagination," Nicholas says.

"I don't remember inviting you to our collective," Vivian points out. "You can have an opinion when you stop treating me like a senile old woman. Until that day, I'll thank you to remember this is *my* house."

"Technically, I believe it belongs to—" Nicholas begins, but Fern cuts him off with a dramatic sigh.

"I wish you'd all stop talking nonsense and get this cleared up so we can go back to bed," she snaps. "I need my beauty sleep."

Even though I'm starting to find this late-night conversation of considerable interest, Fern's word acts as law. She watches with a disdainful lift of her nose as the rest of us return the room to rights. I don't love the idea of Nicholas and Vivian pawing through my blankets and personal belongings, but there's no polite way to refuse their offer, so I make do the best I can.

Things appear to be back on track when Cal appears at the door, looking like a bear awakened from hibernation when it was only halfway through. Like his ursine relatives, he's naked save for the massive amounts of body hair that keep him warm, though he's had the decency to wrap himself in a blanket before stumbling our way. A delicate pink blanket, which I can only assume came from Fern's room.

The only noticeable absence is Rachel's, which I observe with interest. While teenagers have been known to fall into a kind of slumber that rivals that of the dearly departed, it's unusual that she'd be the only one undisturbed by tonight's, uh, disturbance.

"What's all the racket?" Cal roars, creating quite a racket of his own. "There was enough bumping and screaming to wake the dead."

"That's because it *was* the dead," Vivian informs him, unperturbed by his outburst. If Xavier makes these kinds of appearances on a regular basis, she's probably used to it. "Xavier has paid Madame Eleanor a visit."

"Is that all?" Cal asks. "I thought someone had broken into the armory and taken down the pistols, at the very least."

Still, he's not without his kindnesses, because even though he's six feet of burly, hairy, pink-bedspread-covered man, he turns to me and asks if there's anything he can do before taking himself back to bed.

"No, thank you." I struggle not to smile. "Unless Xavier returns, I promise to do my best to stay quiet."

Cal manages to calm Fern by wrapping one edge of the blanket around her shoulders and murmuring something ribald in her ear. At least, I assume it's ribald based on the way her face flushes a pink shade to match the blanket. Apparently, the angry bear approach is one that works well for her. Then again, I suppose it could also just be the lateness of the hour.

I wouldn't mind having a word with Nicholas before he retires, but he, too, leaves as soon as I've reassured him that I'm not going to fall into a maidenly swoon.

"I'd stay, but it's late, and it looks as though Fern isn't the only one who needs her beauty sleep," he says from the doorway. I open my mouth to express my outrage at the implication—I'd like to see how rested *he* looks after eight hours on a plane and a welcome like this one—but he forestalls me with a smile. "Do try not to get yourself murdered on the first day, won't you? I'd like to get at least a partial return on my investment."

And with that, he takes himself off. There's no chance for me to ask how he came to my rescue so quickly, or what he meant to say about the ownership of the house, or anything about anything, really. If I didn't know better, I'd say he's making the mystery of this place more mysterious on purpose.

Because he wants the rest of the family to know I'm a fraud? Because he's genuinely interested in my unbiased opinion? Or, I think—remembering him catching me in the dark, almost as though he'd been inside my room all along—could it be that he, like everyone else under this roof, has something to hide?

Chapter 7

The delicious scent of bacon draws me out of my room the next morning.

To build a true sense of mystery and allure, I try to appear in public only in full medium attire, prepared for ghostly behavior at all times. Mystery and allure, however, have nothing on the pangs of hunger currently spiking through my stomach. I'm still in yesterday's leggings and camisole, my hair tossed into a single braid down my back, and an oversized sweater thrown over it all as I make my way through the hall.

"Breakfast smells amazing," I say as I round the corner into the dining room. To my surprise, no one is seated around the table, and there's not a scrap of food to be found—not even a lump of turnip left over from last night's dinner.

"That's odd." I sniff the air experimentally. All hints of pork products are gone, replaced by the damp chill that lends an earthy scent to most of the house. "I swear, if this is another one of Xavier's tricks . . ."

I go back to my room, thinking perhaps someone left me a tray and I simply didn't notice before. But as was the case downstairs, all I encounter is complete and utter desertion. It's only then that I glance at a grandfather clock and note the time: five-thirty in the morning. It's an ungodly hour for *anyone* to be awake, let alone someone who was up most of the night battling a ghost in her room.

Unfortunately, the hunger pangs and exercise have done wonders in waking my body up. As tempting as it would be to dive under the covers and bury my head until noon, I'll never get back to sleep now.

Since food is still very much on my mind, I decide to go in search of the kitchen. A lot of these old homes retain their original cook spaces on the bottom floor. Following the most logical path I can come up with, I start at the dining room and try to remember which of the three doors Thomas used last night to serve our meal. After a false start in an oversized cleaning closet, I find the right one—dark and dank and in keeping with the rest of the house. A narrow staircase leads directly down, and I can't help noticing the heavily nailed wooden step about halfway down.

Aha. That must be Thomas's encounter with the ghost.

I crouch and examine the affixed board. It's old enough that several decades of wear and tear are visible, but the deeply grooved scratch along one side indicates more recent handling. In fact, the tooth-like marks on the edge could easily have been caused by a crowbar used to lift the boards loose.

Then again, it could also have been caused by a man-of-all-work angrily nailing the board back into place after an accidental near-death experience. I'm not ready to jump to any conclusions just yet.

Since there's not much more I can glean from a broken step that's several weeks old, I continue wending my way down the stairs. From the moment I cross the threshold into the tiled kitchen below, I know I've found the best spot in the house. Not only has it been updated to fit in, if not the twenty-first century, then at least the twentieth, but a fire is blazing in the open hearth. To complete the picture of modernity, a cheerful and surprisingly talented male voice has broken into a baritone rendition of "Dancing Queen."

"Thomas?" I call, not wanting to startle the man by appearing out of the blue. Or the black, as seems more apt given the poor lighting in that staircase.

"Benedict," the man replies in a voice that isn't Thomas's.

I'm about to apologize and introduce myself to the new staff member when I realize who I'm talking to. "Nicholas!"

"Ambrose."

I'm cast into further confusion, but Nicholas pulls a chair out from the heavy wooden table in the middle of the room and waits for me to sit in it. As it appears he has an egg in one hand and a whisk in the other, I comply. He looks very much like a man about to make breakfast.

A cheerful, singing man about to make breakfast. This might be the strangest thing I've seen at Castle Hartford yet.

"Have you lost your mind?" I ask.

"Not that I'm aware of. Coffee?"

"Tea, if you don't mind. Who's Benedict?"

"The patron saint of Europe. And of students, I believe, but I never understood the correlation between the two. Do you take cream or sugar?"

"Just lemon. Who's Ambrose?"

"The patron saint of Milan."

I accept the teacup he holds out to me. It smells heavenly, some kind of bergamot blend I'm sure doesn't come out of a box. Trust the eccentric millionaires of England to serve pig slop for dinner and the most divine tea to accompany it. These people have strange priorities.

And strange conversations, it would seem. Trying to follow along with Nicholas's convoluted logic, I ask, "But isn't Milan in Europe?"

"Last time I checked, yes."

"So one guy gets to be the patron saint of all Europe, and the other one only gets a city?"

"Seems like a rather unfair division of labor, doesn't it? Do you want to keep playing?"

Playing what? Mind games?

"Naming saints," he prods as if I'd spoken aloud. "I assumed, when you walked through the door shouting 'Thomas' at me, we were playing a game. I should probably warn you that I had to memorize them all as a young boy. There's no way you can win."

I believe him. Religious education has never been something I've worried too much about. If he wanted to start naming Victorian spiritualists, however . . .

"Where's the food you already made?" I ask, glancing around the kitchen for evidence of the bacon. "It smelled amazing. Believe me when I say few things will get me out of bed this early, but pork products always do the trick."

"Interesting. And what sort of things will get you into bed this early?"

I strongly suspect him of mocking me, so I answer the exact same way he would. "A concussion. Sleeping pills. Possibly a head cold, but it'd have to be a pretty bad one. A medium's work is rarely done."

He flashes his deep, rare smile before resuming his cooking. I'm so caught up in watching him—the efficient neatness with which he works, the way his close-fitting sweater hugs his shoulders—that I almost forget he never answered my question.

"Seriously, though. I woke up to the smell of bacon, but when I came down to the dining room, it was empty. Did trays go up to everyone else already? How come you didn't send me one?"

"Trays?" He tsks gently. "I'm afraid you're in for quite a bit of disappointment if you think my mother sends breakfast up to her guests. Or if she serves them anything other than cold toast and weak tea. Sometimes, if she's in a particularly good mood, she'll make porridge."

"But I could have sworn I smelled it."

"Most likely you dreamed it. I suppose there *is* a chance Cal installed a hot plate in his room—he's much more intelligent than he looks, our Cal—but he rarely rises this early."

I continue staring at Nicholas's broad back as his meaning seeps through the early morning fog of my mind. It's the way he says *our Cal* that does it, the heavy mockery back in his voice.

"You think it's him, don't you?" I ask. "You think Cal is behind it."

He pauses in the act of stirring, but it's a brief pause, so quick I might have imagined it. "I thought we were going to allow you to come to your own conclusions," he says. "An untainted investigative process, as it were."

"He's very rich, isn't he?" I ask.

"Obscenely so."

"And he makes his money buying up old English properties and selling them to foreign investors?"

"Which is equally obscene, if you ask me."

Asking him is precisely what I'm trying to do, but I can recognize evasive tactics when I hear them. "This is an old English property, isn't it?" I ask.

But it's no use. Nicholas turns and, with a social smile that doesn't touch the deep lines of his face, he says, "Ancient."

The subject is one I'd like to keep pushing, but it's difficult to care much about work when Nicholas slides an herb omelet onto my plate. The glistening eggs cause my mouth to water and my stomach to rumble a warning that would make Xavier proud. I *am* in the presence of a gentleman, however, so I wait until he seats himself and accepts half the omelet before I start shoveling it in.

"Oh, God." A moan escapes my lips. "This is so good. How did you learn to cook like this?"

"Self-preservation." He cuts a delicate piece off his omelet and chews it thoughtfully. "Hmm. Too much tarragon. That must have been when you distracted me with all your talk of saints. By the way, this meal is under no circumstances to be discussed with my mother or any of her dependents. If she knew me to be capable of feeding myself, she'd put a padlock on the larder or install a family of mice in the pantry."

My fork stops halfway to my mouth. "You mean she's starving us on purpose?"

"You didn't suspect? It's the oldest trick in the book. Half of the families in this godforsaken county are known for serving deplorable meals and dampening the bedsheets. It's the only way to dissuade houseguests."

I shake my head. "She has to know it'll never work. Cal's onto her. He slipped me some biscuits before dinner last night."

"Did he? How fascinating. He must like you."

I open my mouth to tell him that lots of people like me—present company excluded—but he continues on in his bland way. "My mother likes you, too. She seems to think you're the real deal."

"Yes, well. That's kind of the point, isn't it?" I retort. He doesn't have to sound so snide about it. As far as Vivian knows, I *am* the real deal. "Are you really not going to admit you think it's Cal?"

"No, I am not." He pats his mouth with a napkin. "You'll be much more effective if I give you your head, so to speak, and let you make your own way through this investigation. I'm not sure why, to be honest. Call it a feeling."

"Ooh, a feeling. I bet that's thrown you into all kinds of disorder."

His gaze meets mine and holds it for an uncomfortably long time. I want to shift and struggle against the heat of it, but I'm trapped. A deer in headlights, if you will. Or one mounted on the wall.

"You have no idea," he finally says.

I force myself to blink and stay focused on the task at hand. "At least tell me this much," I say, "do you think he was the one responsible for last night? 'Cause I gotta say—I like Rachel for this one."

"Hmm. Because she didn't come into your room to investigate?"

"Well, yes."

"She's young. She might have been sneaking out with a boyfriend."

"True. She could have also been escaping through the hidden passageway leading out of my room to cover her tracks."

He doesn't miss a beat. "What makes you think there's a hidden passageway out of your room?"

I don't—or, rather, I *didn't*. But the quick response and lack of eye contact coming from Old Nick over there have me rethinking my position. I place a hand to my temple. "The vibrations from the house . . . They're telling me something . . . If only I could confirm . . ."

Nicholas coughs. "Nice try, Madame Eleanor, but I'm not about to give up the house's secrets that easily. Not unless you give me one in return."

I look at him in alarm. He already knows I'm not really a medium. What more could he want? "What are you talking about? I don't have any secrets."

"Everyone has secrets." He pauses, his head cocked sideways as he watches me. I don't know what it is about that quiet, intense look of his, but I'm finding it more unnerving each time he pulls it out. I have to fight the urge to adjust my hair and posture, to retreat behind the ethereal façade he already knows is a fake. "Like why an otherwise intelligent and beautiful young woman believes in magic, for example."

"I don't believe in *magic*," I protest. "I don't believe in anything. Well, except for science. And money."

He shakes his head ruefully. "I don't buy it. You can't be this convincing as a medium without buying a few of your own lies. Admit it. There's a part of you that thinks all this flitting-through-the-afterlife nonsense could be real. Part of you believes in the possibility of . . . the miraculous."

I rise to my feet, my heart thumping at the implication. He's wrong. He's wrong on so many levels. My belief in the miraculous died the day I realized that no miracle, no mystery, no *anything* was ever going to reach the place where Winnie now resides.

"You don't know what you're talking about," I say. "You brought me here because I *don't* believe in ghosts, remember?"

"Did I?" he muses, watching me with the intensity of a wolf and its prey. "I'm starting to wonder."

Instead of calming my heartbeat down, his response only causes it to pick up in earnest. "What's that supposed to mean?" I ask.

"It means, Madame Money, that you'll have to find any hidden passageways for yourself. You are the expert, after all."

It's enough to make all his blessed saints of Europe swear. "You know, if you want me to exorcise your demons, you *could* be a little more helpful."

"I could, couldn't I?"

Gah. I don't know why I bother. I'd have better luck trying to pry blood from a stone.

"You and your family have some serious problems, you know that?" I don't expect a response, so it's just as well I don't get one. Instead, I rinse my empty plate in the sink and drain the last of my tea. "But I'm going to get to the bottom of this— don't think I won't."

He holds his coffee cup up and nods once. "I expect nothing less. And if you don't already have plans for the morning, might I suggest you explore the grounds? The garden is particularly nice this time of year."

I do have plans for the morning—lots of them, including another search for secret passageways and installing a video surveillance system under the guise of electromagnetic field resonance—but I don't mention them. Considering my growing suspicion of this man, the less he knows about my activities, the better.

Besides, given how late it is in the year, the garden isn't likely to yield anything except permafrost. If I didn't know better, I'd say it sounds as though someone is trying to get rid of me for a few hours.

"Thanks for the tip," I say blandly and, almost as an afterthought, "and for making me breakfast."

He nods once and turns his attention to his plate. I can sense the dismissal in his silence and beat a hasty retreat. I don't mind. For now, my stomach is full and the house is silent.

Two conditions I intend to put to excellent use.

I spend the next hour setting up a network of simple audio-visual recording devices in the most obvious places for a castle haunting: the yellow bedchamber, the parlor, Cal's armory, and the main foyer. The two hours after that are spent placing more sophisticated equipment in less obvious, but much more important places. This includes the hallway where our bedrooms are located, all the entrances and exits to the castle, and, because I'm still curious about Thomas's fall on the stairs, at the landing where the steps turn into the kitchen.

The obvious devices are mostly for show. I use these huge black boxes with pentagrams drawn on them, and I always fabricate some evidence, whether it's spilled ectoplasm or scratchy moans interspersed in hours of white noise. People love this murder mystery type stuff, even if it doesn't help me solve anything in the end.

Which is why I also have the hidden mini camcorders and spy gear. I only hope Nicholas didn't see me as I inserted a surveillance device in the wall across from his room. I thought I was alone in the hallway, but he started talking about the pattern on the wallpaper while I was still trying to get the pinpoint camera into the swirling stem of an artichoke, leaning against the wall as though he'd been there the entire time.

Which, for all I know, he might have been. The man makes about as much noise as a ghost when he walks.

Because of the ungodly hour of my morning wake-up call, all of this has been accomplished before ten o'clock, when the rest of the family can finally be seen stirring to life around me.

"Good morning, Madame Eleanor," Vivian says pleasantly when I wander into the dining room to find the promised tea and fingers of dry toast. "I hope you were able to get some sleep after your intrusion last night."

"Enough, thanks." I sit down and accept a cup of the ice-cold brew, and I even manage to nibble a few bites of the toast. "I hope you don't mind, but I set up some technological equipment around the house to see if we can get something concrete on Xavier's activities. EVP has come a long way in recent years."

"Has it?" she murmurs vaguely.

"Electronic voice phenomena," I explain, even though she doesn't ask. I rarely miss an opportunity to show off. "Xavier could be communicating on frequencies inaccessible to the human ear. By setting up recordings, we might be able to tap into more than what he tells you."

"Of course, of course. Do whatever you think is best."

"And if there's anything like a library, somewhere old family documents might be kept that could shed light on his origins . . ."

Vivian tips her head to the side, her brow furrowed. Today's attire is some kind of hunting and/or racing outfit. Possibly both. Jodhpur pants have been layered with a tweed jacket, and she has a pair of galoshes on her feet. Against all reason, the look seems to work for her. "I'm afraid you'll have to talk to Nicholas about that. We used to have a well-stocked library, with first editions of Romantic poetry and everything, but he moved most of the materials to the village museum a few years ago. He felt that the dampness of the house was ruining the integrity of the materials, though I don't see what a few more years of moisture are going to do when they've been sitting inside this tombstone for centuries."

I'm on Nicholas's side for this one—eighteenth-century books of poetry in this decaying icebox?—but I nod my head in agreement so as to avoid Vivian's bad side. "I didn't know there was a village museum."

"Every village has a museum. Some just know better than to call themselves by that name. I suppose ours is better than most. There were some interesting Roman ruins here back in the day, and you'll find several of the coins and examples of pottery on display. Dusty pottery and moth-eaten books. What a treat for you."

"Is it within walking distance?" I inquire politely. "I'd like to go there and look around, if it's not too much trouble."

"No more than a mile or two, provided you cut across the cow pastures."

"That sounds lovely."

"It's not. It's mostly manure. Here." She reaches down and slips the galoshes from her feet before plopping them unceremoniously in my lap. "You'll want these."

As much as I generally dislike wearing other people's recently discarded footwear, I suspect I'll want the boots, so I nod my thanks and finish my second breakfast.

It's my intention to make the sojourn to the village with nothing more than my notebook for company. However, as I exit the dining room, Rachel comes bounding through the door. As was the case yesterday, she's dressed for arctic temperatures in several woolen scarves and sweaters, the top layer of which is old enough to be eaten away in several places. I assume, from the size and state of them, that they belong to her grandmother. Mrs. Hartford must have heaps of those ratty clothes tucked away. At least I know no one here will die of frostbite.

"Oh, are you heading into the village?" she asks somewhat breathlessly, catching sight of the boots in my arms. Then, as if suddenly thinking of an alternative, she wrinkles her nose. "Or are you one of those outdoorsy people who takes a morning constitutional?"

"I've never taken a constitutional in my life," I promise. "Your grandmother was kind enough to point me toward the village museum. I thought I might stop by and see if there's anything related to your ghost there."

"Like what?" she asks suspiciously.

"An old journal that references Xavier—either as a living man or as a ghostly presence. Folklore about the area." *Castle blueprints*, I don't add. I'm going to find a secret passageway if it's the last thing I do. "I'd like to get a feeling for your family's history to see if I can discover whether Xavier has any direct ties. He might be more willing to open up to me if I can make a personal connection."

"Can I come with you?"

Visions of my plans to uncover all the Hartford secrets disappear in a flash. "Of course," I lie. "I'd love the company."

"Brilliant. Just give me a second to get rid of some of these." Her last words are muffled, as the *these* in question are the top three or four layers of sweaters. It's a sad state when the English countryside in November is warmer than someone's home.

"There. That's perfect—and this way, I can show you how to get there." She winds her arm confidentially through mine, and I resign myself to her cheerful company. At least I might be able to discover what she was doing last night when Xavier hit. "I'll also show you the tea shop just on the edge of town, if you want. They make the most heavenly pound cake. You can treat me to a slice."

I stifle a laugh at the true motive for her generosity and agree to her plan. What else can I do? It seems that Nicholas and Cal aren't the only ones with a few culinary tricks up their sleeves.

"Of course, there's nothing to do here, and all my friends are in London having the time of their lives, but Mum refuses to leave while Uncle Nicholas is in residence. She says he's trying to steal her birthright out from under her nose, but there's that—what's it called, again? I read it in a book once, where the eldest child gets to inherit everything? Oh! Primogeniture."

Rachel, as it turns out, is not the type to refuse to sing for her supper—or breakfast, as the case may be. No sooner had we shaken two miles of mud from our boots and seated ourselves inside the tea shop than she became all smiles and chatter, much of which was helping to cast light on the family situation.

Nutrients will do that to a person, apparently. Who knew?

"I thought primogeniture died out centuries ago," I say and make a motion for the waitress to pack up an additional pound cake to go. I get the feeling we're going to need it. "Surely they've improved the inheritance laws since the Middle Ages."

"Yes, but it's always been our family's custom to leave the property intact." She takes a huge gulp of sweet, milky tea. "That's why it's one of the only estates still under private ownership. The firstborn gets the property and all the income associated with it. The rest of the children have to go out and get jobs."

"Oh? And what does your mother do?"

"She's an actress."

"Of course she is." The sarcastic words are out of my mouth before I can help them, but Rachel nods in agreement.

"You've seen her work?"

"Um, I believe I saw her in . . ." I fumble for a vague reference to a movie. Television show? Stage production? Oh, dear. What if it was a commercial? "It was a few years ago. She played the romantic lead."

"Well, it's nice of you to call it a lead, but she was only on-screen for twenty minutes. And she only had those three lines. It was very romantic, though, wasn't it? When he died of cancer and the shop girl who'd been in love with him all that time adopted his five children?"

That sounds quite horrible, actually, but I don't say so out loud.

"Of course, she retired as soon as she started dating Cal. I think it's disgusting, don't you, the way men demand that the women in their lives stop working like that? As if my mum's sole job should be catering to *his* needs, day in and day out."

"I have a hard time imagining Cal making that sort of demand," I muse aloud. "He seems to really care for her."

She puts her teacup down sharply, filling the air with the clang of china. "You shouldn't believe everything you see, Madame Eleanor. I would have thought a medium knew that already."

"You don't like him?"

"I *loathe* him," she says with all the aggressive certainty of youth. Her violet eyes turn cold. "And even though he pretends not to, he loathes me right back."

I'm tempted to ask her to elaborate, but I know enough about teenagers to keep my questions to myself. Nothing pushes them away faster than honest human interest—or hugs. Rachel reminds me a lot of myself at that age, actually. At least, she reminds me of myself before the accident. Between planning my mom's funeral and becoming Winnie's power of attorney, there wasn't much time for ordinary angst.

"Where do you go to school, Rachel?" I ask instead.

"I don't."

"Oh? Are you a genius?"

"No. I'm delicate—or at least that's what Mum tells the school board so I don't have to attend." She makes a moue of distaste. "But Uncle Nicholas makes me have private tutors so I can still go to university. Mum tried to fight him on it, but no one fights him for long."

"A born autocrat," I say with a nod. I recognized that about him from the start. Autocrats always try to stifle free spirits like mine.

She shrugs. "He's in charge—or, at least, he will be once Grandmother dies. That means he gets to make the rules."

I mentally fill in the rest of that statement: it will be once Grandmother dies or is carted off to a group home in Crawley. He never denied it in so many words.

"What does your uncle do, exactly?" I ask. "For work, I mean. He doesn't talk much about it."

She shrugs again. "Runs the estate, mostly. And manufactures educational materials? I remember there being something about educational materials."

It's not much to go on, but it's more information than I had when I woke up this morning, so I count it as a win. Besides, I've already spent too much time on the practical details. If I keep this up, Rachel will realize I'm a fraud before the day is over.

"That would explain why he and Xavier are natural enemies," I say. "The business world and the spiritual world rarely mix. It's like combining hydrochloric acid and holy water. More tea?" I hold up the pot.

As I'd hoped, the mention of unpleasant liquids causes her to lose her appetite. "No, thank you," she says, still polite, her good breeding ingrained so deeply I doubt she's aware of it. "If you don't mind, I'll head back to the house now. The museum is just at the end of the street. You can't miss it."

"I don't mind at all," I say, pleased at the prospect of exploring the museum on my own. A few hours of uninterrupted research is exactly what I want, especially now that I've gained some more insight into the inner family workings.

Rachel doesn't care for Cal Whitkin—and more importantly, she doesn't care for Cal Whitkin leeching from her mother, though I suspect it's actually the opposite that's taking place. I recognize a sugar daddy when I meet one. Add that to Fern's wish to inherit the castle in place of her brother, Nicholas, and Nicholas's desire to wrest the house from out of his mother's hands, and the mysteries of Xavier the Ghost are starting to unfold quite predictably.

Ah, haunted houses. At their core, they're really all the same.

"Thanks for the company, Rachel," I say as she takes the extra pound cake I ordered for myself and stows it under her arm. "And try not to worry too much—there hasn't been a family yet I haven't been able to help."

She casts a look back over her shoulder, wearing a mocking smile so much like her uncle's, it's uncanny. "True. But then, you've never met a family like ours before, have you?"

Chapter 8

⚛

I'm accosted almost as soon as I walk through the museum door.

"So, it's not as if I'd be asking you to do anything to him that's cruel or hurtful," says the woman following me through the rows of Roman pottery shards, her voice loud in the way of people who try—and fail—to whisper in public places. "Or even anything he hasn't already done, although it's been at least ten years since he's looked at me that way. You know what way I mean, don't you? When his eyelids grow heavy, and he can't seem to stop himself from—"

"I'm familiar with the traditional signs, yes," I say, not bothering to lower my own voice. "But I think you're mistaken regarding what it is I do. I don't know who you've been talking to or what kind of rumors are going around the village, but I don't make love potions. I'm a medium, not a witch."

She flaps her hands at me as if to disburse my words. "Of course not. No one said that. In fact, you don't look anything like I imagined. You're so young, so pretty, so . . ."

"Human?"

"Yes! Yes, that's it exactly. So you'll do it?" The woman's

pleading eyes meet mine, and I take a moment to look her over. It doesn't take long to assess what I see. I'd put her age at somewhere in the early fifties, her once-brownish hair now brindled with gray, her cheeks rosy and well-filled in that way that only exists in the good country air. She could easily wipe a decade off with the magic of a brow pencil and some concealer under her eyes, and her well-cut suit jacket indicates she has the resources to do just that. However, the fact that she's turning to me for help rather than her hairdresser suggests she's susceptible to mystical influence.

In other words, she's the perfect client. Gullible, well-to-do . . . desperate. It's the last one that compels me to act. Not because I'm going to take advantage of her desperation, but because it strikes a chord of sympathy deep within me.

I know how it feels to reach the point where hope begins to die. It's a slow death, a painful one. And just like the real thing, there's no crossing back once it's over.

"It's not easy, rekindling a flame that's been allowed to burn out," I warn as I pull her aside. The potsherds are giving way to fossils, which leads me to believe we're moving back in time, chronologically speaking. "I'll need a few days to gather the necessary supplies. And so will you."

"Of course," she says. "I completely understand. And I can't thank you enough. I know how this sort of thing looks, a woman my age—"

I cut her off with a wave of my hand. "Explanations aren't necessary. It's not my place to judge the mysteries of the human heart."

As I happen to have my notebook handy, I scrawl a few tasks for her to carry out. It seems cruel to send her on errands I know are fruitless, but she'll feel more like an active participant this way. Besides—it'll be fun for her, trying to sneak locks of her husband's hair by the moonlight and getting him to drink the root of a hibiscus from a golden chalice. More than any-thing else, I suspect this woman needs a little fun in her life.

"You have one week to complete this list and bring the nec-essary items back to me." I cast a furtive look around the mu-seum. No one is nearby, not even the bored young man who collected my two-pound entrance fee as I came in. "But let's not meet here. Do you know the tea shop leading into town?"

"Of course."

"When the sun touches the top of the evergreens on the twelfth day of the month, meet me there."

Her brow furrows. "When the sun . . . ?"

"Eleven o'clock or so. On Tuesday."

"Oh, yes. Yes, I see."

I press the paper into her hand. "And tell no one of your plans. I don't want word getting around, you understand?"

"What if I need to get in contact with you before then?" She shoves the paper down the front of her bra. It's all that's needed to convince me I'm doing the right thing. Women who smuggle secret witchcraft recipes next to their breasts are the type of women who need regular doses of adventure in their lives.

"You won't," I say with perfect sincerity. "Now go."

I'm half afraid that as soon as I see the back of her brindled head in the distance, another local resident is going to come popping up with a request for wart removal, fertility tonics, or, one can only hope, a necromancer spell or two, but the cheerful chime of the door closing is followed by nothing but silence.

Well, silence and the gentle pinging of the guy at the front desk playing games on his smartphone, but one can't have everything. I use the moment to find the location of the Hart-ford treasures, which, according to the map, is downstairs in the documents section.

I pick my way down a creaky set of wooden steps, wonder-ing how shortsighted it was of Nicholas to move his family's personal effects from the safe, if damp, setting at the castle to the less safe, and still damp, setting here at the museum. But as soon as I pull open the door at the bottom of the steps, I realize I couldn't have been more wrong.

No expense was spared in the renovation of the downstairs space, and I don't have to look at the plaque near the door to know that this particular wing of the museum was funded by a generous donation from the Hartford family. The hiss of the air-sealed door closing behind me is matched by the bright illumination of incandescent lighting and items carefully arranged for display.

Whatever is kept down here is obviously valuable enough to protect at great personal cost to the Hartfords. *Interesting.*

The research aspect of the job isn't always my favorite, especially when I have to scour through dusty libraries in the middle of the night, but peering through the Hartford family history spyglass ends up being a real pleasure. Whoever Nicholas hired to organize and oversee the content was amazing. Not only is there a log of all the files open to the public, but everything has been catalogued and alphabetized for maximum efficacy.

Unfortunately, there's not much information related to my specific needs. There are entire books of agricultural documents dating back to the eighteenth century, not to mention deeds of ownership and real estate transactions that prove the Hartfords came by their riches honestly. There's even a private diary of someone named Matilda, who appears to have been determined to list every ripped sheet she ever repaired.

But no mention of Xavier. Not as a first name, not as a last name, not even a passing mention in the moldering family bible, where all the names have been carefully listed as far back as the seventeenth century.

I do note, however, that a few other names are absent from the bible, most notably that of my generous hosts: Vivian and

Nicholas, Fern and Rachel. The answer could be a simple one—namely, that it's an antiquated practice few people adhere to anymore—but as I peer closer, I can make out the jagged line of a page that must have been taken from the book at the seams.

A shiver works through me as I run my finger over the torn paper's edge. I'm not enough of a documents expert to know if it has been recently ripped away or if it's an accident of ancient origins, but its absence does seem portentous, especially given the conversation I just had with Rachel.

Driven by an urge to discover more, I return to the files in hopes of finding anything related to the current ownership of the castle. It's a fruitless search. As generous as the Hartfords have been with historical documents, there's not much related to the current generation.

For whatever reason, the Hartfords, like the Wildes, value their privacy. No emphasis on *priv* this time.

A quick glance at the clock warns me that I've already spent far too much time in the museum—and in the land of the living—so I shut the bible and return it to the shelf. As much as I'd like to explore this room and its contents further, Madame Eleanor is going to need to make a few forays into the netherworld if she intends to maintain her reputation.

"Thanks so much for letting me in," I say to the young man at the desk on my way out. He's just as bored and distracted as before, his attention riveted on his phone. He uses a black-painted fingernail to scroll up and down, pausing every so often to push his overly long hair out of his eyes. "It's so quiet down there. Do you get many visitors to the Hartford collection?"

He responds with a grunt. "Dunno. Sometimes."

"Probably more around this time of year than in the summer, I bet," I say. "The cooler weather always seems to drive people indoors."

"Sure. Whatever."

Helpful this boy is decidedly not. "Is there a guest book or something I should sign before I leave?" I ask, making a last grasp. "I'd love to let the family know how much I appreciated my visit."

With a sigh, he extracts a leather-bound portfolio that looks as if it's never been cracked open. I don't expect to uncover much in the way of clues inside, which is why I'm not surprised to find that I'm the first to sign it. In defiance of the young man's ennui, I pen my name with a scrawling flourish, along with a note about how friendly and accommodating I found the staff.

He looks at it with a scowl. "You took up half the page."

"I prefer to leave a mark," I reply. "That way you'll remember me the next time someone comes in here asking questions."

"I liked the last bloke better. He just paid his money and didn't say a word."

"Oh, really?" I say disinterestedly. "I bet it was my friend Cal. About yay tall? Loud? Partial to linen?"

"Um, no." The boy holds his hand up a good foot below mine. "He was up to here and had dark hair. Real skinny guy. Had one of those twirly mustaches."

"My mistake." I bestow a bright, sunny smile on him. "Thanks again for letting me in."

I glance up as I begin the walk back to the castle, happy to note that the dull bulb of the sun is about a quarter of the way above the horizon. A little past three, is my guess, which makes for a decent day's work.

Telling time by the position of the sun isn't the most accurate way to go about things, but I've found that it impresses the families I work for. Even though ghost-hunting technology has moved forward by leaps and bounds in recent years, it's the antiquated mysticism that always dazzles people the most. I can tell time by the sun, direction by the stars, and, in a pinch, make painkillers out of tree bark.

I'm nothing if not thorough.

I'm also nothing if not prepared, so I make sure to stop by the tea shop on my way back. Rachel isn't the only one who's going to smuggle a whole pound cake into the castle for later.

Chapter 9

In my line of work, a home the size of Castle Hartford is both a blessing and a curse. A blessing because the number of hiding places for my tricks is in the hundreds, a curse because it's almost impossible to keep an eye on everything that's happening all the time. The amount of ground to cover is downright ridiculous, which is why I decide to walk around the perimeter to make sure I've mentally logged all the windows, doors, and outbuildings before I head inside.

I've made it almost all the way around before I stumble onto the garden, which Nicholas had been so kind as to invite me to explore. Considering that "garden" appears to be a euphemism for "mud pit and cesspool," I'm starting to believe he was playing a trick on me.

There is, however, an interesting cylindrical stone structure standing off to one side of the garden wall. The roof of the building is in need of repair, and a good washing would go a long way in eliminating the acrid tang emanating from it, but I'm otherwise delighted to find that it's a dovecote in the full British tradition—and by *British tradition*, I mean the Hartford ancestors probably used it to raise entire flocks of pigeons to roast for dinner.

There don't appear to be any birds currently residing inside. That would account for the state of the kitchen cupboards, but I don't know enough about aviaries to be sure, so I draw closer. The sudden urge to get my hands on a white pigeon or two is a strong one. Not because I'm hungry—not even a week at this castle would drive a city girl like me to eat a pigeon—but because inspiration has struck once again.

"I'd be careful if I were you," a voice calls from behind me. "Parts of the mire are less like mud and more like quicksand. One wrong step and you could be stuck forever."

As if to prove it, my pause allows the mud to take over, suction holding one of my borrowed galoshes fast.

"Does gardening fall under your man-of-all-work title?" I ask, glancing back at Thomas. He's sitting casually on the rock wall, watching as I struggle to free my foot. I have no idea how long he's been there, but I could have sworn I was alone out here a minute ago. "I hate to pass a judgment on someone I've just met, but if it does, I think you might want to consider a new career."

"You'll have to acquit me." He laughs and leaps down, extending the long handle of a rake in my direction. "Nothing has grown here for at least twenty years. Here. Hold on. I'll pull you in."

I'm fairly confident in my ability to escape the quagmire without assistance, but I've been hoping for another opportunity to speak with Thomas, so I grab hold and let him haul me in. At the last step, my toe hits a submerged rock of some kind, and I propel forward, falling—literally—into his arms.

My first thought is that it's not going to do my ethereal reputation any good to be caught covered in something so ordinarily earthy as mud. My second thought is that Thomas smells like a decaying forest. It must have something to do with all the damp English greenery—it's seeped into his pores like an immersion bath of ferns.

"Careful there." His arms linger around my waist as he rights my position, waiting until I'm standing solidly on two feet before letting go. Even then, his fingers brush over the small of my back and along the upper curve of my hip, the work-worn surface of his hands evident despite my layers of wispy, trailing scarves.

Like Kevin of Mexican restaurant fame, I find Thomas's bland solidity highly attractive. Unfortunately, being attracted to a man isn't the least bit conducive to my image as a mysterious medium who's above such ordinary things as human desire. Women in my position don't fornicate; we prognosticate.

"Sorry," I say and hold a hand to my temple, as though I'm feeling either a migraine or a premonition coming on. "I'm not usually so clumsy. It's been a trying afternoon."

"Oh, really?" he asks, falling easily into my trap. If anything, that only makes me more interested in him. Bless the sturdy and simple folk of this world. "Did you find something interesting in the village?"

I adopt my most thoughtful Madame Eleanor pose. "Not directly. But one never knows what will come in handy with spirits like Xavier. It's likely he's been here longer than any of you, so it could take some time to unearth all his secrets. I may need to look centuries back."

"As far as all that?" he asks, impressed. He also begins walking toward the house, compelling me to follow. Alas, my survey of the dovecote will have to be resumed at a later date. My to-do list is growing by leaps and bounds.

"Of course. No one I talked to seems to recall a throat-cutting victim any time in the past three or four generations, so Xavier probably pre-dates common memory." I feign a thoughtful pause. "You and your family have a long history here. Is the name familiar to you at all?"

Thomas stops on the threshold to the house, our entry a doorway I failed to notice during my earlier investigations. From the looks of the sagging wooden portal, which hangs askew on rusted hinges, I'm guessing this is some kind of servant's kitchen entrance.

"Do you mean, are there any Xaviers in my family tree?" Thomas laughs and shakes his head. "Not that I know of, but then, my family never kept track of that sort of thing the way the Hartfords did." His smile is self-deprecating and, if the fluttering in my lower belly is any indication, all the more powerful because of it. "Most of us couldn't read, let alone keep careful birth records. Besides, what use would a relative of mine have for haunting a place like this?"

"Maybe he likes the square footage?"

He laughs again. "I've always preferred something cozier and easier to maintain, myself. But if you want my opinion, I think you should spend less time looking at books and more time trying to find the smuggling tunnel."

I swivel my head to stare at him, not bothering to hide my excitement. My interest in smuggling tunnels is second only to my interest in secret passageways. "I'm sorry. Did you just say smuggling tunnel?"

"I reacted the same way when I first heard about it," he says with another one of those devastating grins. "Of course, I was six years old at the time, so that might have had something to do with it. Legend has it there's one that leads from somewhere in the castle to the caves over there."

He points in the direction opposite the village, where a series of hills rise up through the greenery like rocky pustules.

"But don't get too excited. I spent the better part of my youth trying to find it with no luck. Nicholas—Mr. Hartford, I mean— and I both did." He hesitates, as if he'd like to say more on the subject of his employer, but he doesn't. Instead, he looks a question at me. "They say it was used to move brandy up from the coast during Napoleon's reign. Xavier is a French name, isn't it?"

It's French enough to suit me—or, rather, to suit whoever is trying to pass off a legitimate ghost backstory.

"And you say Nicholas knows about this tunnel?" I ask.

"Everyone does. It's a popular story hereabouts."

That's less helpful than a mysterious tunnel known only to a select few, but I'll take anything I can get. The number of things Nicholas *didn't* tell me about this place are starting to add up to a whole lot of something, or my name isn't Eleanor Wilde.

"Would you be willing to show me some of the area?" I ask. "Since Xavier has already shown himself to be . . . sympathetic toward you, he might be willing to aid in our search."

"Anytime," he promises. Just as I'm about to suggest a short walk, he adds, "Except for this afternoon. I've got heaps of chores still to do, and Mrs. Hartford wants dinner pushed up to five."

"That sounds promising," I say. Maybe she's finally been bitten by the hospitality bug. "What are we having, if you don't mind my asking?"

Thomas's laugh portends all kinds of doom—and that's not my paranormal senses speaking. It's my stomach. "I heard mention of something involving canned ham and aspic. But don't worry—I'll slip you a sandwich when the lady of the castle isn't looking. You look like you could use it."

Visions of gelatinous meat products wobbling across the Hartford dining table send an unearthly shiver down my spine.

"A blessing on you and all your future offspring," I say in an appropriately mystical voice. "Make it two sandwiches, and I'll bless your grandchildren too."

The birds make an appearance after dinner.

Their arrival couldn't have been better planned. Spiritually speaking, white pigeons are a great way to get things moving, since they're well-known as harbingers of doom. Many an urban legend tells the tale of a white bird landing on a doorstep to the delight of the family inside . . . only to find them devastated by a sudden death within the week.

As there are more than a million pigeons in New York City alone, there's not much science behind this correlation, but my audience doesn't know that. Especially since the birds pour out of the chimney in a flurry of feathers and mayhem.

"Take cover!" Cal cries as he leaps to his feet and shrugs out of his jacket—this time fabricated in a more ubiquitous gray. I think, at first, that he's going to use the jacket to shoo the birds away, but he wraps it around Fern and presses her head against his shoulder to protect her from an incoming swoop.

It's an unquestionably gallant gesture, and a pang of what I suspect might be jealousy fills me at the sight of it. I value my independence as both a woman and a professional—and Cal is hardly the man I'd choose to protect me from *anything*, let alone a few harmless birds—but there's no denying that the person I love most in the world can't save me from a paper cut. Even Liam would run screaming from the room before anything approaching a protective instinct kicked in.

Without a Cal of her own to shield her, Rachel dives under the nearest chair with a declaration of "I bloody hate birds!" Nicholas goes so far as to raise an eyebrow at me, but I don't have time to reply in kind before Vivian starts laughing and clapping her hands like a delighted child.

"It's Xavier!" she cries. "You see, Eleanor? He's playing more tricks on you. Look at them go!"

I do watch them go, all four of the white birds covered in soot, none of them particularly pleased at having been cannoned out of a chimney and into a room full of screaming humans. Common sense warns me to tell everyone to calm down and open the windows to give the poor creatures a chance to escape, but that doesn't fit in with my persona. Instead, I stand up as quickly as I can—the better to force the blood away from my face and fill my visage with a ghostly pallor.

"This is no trick," I say in a low voice. I stand perfectly still as one of the birds lands on the seat of my chair, its beady eyes staring up at me. Like Nicholas, the bird's gaze is both mocking and inquisitive. "It's death, destruction, and despair."

Cal's jacket doesn't protect Fern from the weight of my words, and she looks at me with wide, horrified eyes. At least, I *think* they're wide and horrified. She came down to dinner in a silver ball gown and fake eyelashes so thick she can barely see through them. "What are you talking about?"

Lifting a single finger, I point at the bird on the chair. "A white dove is a warning of imminent death. I repeat, this is no trick. It's a message."

I have more to say on the subject, but my warning is interrupted by a loud crash as the well-oiled door of the parlor hits the wall. Thomas appears in the flannel and work boots I'm quickly coming to realize are his standard uniform. He's also carrying a large net, which leads me to believe he's come to save us.

"Ah, Thomas." Nicholas seems to share my pleasure at the sight of the man-of-all-work. "Your timing is impeccable. We appear to have an infestation."

"Not an infestation," I correct him. "A premonition."

And then, because there's something uncomfortably ordinary about the act of catching animals with nets, I go ahead and open the windows. From what I know of pigeons, they're likely to find their way home just fine on their own.

I also take a moment to mutter a pigeon-cleansing spell. Since I don't actually *know* any pigeon cleansing spells, it amounts to a low-voiced loop of "peas and carrots rhubarb; rhubarb carrots and peas," which is the go-to for both fake mediums and movie extras when you need to mimic speech but don't have anything to say. I make the motion of the cross and step back to wait for the birds to depart.

It's all very theatrical, and three of the birds gratify my vanity by leaving almost immediately. The fourth, however, is a cheeky little bastard. He remains on the chair I vacated, staring up at me with his wee beady eyes.

"Why isn't he leaving?" Rachel asks from the safety of her chair cover.

"It's filthy," Fern says. "Get it out of here, Thomas. And do hurry."

"Let's keep him as a pet," Vivian suggests. She turns to Nicholas. "Don't we have that old dovecote in the garden, darling? Surely we could install him out there."

At the mention of the dovecote, Thomas casts an inquiring and—dare I say it—suspicious look my way. At the mention of the garden, Nicholas does the same, though there's more amusement than suspicion in his glance.

"This bird is not a pet," I say, my tone firmly ominous. "He's a messenger sent from beyond."

Rachel peeks her head out from under the chair. "What for?"

Allowing my gaze to wander the room, I linger a moment on each face. "I told you already. Death. Destruction. De—"

"Despair," Nicholas finishes for me. "Yes, yes, we understood the first time. Thomas, please extract the animal and dispose of him as you see fit. Rachel, stop acting like a child and get out from under that chair. And Fern—" He looks at his sister and sighs. "Get her a stiff drink or something, won't you, Cal? They're only birds. They've probably been nesting in that chimney for months."

Put like that, it's all very reasonable and level-headed, which is the last thing I want right now. This family needs to be shaken out of its comfort zone, forced into a place with fewer avian intruders and more confessions.

"You won't catch it," I say, mentally willing the bird to take flight and follow its more accommodating brethren. "It's not of our world."

And then, before anyone can notice, I nudge the chair with my foot. As I hope, the movement is enough to jostle the bird into flight. Although he doesn't fly in an *exact* straight line out the window, it's close enough to count as a success.

Like horseshoes and atom bombs, being a psychic offers a little leeway in that department.

"Prophetic birds, Madame Eleanor? Surely we can do better than that. A mystic apparition, at the very least."

I don't need my hidden surveillance equipment to tell me that Nicholas has followed me up to the hallway outside my bedroom.

"I can only work with what I'm given, Nick," I reply somewhat tartly. I turn to find that he's not the least bit breathless from the stairs, once again leaning on the artichoke wallpaper as though he's been installed in place for hours. Did he fly up here? *Or use the secret passage?* "I thought it went rather well, all things considered. I would have chosen a more opportune time to release them—an early-morning fog or during a séance, perhaps—but I suppose tonight's performance was sufficient."

For what might be the first time, a look of perplexity crosses Nicholas's face. It's evident as a slight frown, which makes the heavy lines of his face seem almost lugubrious. "You would have chosen a more opportune time?" he echoes. "Do you mean you would have kept the poor creatures wedged inside the chimney until you were good and ready?"

"I don't know that I would have chosen the chimney at all," I say with complete honesty. I can't help thinking how much more ominous the birds would have been without those sooty spots on their wings. "The logistics were under consideration, obviously, but a chimney is rather pedestrian for my tastes. Still. Any progress is good progress. I'll overlook your interference this time."

He blinks. "My interference?"

"Yes. That is what you sent me to the garden for, isn't it? To find the dovecote? You could have just informed me of your plans like a normal human being, you know. Mystery is supposed to be my thing."

He blinks again. "You mean you didn't plant those birds?"

Understanding begins to dawn—and with it, an eerie suspicion that I'm being had. "Are you trying to tell me that *you* didn't plant them?"

He doesn't bother to blink this time. Instead, all I get is a gray-eyed stare that could turn a lesser woman to ice. Unfortunately for him, I'm no lesser woman. If I could be turned away by something as trifling as stony silence, I wouldn't have a job.

"Xavier," I say with a sigh. I should have known. After that haphazard stunt in my room last night, angrily flapping birds are the next logical step. Sophisticated, this ghost is not.

"You mean the human alternately known as Xavier," Nicholas counters.

"Cart-o-mancy, cart-a-mancy," I say, adopting the singsong tone people use when discussing the correct pronunciation of tomatoes, potatoes, and other foods I'd give my left kidney for right about now. I find it works just as well for fortune-telling terminology. "Who has a dovecote around here?"

"We do."

"Yes, thank you. I noticed it in the, ah, garden. Who has an *active* dovecote around here?"

"We do," he repeats, more firmly this time.

"Um." I examine him closely, looking for evidence that he might be lying or trying to lead me astray. I'm starting to feel that both of these things are a distinct possibility, even though he's the one who asked me to come out here. A man who would hire a medium knowing she's a fake as a means to eliminate a ghost he also knows is fake isn't a man who's at peace in his soul. That's a fact.

Not to mention, there's that whole primogeniture thing Rachel mentioned earlier. If what she said is true, then the only thing that stands between Nicholas Hartford III and this gorgeous, decaying castle is a vivacious older woman who's partial to athletic clothing and terrible food. I'm not sure how Xavier fits into the picture yet, but I don't doubt he's in there some-where. Maybe Nicholas wants me to lend credence to the idea that his mother is unfit to make sound business decisions? Per-haps I'm being used as a means to convince her to hand over the reins?

No answers are immediately forthcoming, and if I'd hoped to find anything in that stern, handsome face, I'm bound for disappointment. Nicholas doesn't even bear the heavy look of bemusement anymore. He's back on solid ground and clearly enjoying his position there.

"I didn't get to examine the dovecote as closely as I wanted, but it seemed pretty empty when I visited earlier today," I say in my defense. "Someone must have extracted the birds before I got there."

"The question is, who?" he asks.

Thomas. He was there, ready with the rake to save me. He was there, smelling of earthy things and outdoor pursuits. He was also keen on pulling me away from the garden and distract-ing me with secret smuggling tunnels.

But I don't say anything. Not yet. Like any good investiga-tor—paranormal or otherwise—I don't intend to start making accusations until I have proof. Or, at the very least, a motive. Other than full access to the pantry and the right to restock it at will, I can't imagine what Thomas would have to gain from running the family out of the home with a fake specter.

"I see it's begun already," Nicholas says after only a brief pause.

"What's begun?" I ask, wary.

"The suspicions. The secrets. I'm not going to lie—I've been looking forward to this part." He pushes himself off the wall, hands deep in his pockets. "But since neither Rachel nor Fern has ever handled livestock with anything but a fork, and I can't see Cal running after live fowl, I'm guessing the person we're tacitly avoiding accusing is Thomas. Either that, or it's me."

I open my mouth to protest, but he interrupts with a mild "I have an alibi, if it helps. I was in London on business for most of the day."

Ah, yes. The educational materials. "I thought you liked Cal for the ghost. Does this mean Thomas falls under your suspicions now?"

"Until these antics stop and we can all get back to our regularly scheduled lives, I suspect everyone." He grows silent for a moment before adding, "Except *you*, of course."

I don't care for the way he says that, as if I, too, am on his list of potential saboteurs. So far, I've done nothing but what he asked—and, given how little I have to go on, I think I've done it rather well.

I'm about to say as much aloud, but he forestalls that, too.

"Good night, Eleanor, and thank you for a most intriguing day," he says and begins to saunter away. "I'm curious to see what the morrow will bring."

Despite myself, I nod at his retreating back. Given everything that's happened so far, I'm rather curious on that subject myself.

Chapter 10

⊸⦦⦧⊸

"*How* much are these people paying you, again?"

I don't care for Liam's tone, which falls on the wary side of disdain. "You're the one who's always accusing me of robbing people. I thought you'd be pleased that I'm actually earning my fee for once."

"I just don't understand, that's all," he says. "Why doesn't this Nicholas guy hire a private investigator like a normal person? Or, even better, kick everyone out of his house and go on his merry way?"

"Technically, it's not his house." I pause. "Yet."

"That still doesn't explain the private investigator part."

I sigh and switch the phone to my other ear. I need my hands free to continue setting up separate trip wires over the window, door, and fireplace in my room. Each one is attached to an independent alarm that will get sent to my phone in the event of unauthorized entry. Anyone coming in through one of those portals tonight will find that I'm not so easily scared off.

Anyone coming in through a different, *secret* entry point is okay with me, too. That will only confirm my belief that there's a passage leading somewhere into this room. I suspect there might be some kind of crawlspace under the bed, but I can't move the massive thing by myself. I tried, but it looks to be Elizabethan and weighs about two tons.

"He doesn't want his family to know they're being investigated," I explain.

"They know *you're* there investigating."

"Yes, but I'm looking for a ghost, not a person."

"There's no such thing as ghosts."

"Yes, but they don't know that."

"They—" he begins again before cutting himself off with a muttered curse. "Never mind. I don't know why I bother."

"I don't, either." I finish setting up my alarm system and step back to admire it. The wires are made of high-tensile steel so thin you can barely see it with the naked eye. Once I flip the lights out for the night, no one will be able to tell they're there. "And it's not nearly as bad as you're making it out to be. I'll admit, this job's a bit trickier than my usual work, since I can't purge the ghost until I find out who it is, but I like it. It's fun."

Liam's voice is incredulous. "Nocturnal visits from strangers and birds pouring out of chimneys is fun?"

"No one got hurt."

"So far." He pauses again. "Did you finish booby-trapping your room?"

I try one last time to shimmy underneath the bed, the phone still tucked under my ear, but there's barely enough room there for dust bunnies, let alone a human woman. "Yep," I say and give up. If I can't get under the bed, then I think it's safe to assume no one else is sneaking in that way. "I'm snug and secure in here now. There will be no strange ghosts—or men—molesting me in my sleep."

A sigh that sounds about a thousand years old hits my ear. "I don't like it. I looked a little into this Nicholas Hartford guy—did I tell you that?"

"Nooo." I don't want to ask, want even less to give my brother a chance to show off, but anything that might be pertinent to my ghost search seems worth looking into. "What did you find?"

"He's a gazillionaire. Like, a legitimate Scrooge McDuck, rolling around in his pit of money."

"There are no pits of money around here. I checked."

Despite himself, Liam snorts a laugh. "I mean it, Ellie. By all accounts, he's a pretty big deal. He runs like three textbook companies and also sells lab equipment to private schools."

"Everyone has to make a living," I say.

"To the tune of ten million a year?"

"Some of us live better than others."

Liam sighs. "Just be careful, is all I'm saying. People can do terrible things when that kind of money is on the line."

But that kind of money isn't on the line, I want to say. Nothing about the Hartford ghost has been the least bit malevolent. No one's life has been put at risk; no one is making threats. If I had to make a firm guess right now, I'd say this house is being haunted by a bored, unhappy teenager—Nicholas's concerns about Cal and Thomas notwithstanding.

"I promise to leave the moment I feel I can't handle things," I say. "Though you could do me a favor and use those Google-fu skills to discover anything you can about a real estate developer named Cal Whitkin."

"What am I, your personal assistant?" Liam grumbles, but I know he'll be good for it. "Why? What's the matter with him?"

"Poor volume control and terrible taste in clothing," I instantly reply. On a more sober note, I add, "Nicholas also seems to think his real estate plans might include the acquisition of the Hartford family lands—at a discounted ghost rate, of course."

Liam's low whistle says it all. "Are you sure you want to get caught in the middle of that?"

Even though he can't see me, I shrug. "From what I've found so far, I'm almost certain I'm dealing with a typical domestic squabble. You know how families can be."

Liam falls silent. Although I'd hesitate to call it a sixth sense, I know, without the need for speech, what he's thinking. For Liam, any mention of a *typical family* is a reminder that those ordinary arguments and cheerful disagreements are something we'll never have.

See, for me, Winnie never really went away. Like a phantom limb, I can feel that she's still a part of me. Of *us*—of Winifred and William and Eleanor, siblings united by blood and bone, separated by something much less tangible than that. But for Liam, the loss has always been final. Unlike me, he can't stomach the murky in-between where life and death intersect.

I'm the only one who likes it here, who *thrives* here.

"I know I don't say it very often, but I'm proud of you, Ellie," Liam says. He sounds so serious, so solemn, that a shiver runs down my spine. In the burst of melancholy that follows, I'd almost say the house shudders with me.

"No, you're not. You think I'm one step above a con artist."

"Um, I think you're exactly on par with a con artist." He hesitates. "But you take good care of her. I appreciate that more than you know."

"Well, it's only fair, since you take good care of me," I reply somewhat mistily. Then, because I can't bear to end on such a somber note, I add, "Which is why I'm taking you with me to Mexico when this is over even if I have to drug you and stuff you in my suitcase to do it."

Chapter 11

My late-night visitor is much quieter the second time around.

I'm not sure what causes me to awaken—if Xavier makes a sound or nudges my sleeping form, or even if my own unease after Liam's phone call causes me a more restless night than I'm used to—but my eyes pop open while the moon is still high enough to cast luminous rays through the gap in the curtains.

My first thought is that the flittering, filtered light is beautiful in an otherworldly way—the kind of moonlit darkness that can only exist miles away from a large city. My second thought is that it would be a lot prettier if there weren't a man standing at the foot of my bed, watching me sleep.

"Nicholas?" I bolt upright and jump to my feet, taking the sheet with me. It's a maidenly gesture—and one that's not in the least necessary, since I'm wearing shorts and a T-shirt—but there's something about strange gentlemen sneaking over floorboards at night that calls for a little Victorian flair.

It's not Nicholas, though—or, if it is, he doesn't intend to answer to his name. With a start of surprise, the man steps to the other side of the bed and disappears.

There's no flash paper this time, no moaning sounds or the hurried footsteps of the entire family coming to my aid. Just a brief moment, a shadowy figure, and then nothing but the ringing silence of my solitude.

"Where did he go?" I turn and reach for my space-age lamp, yanking the cord and scattering illumination to all corners of the room. There's no sign of anyone, shadowy or otherwise, as I whirl in a full three-hundred-and-sixty-degree rotation. The next logical step is to check the window to determine if the man is hiding behind the floor-length curtains.

He's not, and in the process of investigating, I set off my own tripwire.

The window alarm is set as pigeon sounds, since it seemed the most apt at the time. Almost instantly, the sounds of coos and clucks fill the air. It's followed soon thereafter with my own muttered curses.

"Clumsy, foolish, where's the stupid off button for this thing?" I demand. The first two I have no excuse for, but I eventually find the alarm button on my phone and press it. Once again, the room plunges into silence. I'm prepared for it this time, and I hold my breath, hoping to hear retreating footsteps or the muffled thumps of someone hiding in the wardrobe.

Nothing.

Sound alone isn't enough to convince me that my guest has departed, so I follow through by checking inside, underneath, and around every piece of furniture in the place. It's a dusty search and a fruitless one.

Still nothing.

Once again, I'm entirely alone in the room, left with nothing but what appears to be an overactive imagination and the half-fog of sleep. Instinct urges me to put up another hue and cry to see who comes running—and the direction from whence they come—but I notice a scrap of paper peeking out of one of the weathered floorboards and stop.

I inspected the floorboards during my initial poke-fest of the room, even going so far as to test each edge to see if I could lift them. It seems excessive, I know, but I once found a hold containing a family's hidden cache of heirlooms this way. They'd been missing for months and presumed to be the work of a ghost's kleptomaniacal leanings. In reality, the credit for its loss went to the woman of the house, who showed a marked tendency to overdo it on the Vicodin and vodka and who, when under the influence of this dangerous cocktail, gave in to her hoarding tendencies. I also found a wallet in the deep freezer and several sheets of collector's stamps behind a family portrait.

This slip of paper pulls out easily, secured along one edge by a brittle, yellowing piece of tape, and it reveals no such hiding place underneath. I try to leverage the board up with my fingernails and even a pocket screwdriver I carry in my bag, but it doesn't budge. The hole, if it can be called such, is just the natural gap between boards of wood.

And Xavier was trying to secretly extract the paper from it? I wonder. The timing doesn't feel right, as he's had ample opportunity to take it out of this room without fear of being caught. Besides, his activities weren't that of a sneaking, slinking intruder. He'd just been standing there, creepily staring at me.

Since it seems the most obvious course of action, I unfold the paper and scan it. From the soft, feathery texture and the heavy creases, I'm assuming it's old. The handwriting is old, too, slanted and flowery in a way that few people bother with in this day and age.

> *The Dead walk at Night.*
> *The Spirits ever fight.*
> *Those who Betray will step into the Light.*

I turn the paper over, wondering if there's any other relevant information to be found, but there's nothing. No address, no date, no names—definitely not a lock of hair I might be able to send in as DNA evidence. Just a bizarre misuse of capital letters and a feeling that someone is setting me up to be duped.

"Oh, come on," I say and give the edge of the paper a healthy lick. As I expect, it tastes like tea. Earl Grey tea, to be exact, eerily similar to the cup offered me by Nicholas yesterday morning. It's the oldest trick in the book, aging paper with tea.

Not to mention, whoever affixed it to the edge of the floorboard—no matter how old they made the tape look with dirt and a heat gun—failed to take into account the fact that Scotch tape wasn't invented until the twentieth century.

Honestly, it's as if Xavier isn't even trying at this point. I'd call him the biggest hack known to man- and ghost-kind—except for the fact that he managed to get both in and out of this room without my knowing it. That makes at least one mystery worth figuring out.

And *figuring it out* is exactly what I intend to do.

Since I'm no stranger to prowling dark corridors in the dead of night, I decide to take advantage of my rudely awakened state. Of course, I have to get dressed first, since it won't do to get caught snooping in my street clothes.

Ellie Wilde, peering around corners in a T-shirt and yawning into her fist, is nothing more than a bad houseguest. But Madame Eleanor Wilde? Sleepwalking in a trancelike state, clad in a floating white nightgown with her dark hair streaming behind her?

That, my friends, is exactly what these people are paying for.

My transformation takes no less than half an hour to accomplish. By the time I'm appropriately attired and my hair has the texture to make it look as though I recently climbed out of a well, the moon has slipped behind a cloud.

I couldn't have staged it better if I tried. Darkness envelops every inch of the castle, making the shocking white of the vintage nightgown I'm wearing stand out like a ghostly beacon. It's never my primary goal to run into anyone else while running a nocturnal investigation of this sort, but it can happen. And in this instance, I halfway hope it does.

If *someone* thinks I dropped the ball by not making it to the pigeons before Xavier did, then he'll have much to be sorry for. Especially if he's the one who was hovering over the foot of my bed and planting fake notes in the floorboards.

I click open my door as quietly as I can, but any sound seems loud in the quiet tomb of the castle. The silence has the benefit of heightening my other senses, but it's still difficult to see around me—mostly because the only light I've brought with me is a single lit taper.

The candle isn't, as it first appears, for aesthetics. While the picture it makes is spooky enough to appease the most exacting of haunted house connoisseurs, the flame has the additional benefit of catching every draft that whistles down the empty hall. Somewhere in this godforsaken wing, there's a secret doorway that leads to my room. Since I doubt that door is hermetically sealed, it will create a draft where there should be none.

With this in mind, I begin a slow shuffle back toward the far end of the hall, where the rest of the family is sleeping. I pause at every painting, every fixture, every inch of molding—if it could feasibly be pulled aside to reveal a portal, I refuse to leave it unchecked. As a result, my progress is necessarily slow. A good fifteen minutes of steady, unwavering flame-bearing passes before I reach the area outside Nicholas's door. I pause at the threshold, my ears alert for any sounds of movement within. Nothing but the gentle crackle of my candle reaches my ears.

Well, if he's in there, he's not a snorer, I'll give him that much. Tempting as it is to try my hand on the brass doorknob and examine his room, I dare not risk it. I might be able to convince Vivian or Cal that my nocturnal wanderings are done on a subconscious level, but Nicholas would never buy it.

I turn on my heel and lift the candle, prepared to resume my search. At first, I think that the shadow cast on the opposite wall is a trick of the light. It's not at all what I expect it to be—flat and oblong and like, well, a normal shadow. Instead, the light is broken off in several directions, glints of it like shards of glass. With a gasp, I realize that *shards of glass* are exactly what I'm looking at. A broken mirror, to be exact, smashed to pieces and hanging askew on the wall.

Broken mirrors are a great way to spook a family—people who believe in ghosts also tend to believe in superstitions like seven years of bad luck—but I didn't touch this one. Unless, of course, you count the fact that one of my pinhole cameras had been installed directly above it.

"Oh, no," I say, a moan caught in the back of my throat. I run my fingers over the now-familiar artichoke wallpaper, not stopping until I hit the snag in the plaster that had once housed my thousand-dollar pinhole spy camera.

It's gone.

I whirl, holding my candle aloft, but there's nothing to see but empty hallway in either direction. Mindful of the effects of broken glass on bare feet, I make a beeline for the other locations where I planted hidden surveillance devices.

They're not there. In each spot where I installed a camera, there's nothing left but crumbling plaster, ripped wallpaper, and a hole where my equipment should be. With each new discovery, my mental calculator goes higher and my heart sinks lower—especially once I take my investigation downstairs to the main floor.

The tape recorder in the parlor? Smashed to pieces.

The camera at the front door? Crunched under foot.

Even my useless black pentagram boxes have been smashed open and laid to ruins, splinters of black-stained wood scattered all over the cavernous foyer.

"No, no, no, no, no," I say, sinking to my knees. It's melodramatic, I know, but this is one time the situation really calls for it. That's ten thousand dollars' worth of damage to my equipment, at the very least, and it's not as if I have any of it insured. There's not a big business for covering high-end spy gear. Insurance companies tend to want to know *why* you're outfitted like James Bond getting ready to take over a safehouse—and the answer is rarely what they want to hear. Which means I'm looking at years of my savings, months of Winnie's care. Gone, just like that.

Snuffed like this candle. Or a human life.

"The kitchen," I announce to the empty room, my voice echoing over marble and stone. For the first time, I don't delight in the atmosphere of it. Maybe whoever did this forgot to get the one I installed down by the back stairs.

It's the only hope I have of finding any information about the perpetrator of this particular crime, so I lose no time in heading toward the dining room. There's no light to speak of, but my rage provides an inner glow that moves my steps along. If it weren't bad enough having a fake ghost creep into my bedroom at night, now it's destroying my personal property, too. Nicholas never said anything about *that* in the job description.

"He'll have to reimburse me for every penny," I mutter, my words echoing hollowly off the walls. I yank open the door and start descending the staircase. "Plus damages. Substantial emotional damages."

I'm so caught up in my plans of vengeance—I'll create a real ghost, destroy the castle's value from the ground up, leave a bad Yelp review about the village museum like you wouldn't believe—that I don't notice the broken step until my bare toe hits it. Since I've been moving at an angry, stomping pace, it catches me at full speed. The slice of a splinter stabbing under my toenail is second only to the feeling of weightlessness as my knees buckle and I go flying the rest of the way down the coarse wooden steps.

So this is what it's like to die, I think, right before the world comes crashing down around me.

Okay, so I suppose it's more accurate to say that I come crashing down to the world, but the idea is the same. There's gravity and there's pain in equal proportions.

There's also something at the bottom of the steps to break my fall. At first, I'm unsure what it is—a large, knobby bulk, both hard and soft at the same time. And warm, but that could just be my own body's reaction to realizing what the object is.

Not what, Ellie. Who.

It's the same voice from before, the one that called me silly and told me the house was shivering in anticipation of my arrival. As before, my instinct is to push that voice away, to refuse to yield to the idea that this world is made of anything but hard, callous facts.

But I don't.

Maybe Nicholas was right about that. Maybe I do still believe in magic and miracles. A bizarre thing to realize when I'm lying on top of a dead body, but then, I've always walked a little on the dark side.

I jolt to my feet, my movements jerky as I push myself as far from the body as possible. It's impossible to tear my gaze away, though. As the voice suggests, I have no idea who it is—he's a stranger in an even stranger place—but there's no mistaking the odd twist to his neck or the way his blank eyes glaze upward.

"Xavier?" I ask, my voice coming out thin.

I don't know if I expect an answer or not, but I don't get one. Not a voice, not a laugh, not even a whisper of a breeze tunneling down the kitchen stairs. I'm alone with a dead man. For some reason, I find that worse than the idea of sharing the space with an unknown entity from beyond the grave.

Despite the lack of breeze, I shiver. I also turn on my heel and, throbbing toe notwithstanding, flee back up the stairs to find someone—anyone—who can help me.

Chapter 12

One of the nice things about working in the realm of paranormal fantasy is that nothing can scare me. All mysteries have a reasonable explanation; all ghosts can be subdued with common sense. There's nothing in this world—or the next—that can rattle me.

Or so I thought.

"But he was just here!" I cry, staring at the spot where the body had lain less than fifteen minutes ago. In place of the crumpled form of a complete stranger, there's nothing but empty flagstone. "For the sake of everything that's good and holy, this is exactly where I found him. He broke my fall."

Cal makes a show of searching the immediate area for the body, as if it were a mislaid earring rather than an entire human being.

"The sake of everything good and holy?" Nicholas asks, watching me. "Are you certain you should be taking such liberties?"

I turn to glare at my host, but it's difficult to stare down a man who's wearing monogrammed silk pajamas. "Laugh all you want, but I'm telling you, there was a body here." I stab my finger at the step above Nicholas's head. "He must have tripped on the broken stair on his way down. He broke his neck. I *saw* it."

"You saw him break his neck?" Cal asks and begins his search anew. When he once again comes up empty, he says, "Are you sure he didn't just . . . sprain it?"

Nicholas's mouth twitches, but I don't find much to be amused at about this situation. Both of them had been sound asleep when I'd gone upstairs to summon assistance of the strong, male variety. No one had been up making secret breakfast meat, and no one had seemed alarmed when I told them what I'd found.

"Couldn't you have found a body *after* three o'clock in the morning?" Nicholas had asked with one bleary eye on the clock. It had been a short-lived bleariness, though. For all his languid annoyance, he'd gotten up and joined me in the hallway after only a brief pause.

Cal's room had been my second stop, and a much lengthier one it was, too. He hadn't wanted to disturb the huddled, sleeping Fern next to him, so we'd been asked to wait in the hall while he got dressed, located his phone, donned his favorite slippers, and finally emerged to join us.

"After all," he'd said with a hearty laugh, "it's not as though the poor guy's going anywhere, is it?"

This was the result. An empty space where the body had been, a fake medium growing more overwrought by the minute.

"Of course I didn't see him fall. By the time I got here, he was already dead." I shove my foot out as if to prove it. My big toe feels swollen and throbbing, even though the wound is only visible as a slight puncture under the toenail. "I hit the broken stair. I came tumbling down. I would have probably broken my neck, too, but . . ."

"He saved you." Nicholas's flat tone gives nothing away.

"He saved me," I agree.

"And then he disappeared. Vanished into thin air. Like a, er, wayward spirit, perhaps?"

I could scream in frustration, though I'm not sure who would be the intended recipient. These two blockheads aren't helping matters any, but I can hardly blame them for not taking me seriously. After all, I've spent most of my adult life spinning wild fantasies about death and the afterlife. I'm literally the woman who cried ghost.

"What about all my equipment?" I ask, almost desperate. "And the stair?"

"Xavier," Cal says with a cluck of his tongue and a shake of his head, his jowls wagging. "Always up to something. D'you think I should take Fern to stay in a hotel for a few days? She's not up to this kind of emotional upset—fragile, that's what she is."

Nicholas must sense that I'm nearing the brink of my patience, because he asks Cal to go upstairs and inform the rest of the household that the dead body has turned out to be nothing more than the hysterical ravings of an overpriced medium.

"I'll tell them you were sleepwalking," Cal says in a kind voice. He pats me awkwardly on the shoulder, and I notice there's a bandage on his thumb that I could have sworn wasn't there last night.

An injury incurred while smashing electronics, perhaps? Pulling up broken stairs? *Pushing strange men down them?*

He sees my look of interest and quickly pulls his hand away. "One of those blasted birds pecked me," he says. "Fern thinks I should get a tetanus shot."

"But—" I begin, about to point out that the birds had gone nowhere near him.

Nicholas doesn't let me finish. "But tetanus shots are for rusty nails, not animals. We'll have the doctor out to take a look at you." He casts an obvious glance down at my toe. "You and Madame Eleanor both."

"No need," Cal blusters as he backs away.

"Don't be ridiculous," I say at the same time.

Nicholas just laughs. "I thought as much."

His diversionary tactic works, however, and Cal makes his escape. Nicholas waits only until the other man's heavy tread leaves the top step before turning to me with one quizzically raised brow.

I don't need him to voice his question aloud.

"This isn't part of any kind of mystical plan," I protest and hold my hands up as if to ward him off. "I woke up and found all my stuff smashed. I came down the stairs in the dark. I tripped on the broken step. I landed on a body. A *dead* body, Nicholas. I'm as sure of that as a person can be. He was still warm and . . ."

I want to tell him about the voice—about how it spoke to me, laughed at me. But, of course, I don't. I'm trying to make myself *more* credible in his eyes, not less.

Unsurprisingly, my plea doesn't work. That same brow remains raised, Nicholas's pose casual in a way that seems one hundred percent fabricated.

"I swear it on my sister's life" is all I say.

There's no way of knowing whether or not he believes me. I've only been acquainted with this man for a few days, so he doesn't realize what it means for me to invoke my sister in this way. Liam would know, and maybe Peggy from Happy Acres, but that's about it.

And Winnie. Winnie would know.

"Alright," he says before I have a chance to decide whether that voice comes from inside me or from the castle. He nods once. "Let's say I believe you. You woke up and found your equipment broken to pieces and immediately decided to come downstairs. Why?"

My eyes widen in surprise at my own stupidity. "The camera," I say. In all the drama of finding the dead body and rushing upstairs to get help, I'd forgotten the reason I came this way in the first place. "I installed a camera just across here."

Without waiting to see if he follows, I hightail it for the small shelf where I'd placed the last of my devices. It's the best of all my hiding spaces, an inset in the rocky basement wall that I like to imagine once held all manner of herbs hung to dry. Whatever its past incarnation, it's now a catch-all in the manner of kitchens everywhere—rubber bands, an unused glow stick, lonely playing cards with the corners nicked off.

And, of course, my little handheld spy camera. With any luck, it will contain footage of the grisly scene I recently fled.

"I ought to have Thomas clear that junk away," Nicholas says over my shoulder. He's standing much closer than I at first realize, his body warm and substantial in a way I find far too comforting than is good for me—especially since the last warm and substantial body near mine was no longer living. "Well? Do you see it?"

Oh, I see it. I pull the camera out from among the debris, the cracked plastic pieces trailing a frayed black cord.

I can't understand why the sight of that cord makes me want to cry. Of all my broken and missing devices, this camera is the least expensive. It was the first piece of tech I owned, bought before I had any idea what I was getting myself into, a down payment on a lifestyle it's too late to quit now.

But there it is, a bubble of anguish in my throat, a prick of tears not far behind.

"So much for that idea," I say, dashing a furtive hand against my eyes. "Whoever killed that man was sure not to leave any trace behind. Look at the lengths he went to—he even took the body."

Nicholas takes the broken camera from me and folds it in a

handkerchief extracted from the pocket of his pajamas. I'm not sure what to make of that—either the gesture or the fact that this man sleeps with handkerchiefs within reach—but his voice is kind. "It can't have gone far. You left for—what? Ten minutes? Fifteen? Where did he go? How far can a body be moved in that amount of time?"

"Half a mile?" I guess. "How should I know? I've never moved a body before. He wasn't very big."

To Nicholas's credit, he begins making an earnest assessment of the area. From the start, his search is more useful than Cal's; he actually gauges the distance from the bottom of the stairs to the kitchen, and then from the kitchen to the servant's entrance leading outside. Following his logic—that a body moved from its spot would most likely be dragged out the nearest door, I follow him. But my look of doubt matches his own when we find the door firmly shut. Opening it doesn't help matters any, as there's a heavy pile of mud on the doorstep that still bears the footprints Thomas and I made coming in yesterday. If anyone—living or dead—exited this way, they had to float to do it.

Now, floating entities aren't as rare as you might expect. There's a lot that can be done with wires, hooks, blasts of air, and the magic of angles—especially when it comes to levitation photos. Give me twenty minutes, a working camera, and a footstool, and I could make any number of bodies float out that back door.

The real deal, however?

"Up the stairs?" I suggest doubtfully. They're too steep and dark and, at the moment, broken to make the idea a reasonable one. A new thought hits me and I groan. "Oh, God. You don't think . . . the oven?"

Nicholas laughs outright. As if to prove how ridiculous I'm being, he systematically opens every cupboard door and pretends to look for a hastily hidden body. By the time he reaches the crisper drawer in the refrigerator, I've just about had enough.

"Yes, yes, it's all very funny to you, but I know what I saw." I know what I landed on, know what I heard. "He has to be around here somewhere."

"Did you check the secret cubby?"

I whirl to find Rachel standing in the doorway, her feet planted in the exact spot where the man had lain less than half an hour ago. A gray woolen blanket is wrapped around her shoulders, and she suppresses a wide yawn, but her eyes sparkle for all her apparent sleepiness.

"Cal told me what happened," she says by way of explanation. "I couldn't resist. Did Xavier really murder someone?"

"No one has been murdered," Nicholas says with a sigh. "Even if there was a body—"

"There *was*," I put in forcefully.

"Even if there was a body," he repeats carefully, "there's no saying his death wasn't an accident. You were careful on the step?"

She nods, still with that excited gleam in her eye. "I'm always careful on that step. Thomas warned me about it ages ago. Xavier likes to pop it up in the middle of the night when no one is around."

"He's done it more than once?" I ask, frowning. That isn't in keeping with the rest of Xavier's antics. I wasn't kidding before when I ascertained that Xavier's manipulations were mostly benign; it's what makes me think Nicholas is right about this being an inside job, that someone in this house is playing tricks on everyone else. Those stairs, however, really are dangerous. Someone could get hurt.

I think of the man's body and gulp. *Someone already did.*

Nicholas seems to share my concern, his brow lowering. "Have you ever seen it up like that before?" he asks.

"Well, no. But you know Xavier mostly leaves me alone."
She shoots me a look of triumph. "He likes me best of all the
family. I'm his favorite."

"You're everyone's favorite, brat," Nicholas says with real
warmth. "Now go back upstairs and mind your own business."

There's that pang again—the almost-jealousy, the feeling that
I'm all alone in this world of my own making. I've been around
a lot of dysfunctional families in my day—including my own—
and this one is proving itself to be just as strangely antagonistic
as the rest of them. Yet I can't help recognizing that there's genuine love here, too.

"Does that mean you've already checked the cubby?" she
asks, ignoring his command. "I used to hide there all the time
when I was a kid. I think there might even be a stack of Nancy
Drews and a flashlight still inside."

"What cubby is this?" I ask.

Rachel turns her wide, blinking violet eyes on me. "The one
under the stairs, of course. They used to keep wine under there,
I think. There are panels all along one wall with racks built in.
It's where I'd hide a body, if I needed to in a pinch."

I expect Nicholas to be laughing again, mocking us for our
romantic flights of fancy, but he's watching Rachel with an intensity that sets my heartbeat skittering. "I thought it was bricked
up years ago," he said. "In fact, I distinctly remember ordering it
to be done."

"You did." Rachel laughs. "But Mum took the money you
gave her for the builders and went shopping in Paris instead.
You ought to know better than to give her cash straightaway."

Nicholas tells Rachel to stay exactly where she is as he
pushes aside a shelf lining one wall of the alcove to the left of
the stairs. Given the sharp turn halfway up the steps, it makes
sense that there would be a crawlspace under there. I hadn't noticed it before since the door is located behind the shelf, which

holds various pots and pans that look as though they don't get much in the way of use.

Secret passages, lost smuggling tunnels, kitchen hidey-holes . . . is there nothing this place doesn't have?

Unfortunately, all of my earlier enthusiasm for intriguing architecture has disappeared. Now that the moment has arrived, I find I'm not too keen on coming face-to-face with the ghastly spectacle of death again.

The body itself wasn't terrible. Landing on top of it isn't going to be my favorite memory of this adventure, but I can't overlook the fact that it saved me from serious injury—possibly even my own death. That the body disappeared isn't catastrophic, either. Like most of the mysteries around this house, I'm sure there's a perfectly logical, scientific explanation behind it.

It was his eyes. That's the thing I can't seem to shake, the picture that moves across my vision every time I blink. Those blank, glazed eyes were so much like Winnie's.

Lost. Gone. Dead.

I decide to stay where I am and keep Rachel company at the foot of the stairs, even though the girl is far more excited than terrified at the prospect of Nicholas's search. We listen, standing still, as the door scratches open and Nicholas steps out of our line of vision.

"Uh, Madame Eleanor?" The formality of my name matches the formality of his tone.

"Yes, Mr. Hartford?" I reply, equally precise.

"Could you perhaps join me for a moment?"

I think of those eyes and wince. "Is it an absolute necessity?"

There's a slight pause. "Yes."

There doesn't seem to be any way around it, especially when Rachel looks at me with something approaching disappointment. Of everyone in the house, I'm the one who's supposed to be most accustomed to death, the one who can confront the cloudy organs of vision without shuddering. I take her hand and give it a reassuring squeeze, as though my concern all along has been *her* well-being, not my own.

"You have nothing to fear. Whoever this man is, I don't sense that his spirit lingers."

"Oh, right," she says, as if the thought of another ghost haunting the house hadn't occurred to her. "I'm sure that will make Mum happy."

Nicholas clears his throat in an obvious and commanding manner, so I pick my way over to where he's hunched, peering into the cubby with his cell phone outstretched in flashlight mode. Even in that position, which would make any other man look at a disadvantage, he seems cool and detached, almost as though he's examining a horse for purchase rather than a dead body.

"Do you recognize him?" I ask.

"Er, no. I doubt even his mother could in this particular state."

"What?" I nudge him out of the way. "He was perfectly intact when I landed on him."

Nicholas lifts an arm to hold me back—a gesture I will forever be grateful for. That hand prevents me from barreling into the dirt-lined hole under the stairs, from thrusting my face inches away from a body in such an advanced state of decay it's practically a skeleton.

"Holy hypnosis," I cry, taking a step back with a hand pressed to my nose. I've spent enough time ousting dead rodents out of walls that the sweet, sickly smell of rotting flesh no longer overpowers me, but nothing could have prepared me for this. "What the devil is that?"

Nicholas turns his head just enough to appraise me. "I thought it was your corpse."

I lift a finger and point. The body—the skeleton—in question is little more than a heap of bones held together with fraying, leathery bands of flesh. "You think I landed on top of that only to brush myself off and go in search of assistance? Are you delusional? My corpse was clean. *New.*"

"Oh, dear," Nicholas says and straightens. "This can't be good."

He closes the door mere seconds before Rachel's head pops around the corner. "What's wrong?" she asks. "Did you find him?"

"Rachel, I need you to go upstairs and call the police. No, don't ask questions, and no, you may not open that door and see for yourself. Tell them they'll need to bring the coroner."

Rachel wrinkles her nose. "Why does it smell so awful?"

"I believe that qualifies as a question" is the polite reply. "And if you happen to see Thomas around, please send him down. We'll need someone to stay here until help arrives to make sure nothing is, ah, moved again."

"I can stay," I offer.

The look Nicholas gives me is long and careful and, frankly, insulting. I'm about to tell him that not only do I *not* lie about finding bodies in stairwells, but I also don't move said bodies around, but Rachel pipes up before I can leap to my own defense.

"Thomas isn't here," she says. "Remember? It's his long weekend. He left after getting rid of the birds last night."

"Blast," Nicholas says, even his curse more of a calm rejoinder than an actual outburst. "I'll have to stay down here myself. Madame Eleanor, do you think you could relay the news without alarming the family any more than is necessary?"

"I don't know." I'm needled to retort in a fake, syrupy voice. "It's such a great opportunity for me to create widespread hysteria and panic."

"Then just do your best," he replies, ignoring my sarcasm. "And try not to touch anything on the way back up the stairs, will you? If you happen upon another body . . ."

Despite the fact that this man is doing everything in his power to goad me beyond my endurance, I can't help asking. "What, Old Nick? How would you suggest I deal with the next one?"

He laughs. "Check to see if its throat is cut. One of these poor bastards had better be Xavier, or we're going to end up being haunted forever."

Chapter 13

"Miss—Ma'am—Madame—I'm going to need you to walk me through it one more time." The policeman sitting opposite me in the parlor makes the command in polite tones, but I can tell it's only a thin façade. He doesn't look at all the way I'd expect a small-town English cop to look, which might account for my strong feelings of antipathy toward him. He's neither tweedy nor bumbling. He's sharp and thin, like a weasel, wearing a bright yellow vest and sucking on his fifth cigarette since he got here. Also, his name is Peter Piper. I cannot and will not respect a man named Inspector Peter Piper.

"I'm not sure what else you want to hear." I push my half-empty cup of tea underneath his cigarette to catch the ashes. "I already told you that I woke in the middle of the night to find all my equipment smashed to pieces. There was one last camera in the kitchen, so I headed down to check."

Inspector Piper uses his ash-covered fingers to flip through his notebook. He stops on a page that looks, to my upside-down view, as if it contains a drawing of a donkey. "Ah, yes. That's what has me in a puzzle. Why did you put a camera in the precise location where the body was later found?"

I don't care for the way he phrases the question—or for the way he's captured the donkey's baleful expression. "Well, I put cameras in several different locations, and that one held particular interest to me."

"Why's that?"

"Why did I place the cameras, or why did I choose that one?"

He waves his hand, casting even more ashes all over a threadbare Aubusson carpet, which I suspect is worth more than both his and my life combined. "Either one."

"Well, I placed the cameras in hopes of catching video surveillance of the entity that's been haunting the castle. And I chose the kitchen because Thomas—that's the man who works for the family—told me about a broken step on those stairs when I first arrived. It was one of the first things I investigated."

"As a ghost hunter." It's not phrased as a question—or, if I'm being honest—with much credulity.

"Yes."

"You must not be a very good one if the ghost managed to pull the step up again without you knowing it."

His words rankle more than I care to admit. "Yes, well. You must not be a very good policeman if you think it's acceptable to fling ashes over an active crime scene."

Inspector Piper is not, as I hope, upset by my attack. He glances around the room, as if he's just now realizing where he is. "I don't see any bodies. Or did you find one in here, too?"

"Of course I didn't find one in here. I don't make it a habit to stumble across corpses, Inspector. Strange though it may seem, these two are my first. I tend not to deal directly with the dead. Usually, I just burn some sage and say a few chants."

"Interesting," he says in a tone that implies he finds it anything but. He then takes a different tack, leaning back in his chair as though he has every intention of making a prolonged stay. "You wouldn't, by any chance, be the witch who told Mrs.

Brennigan to steal the sacramental cup from the church vestibule yesterday, would you?"

It takes me a second to realize what he's asking. The name Mrs. Brennigan doesn't mean much, but *sacramental cup* and *witch* have an all-too-familiar ring. A brindle-headed, accosting-me-in-a-public-museum ring, in fact.

"I believe my exact words were golden chalice," I say, rising to my own defense. "And I didn't tell her to steal it—I only told her to get her hands on one for a situation she needed my help with. Gold is a powerful stimulant for positive energy."

He reaches the end of his cigarette and drops the butt in my teacup. "Do you often direct your clients to procure gold for you?"

Oh, dear. This is exactly why I try to avoid things like taxes and government officials. It's so easy to spin the service I provide into something sinister. Especially if the people I help make it a habit to steal from churches.

"No?" I try.

If the way he doesn't even blink is any indication, he doesn't believe me.

"I'm sure she intended to put it back once her task was done," I say. And then, because it seems as though this whole dead-body-under-the-stairs thing is getting off course, I add, "I don't see what any of this has to do with the man I found."

"Ah, yes." Inspector Piper flips through his notepad once more. "Xavier, I believe the family calls him. The source of your ghost."

"He's not my ghost," I protest. I'm starting to feel terribly misrepresented here. Just how much of this village's problems are to be foisted onto my shoulders? "And I'm not talking about the old bones—I'm talking about the new ones."

He studies his notes as if through a microscope. "I thought you said it was a freshly dead *body*."

"It was."

"But there were bones?"

As screaming my frustration doesn't seem likely to get this interview over any faster, I press the fingernails of one hand into the palm of the other. "I was speaking metaphorically," I say. "I meant, of course, the bones inside the body. The fresh one. The one that broke my fall. I don't suppose you guys have located it yet?"

Inspector Piper gives me a sharp look and snaps his notebook shut. "No. But rest assured you'll be the first to hear if we do."

"That sounds ominous. Is this the part where you tell me not to leave the country?"

"Do you have plans to leave the country?"

"Eventually, yes. It was never my intention to relocate here." I pause. "Do you always answer questions with another question?"

Something like a smile twists the side of his mouth. I say *something* like a smile, because the expression falls short of its goal. I get the impression Inspector Piper isn't a man to drop into regular bursts of hilarity. "Why? Does it make you uncomfortable?"

"A little, yes," I confess and extend a hand—the one with the half-moon impressions left by my fingernails. With any luck, he'll take the hint and move on to interrogate the next witness. "I'm sorry that the woman took a cup from the church, and I'm sorrier still that you don't believe me about the body. But there's nothing illegal about me being a guest of the Hartford family or about accidentally stumbling upon an ancient pile of bones buried under the stairs. If anything, I'm the victim here. My equipment—"

"We're looking into it," he promises. Although he seems reluctant to do so, he takes my hand and shakes it. His skin is dry and papery, almost like the withered flesh of a decades-old corpse. "And, ah, if it's not too much trouble, Miss—Ma'am—

Madame, it would be best for us both if you don't leave the country anytime soon."

"I bet the bones could walk." Rachel sits cross-legged on her bed, her face alight with pleasure at the prospect of skeletons rattling down the halls. Her bed, like mine, is some kind of two-ton brick that looks as though it was built with the original home. "That's how they got in the cubby. Xavier put himself there so we would find him and bury him."

"It's possible," I say, unwilling to curb the young woman's tongue. This is too good of an opportunity to get information out of her to point out that perambulating bones stretch even the bounds of *my* imagination. "It wouldn't be the first time a ghost has called on me to find his mortal remains."

She lifts her pencil from the sketchpad on her lap. "It wouldn't?"

"You made his mustache too big." I indicate the long, drooping bit of facial hair off to one side of her drawing. "Think less Tom Selleck and more Clark Gable."

"Who are they?"

I bite back a sigh. Even though I'm only a decade older than Rachel, it feels as though it could be centuries. Nothing ages a girl quite like medical bills and regular communication with the dead. "American actors. Never mind. Give him a little trim, if you don't mind."

She shrugs and begins erasing her sketch. I don't think her portraiture is good enough to turn her into a professional forensics artist just yet, but there's no denying the girl has skills. She's also willing, which is a big plus. I offered to sit down with a specialist from Inspector Piper's team so they could see if my body matches any recent missing persons reports, but all he did was look at me as though I'd offered him a ride on my broomstick.

"His eyes were closer together than that, too," I suggest,

watching as she tilts her pencil and begins scraping it over the notepad. "And his forehead was smaller."

Rachel keeps sketching. "Well, I don't recognize him, that's for sure. And I know every man under the age of fifty who lives in the county."

"Really?" I lean back in my chair. Although our beds are similar in shape and size, the rest of the furniture couldn't be more different. Rachel's is well-worn, comfortable, and most likely worth a fortune. The club chair I'm currently seated in is upholstered in leather that feels like butter under my derriere. I'm starting to wonder if the uncomfortable guest room furnishings are just another in a long line of treats Mrs. Hartford keeps in store for those unfortunate enough to pay her a lengthy visit. "You must have a very photographic memory."

She frowns, her pencil halted in midair. "No. Just a mother who doesn't like to be alone. She's dated most of them."

Her confession strikes me as both painful and pathetic, and I'm hit with a sudden urge to wrap the poor girl in a hug. Teenagers thrust too soon into adulthood have a way of developing the kind of cynicism most people take a lifetime to perfect.

Trust me. I know.

"Where did she meet Cal?" I ask, as though the question has just occurred to me.

"Cal met her" is the automatic response. "At a dinner party about six months ago. He paid the hostess a thousand pounds to seat him next to my mom—and then he made sure she found out about it before the meal started so she'd be impressed. How gross is that?"

"Revolting," I say, but I can't help being secretly impressed. That kind of move requires a suavity unexpected in a man of Cal's caliber. Nicholas was right about him being no fool, despite the eighties clothes and blustering affectations. "She fell for it?"

Rachel's glowering look is meant, I'm sure, to put me in my place. "Wouldn't you?"

"I don't know," I say with complete and somewhat depressed honesty. "No one has ever tried something like that on me before."

"Me either. It happens to Mum all the time, though. It must be nice, don't you think, to attract men the way she does?"

I reply with an airy and vague "There are many different ways of attracting men."

"You mean love spells?" she asks.

Thinking warily of Mrs. Brennigan and the stolen chalice, I linger over my answer. There's no way I'm heading down that path with Rachel if I can possibly avoid it. If a grown woman will resort to theft—and from a church, of all places—for the sake of romance, how far might a moony-eyed teenager go?

"Among other things," I eventually say. "Money is a type of love spell, when you think about it. It calls and seduces, blinds the unsuspecting to a lover's true intentions."

Rachel's eyes grow wide. "I've never heard it put like that before. You think my mother is under Cal's spell? That he's . . . bewitched her?"

"It's difficult to say." I place a hand to my temple. "The human heart is a mystery, even to the spirits. His intentions *seem* pure, but greed is one of the most powerful forces on earth. There aren't many who can resist it."

"I can," Rachel says with all the vehemence of privileged youth. I'd like to ask her how well she thinks those morals would stand up against hardship—*true* hardship, like watching a loved one slowly waste away—but I don't. She's seen enough of the world's horrors today.

She applies herself to her picture with renewed vigor, asking a few questions about the placement of moles and the size of his ears—neither of which I can help her with, since my look at the corpse was cursory, at best. Within a few minutes, she finishes and holds up the completed sketch for me to inspect.

"There. Does that look like the dead man?"

Provided I cover up the eyes, yes. It's impossible to explain to Rachel that she made the eyes too lifelike—gave the man verve and sparkle and whatever that indefinable something is that makes us who we are.

Erase his humanity, I want to tell her. *Take away his soul.*

"It's perfect," I say instead. "You're sure you've never seen him before?"

She wrinkles her nose and studies her own handiwork. It's not at all in her usual style—those grotesque, twisted figures that line her bedroom walls—but I sense that she's proud of the picture in spite of it. Maybe because of it. It's always nice to know you have access to more than one wheelhouse.

"No. If I squint, he looks a little like my art teacher, but Mr. Corigliano doesn't have a mustache. He says he can't grow one. It comes in all patchy."

A knock at the door draws our attention. Rachel bids the guest to enter, and unsurprisingly, Nicholas's head appears around the side. "Ah. Here you are, Madame Eleanor. I've been looking everywhere for you."

There's a question in that remark, so I do him the favor of answering it. "I'm hiding until Inspector Piper is gone. I don't care for the way he looks at me."

Nicholas's face is perfectly grave. "And what way is that?"

"As if there's nothing he'd like to do more than put me in handcuffs and lock me in a cell for the rest of my life."

"Surely he's not the first person to feel like that."

Alas, he's not. He's probably not even among the first dozen. "Did you tell him my idea about bringing in the cadaver dogs to find my dead man?" I ask.

"Er, yes. Unfortunately, he seems to believe the *other* dead body will only throw them off."

"Huh. I hadn't thought of that. I guess that means scouring for a DNA trail is out, too." I point at the picture in Rachel's hand. "Do you recognize that man?"

In this, as in all things, Nicholas acts in a polite, methodical manner, giving my words a weight that any other man—Inspector Piper included—might feel unnecessary. He takes the sketch from Rachel and studies it for a full thirty seconds before shaking his head. "Not to my recollection. But then, I don't live here full-time, if you'll recall. You'd be better off asking my mother. Or Thomas. He'll be the one most in contact with people passing through."

I'm about to ask when Thomas is expected to return, but Nicholas turns his attention to his niece. "You drew this?"

She nods.

"Impressive. Is your mother still refusing to send you on that art exchange?"

She nods again, this time with a growing scowl. "Cal thinks a cultural education is a waste of time. He says all the value these days is in either real estate or tech."

"Spoken like a true Machiavellian," I say with a sad cluck of my tongue. "But then, that's an ironic title in this situation, isn't it?"

When the Hartfords look a question at me, I explain, "Machiavelli might have been mercenary, but he was also Italian. Even he wouldn't have objected to a semester spent abroad there."

Rachel squeaks loudly and allows her bottom jaw to fall. "How do you know the art exchange I want to go on is in Italy? I never breathed a word. Uncle Nicholas, I never breathed a word."

"I'm sure you didn't. Madame Eleanor has her ways."

It's true. Madame Eleanor has a lot of things, including common sense. An art teacher named Corigliano and a tendency toward the baroque in Rachel's artistic style leave little room for anything else. Besides, I remember a fervent wish to visit Italy when I was of a similarly tender age. It was probably the young drinking age that did it.

"For what it's worth, I think you should go," I say. "You're much too talented not to."

"I agree," Nicholas says, startling both me and Rachel. I doubt that's a duo of words that leaves his lips very often. "When all this is over, remind me to have a word with your mother. I'll gladly cover the cost."

"Oh, Uncle Nicholas—do you mean it?"

"Why not? It's better than keeping you sitting around here, dancing attendance on your grandmother."

He offers the promise with a careless air, but I can see the impact it has on Rachel. She shows every sign of flinging herself at her relative's generosity, so I take the picture out of his hand to avoid its being crushed.

I also make a discreet exit as quickly as possible. Intruding on touching family moments always makes me uneasy. My voyeuristic tendencies end where real human sentiment begins.

Since I assume Nicholas still wants that word with me, I hang out in the hallway for a few minutes, waiting for him to emerge. It's not an ideal place for me to linger; the smashed hole in the plaster is a painful reminder that I'm still out several thousand dollars with this day's work. Someone wanted to make sure I didn't see what was going on inside this house, and they went to extreme lengths to ensure it.

That, or someone killed an innocent man and realized there was audio-visual evidence that could pinpoint them as the murderer. I don't like the underlying message either way. I glance down at the picture in my hand and barely repress a shudder.

"Ah, you waited." Nicholas appears behind me, closing Rachel's door with a quiet snick. "Thank you. Could we have a word?"

"To be honest, I'd like more than just one," I reply.

"You're angry."

Angry is hardly the word I'd choose to describe my current state of being. Bewildered, bemused, be-really-freaking-confused, yes. But angry? How can I be, when I don't know who—or what—to be angry at?

"Yes, well," I say primly, "I'd suggest we go to my room to

talk, but I doubt that's a good idea in the current circumstances."

For a moment, I consider telling him about those exact circumstances. In other words, about my nocturnal visitor and the tea-stained note I have tucked carefully away inside my pocket. It doesn't take a psychic to make a connection between the man standing over my bed and the body at the bottom of the stairs. Even in a house as large as this one, there's a limit to how many people can prowl around in the dark at the same time.

But what that connection is, I daren't hazard a guess. Was the dead man in my room? Was the murderer? *Was Nicholas?*

I fight a shudder as the possibilities start hurling themselves at me. The only things I know for sure are that someone died in this house last night, someone else died under the stairs years ago, and the police have asked me not to leave the country until at least one of those mysteries is solved.

I'm not taking any chances.

"Afraid for your virtue, Madame Eleanor?" Nicholas asks.

"No," I reply somewhat tartly. It's not my virtue I'm worried about so much as my life. "I'm afraid of eavesdropping. I still haven't figured out how Xavier got in and out of there without any of us seeing him."

"I wonder, is there anything about Xavier that you *have* figured out yet?"

Even though his question is asked with heavy irony, I have to pause and think about it for a moment, which goes to show what a disaster this ghost-hunting trip has been so far. Usually, I not only have the cause pinpointed by now, but I've developed a firm plan of action for ousting the ghost and breaking as many bottles of wine as possible. To shatter my Châteauneuf du Pape at this particular cleansing would only be to contaminate a crime scene.

"Well, I know he hasn't appeared at all today," I say. "At least, not since—"

"—the mysterious mortal remains under the stairs were removed? Yes, I know."

"I was going to say, since I found a dead man and the place has been crawling with cops, but yours sounds good too." I peer up and down the hall. For the moment, it's empty, but I don't like how exposed we are. "Seriously—could we go somewhere private?"

His brow lifts. "You know something."

"I know lots of things, but that isn't the point. Shall we go for a walk?"

I don't wait for an answer, since a walk is exactly what I need right now. Crisp, clean air. Distance from this house. I've never been much of a one for extolling the virtues of exercise, but the flight part of my fight-or-flight responses appears to be getting the better of me.

In this, Nicholas humors me once again, following me down the stairs and out through the foyer, since the kitchen is still closed off to the family. The sound of voices and scuffling from below indicate the police are still hard at work gathering evidence.

At least, that's what I assume they're doing. For all I know, they could merely be discussing how best to put the blame on the conniving American spiritualist in their midst.

"Is this far enough from the house that the spirits can't overhear, or do we need to keep going?" he asks after we make it past the flashy red car—which, alas, I've discovered belongs to Cal rather than Nicholas. "I doubt Xavier's range is all that great."

"Let's keep going," I suggest. There are too many outbuildings and hiding places around here to make me very comfortable.

Nicholas hesitates but doesn't question me, even going so far as to offer me an arm as we head onto a well-beaten, rocky path heading south toward Thomas's smuggling cliffs. Once again,

I'm surprised at the strength of that arm—the latent power of it. It's a good reminder that I'm completely at this family's mercy out here. Because, honestly, what do I know of them? Their current predicament, certainly, but nothing of their morals, their history. For all I know, they regularly kill people and hide their bodies under the stairs. I could be next.

I make a mental note to check in with Liam before I go to bed tonight.

"The family holdings extend to those hills just over there," Nicholas says by way of conversation. "We used to own most of the county, but bits and pieces have been sold off throughout the centuries."

I glance in the direction he indicates. Farming has never been something I have much interest in—or knowledge of—but the bleak, barren rocks don't look to me to support anything but moss cultivation.

"What's the land used for?" I ask.

"Dairy farming, once upon a time. Nowadays its sole use is keeping neighbors from creeping too close."

I swivel my head to peer up at him. "You mean you don't make money from this place?"

His laugh is short, almost a breath. "No. The Hartfords haven't made income from this estate since the First World War."

I think about what Rachel told me, how Nicholas divides his time between business and running the castle. But how much running could a castle possibly take if all it supports is a crusty old dovecote and a garden that's more mud than vegetation? And more importantly, who pays for it?

As if reading my mind, Nicholas says, "This place is a money pit. Has been for decades."

"Then why do you keep it?"

He inclines his head. "It's *our* money pit. Did you pass the cemetery when you arrived that first day?"

I recall the moss-covered stones that filled me with such excited anticipation in the taxi and nod. "It's yours?"

"My grandfather is buried there. My father." He pauses but doesn't look down at me, his gaze fixed on something in the distance. I glance, but anything he sees on that horizon is purely metaphorical. "I could no more sell that cemetery than I could my own limbs. *You* know what I mean."

Oddly enough, I do. Family bonds are a strange and powerful thing.

I don't know how Nicholas manages it, but when I look back at him, he appears just as much at home out here among the rocky landscape and barren trees as he does inside his stately home. You would think that a man as neatly starched and ironed as this one would only be at ease indoors and among velvet hangings, but he looks very much the lord of the manor as he takes long-legged strides over his land.

His useless land. His useless, money-sucking land. His useless, money-sucking land that everyone in this family is obsessed with in some form or another.

On that thought, I stop. The house is far enough away that I don't fear anyone overhearing us, but close enough that someone will come running if I scream. Or so I hope.

"This is good," I say and detangle my arm from his. "Now. I need you to tell me what you want."

A look of placid amusement crosses Nicholas's face, the beginnings of a smile at the edge of his lips. "We didn't have to come all the way out here for that. I generally prefer to conduct that kind of—shall we say, conversation?—indoors."

"About *Xavier*."

"What about him?"

I can't decide if he's being purposefully obtuse or not. "As I said in the house, Xavier hasn't been active all day. I'm guessing the presence of the police has spooked him—if you'll pardon the pun—into temporary quiet."

Nicholas feigns thoughtfulness. I call it feigned because he tilts his head to one side and places a finger carefully on his chin. No one makes gestures like that in real life. "Either that, or Thomas's absence is telling us something very obvious," he suggests.

I start. In my mind, Thomas's absence indicates his innocence rather than his duplicity. If he left late last night, as Rachel said, then he couldn't have had anything to do with the dead man. In fact, he's the only person with an actual alibi.

"You're missing the point," I say.

"Which is?"

"That Xavier isn't going to do anything while the place is buzzing with police. There are too many eyes and too much at stake. And when the cops do finally leave, he might use the bones being removed as an excuse to disappear."

"Ah. You think that too?"

"Of course," I say. "It's what I'd do if I was in Xavier's place. It's a neat and simple solution to an increasingly messy situation."

"Interesting. I wouldn't have taken you for the neat and simple type."

I suspect there's more insult than compliment in that remark, so I ignore him. "Whoever is pretending to be the ghost is going to be the top police suspect, since he's the only one we know for sure is skulking around in the dead of night." *With the exception of me.* "Regardless of how Xavier is connected to the bones under the stairs—or not—it's too risky for him to keep playing tricks. For good or for bad, I think your ghost just got laid to rest."

"That's rather poor-spirited of him," Nicholas murmurs before flashing me a quick smile. "You'll have to forgive *my* pun this time."

"There's also the small matter of the other body."

"Ah, yes. I imagined we'd get to that eventually."

"I'm not making it up, Nicholas. I *wouldn't*."

He looks me squarely in the eye. For once, his expression isn't veering toward mockery, and it's all the more upsetting because of it. The full force of this man's stare seems a bit like looking at the sun. During an eclipse.

"You asked me to believe you, so I do," he says.

Although it's the response I'm hoping for, the way he phrases it brings me no comfort. He's *choosing* to believe in the existence of the body, as if there's still a question of it lingering in the air. In other words, he's acting on faith.

But I don't believe in faith, and neither does he.

"We have to assume that Xavier destroyed all my equipment and pulled up that stair," I say in as matter-of-fact a voice as I can muster. It's the only way I can think to counteract his uncomfortable conviction about my honesty.

"We do?"

"Which means he probably also killed that man, because I'm ninety-nine percent sure that's how he died."

"Only ninety-nine percent?"

"Which also means that he hid the body while I went to get you and Cal. Which *also* means that Xavier is not only a nuisance, but a killer." I pause, waiting for yet another sarcastic reply. "Well?" I prompt.

"Well, what? Keep going. You were finally starting to make some sense."

I throw a pair of exasperated hands to the sky. "You hired me to come out here and find your ghost," I say. "Not a murderer. No offense, but I'm not equipped for this sort of thing."

A frown passes over his face, almost at the exact moment a cloud crosses over the sun. The day is already heavy and overcast, one of those cold, wet November days that seem ideal for faking ghostly escapades, and the loss of that tiny ray of sunlight does a number on my senses. A shiver works through me, goose bumps breaking out over my arms and causing the hair on the back of my neck to stand up straight.

It's my arrector pili muscles reacting to the chill, nothing more. My body's autonomic response to environmental stimuli.

I *know* this, yet I still can't help feeling the same as when Xavier's voice called to me through the house. Someone is trying to tell me something. Someone is trying to warn me away.

"If what you say is correct—" Nicholas begins, his voice low.

"It is."

"If what you say is correct," he repeats, lower still, "then I don't see how anything has changed. I hired you to help me find Xavier. Now, more than ever, finding Xavier is of paramount importance, wouldn't you say?"

"Well, yes. But—"

"Inspector Piper obviously isn't going to be of help in this regard, and I'm at a loss to explain any of this on my own." In a rare moment of candor, he adds, "You've already figured out that I like Cal for this, but he was upstairs and sound asleep when you stumbled upon the body, so he couldn't have moved it."

I know. He was upstairs. As were Nicholas and Fern, Vivian and Rachel. Only Thomas is unaccounted for, but it's his weekend off.

Or so he wants us to believe.

"Please, Eleanor. Stay." Nicholas gives me another one of those disconcertingly honest looks. "Help me find Xavier. I'm sure the rest will fall into place once we figure that part out."

I don't want to do it. Every instinct I have—mystical or otherwise—is warning me away from this place. I *like* the Hartfords, and I like the money I'm earning even more, but for the first time in my life, I fear I may have stumbled on a mystery that's too big for me alone.

You don't have to do it alone, silly. You have me. I'm on my way.

"Stop it!" I cry, holding my hands over my ears. "Go away."

Not unnaturally, Nicholas assumes I'm talking to him rather than the strange voice that's been plaguing me since my arrival here. "Of course, if you don't think you can—" he begins stiffly.

"Not you," I mutter. "*Him*."

"Him, who?"

I wave a hand toward the castle. "Xavier. The house. I don't know. Don't ask me to explain."

To his credit, he doesn't ask. He also doesn't let me off the hook for his request, looking at me with that same expectant air from before. I have no idea why he has such faith in my abilities, or even why he wants a stranger here during a murder investigation, but I'm not equal to that look of supplication.

I've also been told, albeit in uncertain terms, that England is going to be my home until Inspector Piper decides otherwise. Since I'm hardly in a position to spend several thousand dollars on a hotel when there's a perfectly good—if chilly and slightly murderous—castle to be had, I make up my mind.

"Fine. I'll stay."

At his look of relief, I feel compelled to add, "But if one more body makes a mysterious appearance, I'm leaving on the next flight out of here."

"I'll see to it myself," he promises. "By the by, what are your plans for Rachel's drawing?"

"Get copies made. Post it all over town. Offer a reward for information." I shrug. "Someone must have seen him around the village. How many small, mustachioed men can there be running around a place like this?"

I stop, alarmed, as I realize what I've just said. I don't know about the genetic prevalence of small, mustachioed men in quaint English towns, but I do know that just such a man was described to me in the village museum not two days ago. A man digging around in the Hartford family history, no less.

It can't be a coincidence.

Coincidences can and do happen in this world, and they explain away so much more paranormal phenomenon than people realize, but this isn't one of those cases. Not when there's so much at stake. Not when so many people are hiding something.

I cast a sidelong look up at Nicholas, but his bland expression gives nothing away. Of all the people in this castle, he has the most at stake—an inheritance, in fact. He also knows more about the ghost than he's letting on. He admitted as much from the start.

But I say nothing. I merely allow him to take my arm again and start leading me back toward the castle.

"Make sure you take an extra copy to Inspector Piper," he says with a perfectly calm air, his forearm like stone underneath mine. Or like age-old castle walls. "We wouldn't want to withhold any evidence from the authorities."

"We wouldn't?" I ask, unsure if he's being sincere. I was under the impression his opinion of Inspector Piper matched my own.

"Of course not," he says and smiles down at me. "After all, the last thing we want is for any suspicion to fall on *you*."

Chapter 14

Not even a real psychic could have foreseen the benefits of murder in a place like this.

"This one's from Mrs. Cherrycove." Vivian stomps through the dining room door, the aroma of cheese and potatoes trailing in her tempestuous wake. She slams a ceramic dish down on the sideboard. "The interfering ninny. It took me fifteen minutes and four glasses of sherry to get her out the door again."

"She drank four glasses of sherry in fifteen minutes?" I ask, slightly alarmed. The alarm is only slight because I'm already up out of my seat and piling potatoes dauphinoise onto my plate. I don't know who this Mrs. Cherrycove is, but it looks like she knows her way around a carbohydrate. "I hope she isn't driving."

"She never drives," Vivian replies. She eyes the bulging sideboard with distaste. "She came with Penny Dautry."

"Oooh!" From the other side of the dining room, Rachel sits up, a gleam in her violet eyes. "Did Penny bring her famous chocolate cake? We had it at the old vicar's funeral last year."

"There will be no cake," Vivian says in her most quelling voice.

"I wouldn't have minded a slice or two," Cal says. He pats his stomach. "Or three."

"It does seem a shame for you to make her take it back," Nicholas adds with something like regret.

I'm curious about what kind of cake could move even a man like Nicholas to protest, but we hardly need the dessert at this point. The door knocker has been pounding from the moment we woke up this morning, revealing a succession of inquisitive neighbors laden with food. It's a veritable smorgasbord of condolence casseroles in here, and it isn't even noon yet. I've never seen people eat so much food in such a short period of time.

Well, everyone is eating except for Vivian and Fern. Vivian because she appears to like her neighbors even less than she does houseguests, and Fern because she mostly looks bored. She managed a few bites of salade niçoise about half an hour ago and has been draping herself in various poses over the dining room chairs ever since.

"I don't know what we're doing, sitting around here and accepting mourners like some Victorian family of old," she says, frowning around the table. In direct opposition to our semifunereal atmosphere, she's dressed herself in a white lace pantsuit that's much more elegant than it sounds. She's practically bridal. "We should be packing up and moving as far away from this decrepit place as possible. Who knows how many other people are buried under our feet? There could be thousands of dead bodies lying around here."

Cal's eyes protrude in a moment of alarm. "*Thousands* of dead bodies? No, love. Hardly that."

She waves her hand. "Who would be able to tell, with all the damp and falling bits?"

"I think we'd notice thousands of bodies lying amid the general rubble," Nicholas says dryly.

"It's not rubble," Rachel protests, holding her fork like it's a trident. "It's home."

I keep my mouth shut and let the family wrangle, pausing only to shovel a few more forkfuls of the potato casserole into my mouth. Although I'm not normally one to take a back seat to a promising argument, I'm doing my best not to insert myself any more into the family dynamics than necessary.

Part of it is professional interest, a medium's need to gather information before taking steps to remove a ghost. An even *bigger* part of it is exhaustion. I spent most of last night lying awake in bed, clutching one of the axes from the foyer. I'm not sure whether I was more relieved or disappointed when the sun came up and I'd had no recourse to use it.

No one watched me sleep. No one left me notes. No one tried to murder me. I suppose I should probably consider that a win.

"Well, Madame Eleanor?" Nicholas asks, directing a look of inquiry at me. "What are your plans for the day?"

I plaster a smile on my face and turn to him, determined not to show any of the anxiety I'm feeling. He knows, though. He caught me tiptoeing down the stairs in the early light of dawn to hang the axe back up and has been watching me with a strange light in his eyes ever since.

"I'm going to explore the countryside and gather some herbs," I say with a cheerfulness I'm far from feeling. "Xavier has been awfully quiet since the police removed the bones yesterday, so I'd like to make a summoning draught and see if we can encourage him a little."

"Ooh, a summoning draught?" Rachel turns to me with interest. "What goes in that?"

"It depends on the spell." I scramble to think of which

herbalist-friendly weeds I'm most likely to encounter on the walk over to the village. I'm less interested in draughts and more interested in paying a few visits in town, so the less time I have to spend foraging in the wilderness, the better. "Dandelion roots are good at drawing out spirits. I'll mix it with some mallow and rowan berries to strengthen its energy."

"Berries? Mallow?" Cal scratches his chin doubtfully. "That sounds like a recipe, not a spell. Will we have to eat it?"

"Only if you want to summon Xavier to inhabit your body."

Nicholas covers a laugh with a cough. "I suggest we stick with the food we have for now. At this rate, we'll have enough in the deep freezer to see us through to the end of the month."

"A whole month?" Vivian releases a moan and eyes the sideboard with increased loathing. "That's it. I'm having Thomas take the knocker off the door the second he returns."

At the mention of Thomas, my interest perks. Most of the family is too preoccupied with their own thoughts to notice—Rachel is busy stuffing garlic knots down one sleeve of her sweater, Cal is glancing at his body in contemplation of its being taken over by a wayward spirit, and Fern has taken to examining her nails with interest—but Nicholas watches me with an intensity bordering on the uncomfortable.

"Where are you *really* going, Madame Eleanor?" he asks as he walks me out of the dining room.

"I told you," I reply, my shoulders stiff. "To gather herbs."

"Yes, and I'm sure you'll manage to stuff a few dandelions in your pockets on your way to lend authenticity to your lie, but that's not what I was asking. How did you sleep, by the way? You're looking very refreshed this morning. Murder must agree with you."

I glare at him. I look like I slept with my head under a sink, and he knows it. Even putting in my usual heavy coil of braids was too much to contemplate this morning, so I have my hair pulled back in a ribbon instead, the dark strands falling to my waist like a waterfall.

"If you must know, I was up most of the night in case Xavier stopped by again."

"And did he?"

I speak without thinking. "No, not this time. I wonder . . ."

"Yes?" he prods.

Too late, I realize my error. I'd been about to say that I wonder if the person visiting my room at night was the mustachioed man, meaning that any and all nocturnal wanderings are now at an end. I don't know *why* he would have wanted to scare me away with thumps and fake notes, but it would explain why last night was so quiet.

"I wonder if we've seen the last of him," I say with an attempt at serenity. "I guess we'd better hope my summoning draught works."

"I guess we'd better. But that isn't what you were going to say." Nicholas reaches out and takes one of my long locks between his fingers, twirling it as if in rapt contemplation. No part of him is actually touching me—not my bodily person, anyway—but the gesture feels warm, intimate.

It feels *good.*

"Yes, it is." I jerk away from him—and from that sensation. The path to warm intimacy isn't one I tread with anything but trepidation. Especially where a man as stubbornly mysterious as this one is concerned. "And for the record, I'd like to know how well-rested *you'd* look after an experience like mine. I don't know how many dead bodies you've landed on top of, but it's highly traumatic. It's a wonder I'm able to function at all."

"Of course," he says. "You poor thing. I'm sure your restless night was nothing more than nerves."

"It was," I say and because it seems pertinent, if not entirely truthful, "I wouldn't lie to you, Nicholas."

The flicker of his eyelashes is the only indication he gives that he doesn't believe a word out of my mouth. "I know you wouldn't," he says with the smile that contains only mockery. "After all, if a man can't trust his paid psychic, who can he trust?"

Chapter 15

"Oh, yeah. That's the guy from the other day." The young man from the museum nods over the drawing. "Except his mustache was more—"

"Yes, twirly. I know." Impatience makes my voice terse, so I temper it with, "I tried to get Rachel to trim it back a little, but this was as good as we could manage. Please. It's important. I need you to try very hard to remember anything this man said or did while he was here."

My request appears to fly right over his head. His floppy hair, this time flattened under the weight of his oversized headphones, shifts to reveal one heavily made-up eye. "Rachel?" he asks, his voice sharp.

"Um. Yes?"

"You mean Rachel Hartford? From up at the castle?"

The question is a rhetorical one. From the way his expression changes, transforming him from a caricature of a teenage boy to a living, breathing, hormonal one, it's clear there's only one Rachel in his world. With an intensity bordering on the ridiculous, he studies the picture anew, his hand tracing the line of the man's cheekbones.

"She drew this?" he breathes. "Really?"

I hold back a sigh, once again feeling much older than my twenty-eight years. "She sure did, Lothario."

He looks away from the picture long enough to throw me a puzzled look. "My name's Benji."

I don't bother to explain the reference. His bobbing Adam's apple and starry-eyed rapture are all I need to tell me that anything short of Rachel walking through the door with a box of gold hearts isn't likely to penetrate the lovesick fog of his brain.

Ah, young love. So sweet, so innocent, so . . . easy to manipulate.

"So *you're* Benji," I say with all the air of one pulling a worrisome pebble out of her shoe. "That explains it."

At this, his spine almost approaches a vertical state. "She mentioned me?"

I don't answer, opting instead to tap on the paper, my blood-red fingernail glinting. "She and I are working together to try to discover what we can about this man. I know you said you don't keep any records, but do you recall anything about his visit? The exhibits he looked at? What he found the most interesting?"

Benji, for all his lazy teenage habits, is no fool. "Is Rachel waiting outside? Didn't she want to come in with you?"

"Well, she *did* want to," I say with a casual disregard for the truth, "but she chickened out at the last second."

"Chickened out?"

"Yes. I think she was feeling shy."

A slow, toothy grin moves across his face. "Shy?"

"She said something about needing to pick up a stack of magazines at the newsstand instead. Which is weird, because the Hartfords have several subscriptions delivered."

His grin deepens, and a blush steals across his sharp cheekbones. I should feel terrible for leading him on this way, and a small part of me does, but a larger part doesn't. After all, I'm only doing the exact same thing I do to people every day: give them hope, promise them something more than the banality of the real world.

Hope, for all its false promises, is a powerful motivator. Benji's next words prove it.

"He basically did the same thing as you," he says and points at the stairs. "Came in. Paid his fee. Snooped through the Hartford files. He seemed pretty interested in that fusty old bible."

The one with the missing page. "Oh? Was he?"

"Yeah. It's weird. No one's been down to look at that stuff in months, and then both of you showed up in the same week. What's in there that's so interesting? It's nothing but names and birthdays."

"I like names and birthdays," I say. "Especially when they belong to people I know."

He shrugs, but with a heightened color that indicates he's flipped through the pages on his own search at least once.

"Weird, though, that the page with Rachel's name wasn't in there," I add and wait to see his reaction.

It's everything I hope it will be. His first instinct, to deny having been creeping on an old family bible, is quashed down under a stronger force: curiosity.

"What are you talking about?" he asks. "Of course that page is in there. At least, it was—"

"Yes?" I urge. "When did you last see it?"

"A while ago." His eyes—or eye, rather, since one is still hidden under his flattened hair—doesn't quite meet mine. "I only looked that one time."

We both know his words to be a lie, but neither one of us mentions it. Instead, I lean over the desk the way I imagine Inspector Piper might, should he ever decide to take up an actual investigation.

"*Think*, Benji. Have you been down there since the mustachioed man was here? Can you tell me for sure if you've seen Rachel's page since then?"

"I don't know," he says. "I mean, it's not like I check every day. I'm not . . . weird or anything. I swear."

"But it was there recently? Within the last month?"

"Maybe. Yes." Sweat breaks out on his upper lip. I feel almost cruel, grilling the poor boy, but this is the closest I've come to an actual clue yet. I'm not giving it up so easily. "Yes, within the last month. I was down there dusting and just happened to notice," he adds defensively.

"And can you tell me exactly what was on that page?"

He seems slightly bewildered. "I already said. Names and birthdays. For Rachel and her mum and uncle and stuff."

"Can you remember if there was anyone named Xavier listed on it?"

"No."

"No, you can't remember, or no, there was no mention of that name?"

"No, there was no mention of that name." For the first time, Benji looks at me with an air of suspicion—an air of suspicion I admittedly deserve. From a legal standpoint, there's no reason why he should tell me anything he doesn't want to. "That's kind of a funny name nowadays, isn't it?"

Since there's every chance I'll need Benji's help again, I decide to ease up. "Benji's kind of a funny name, too," I say in a friendly tone that acts as though the past five minutes never happened. "Is it short for something? Benjamin?"

"Yeah." He blinks. "How did you know?"

"A lucky guess." I tug the drawing from under his fingers. "And just so I'm clear—the mustachioed guy didn't do anything else while he was here? He only looked at the bible and left?"

I have the impression Benji would like to keep the drawing with him as a keepsake, but it's my only copy. Technically, I should head straight to Inspector Piper with both it and Benji's confession of having seen the man before, but I'm hesitant to hand it over to someone who takes me as seriously as a hangnail.

"That's it," Benji confirms. "Well, and maybe he glanced at a few other records, but I didn't follow him around the museum. People don't like to be bothered."

People also don't like to be murdered, but look what happens anyway.

"There's one more thing you can help me with," I say, even though Benji didn't offer and my lie about Rachel being too shy to come inside appears to be wearing off. "I'm hoping to find a little more information about the history of the local population. Not just the Hartford family, but everyone. Things that might mention community marriages, births, deaths, that sort of thing."

"Xavier?" Benji guesses.

"Yes, but I'm not sure about the dates when he'd have been alive. It could be a window of several hundred years. I was hoping there might be a way to narrow the search."

"Narrow the search?" he echoes.

"Yes. Do you have anyone on staff who might be able to help me with that?"

He blinks at me and casts a look around the room, as if expecting someone able to answer my questions to pop out of the woodwork. Predictably, we're both disappointed.

"Sorry, lady, but what you're looking for isn't in the village museum."

"It isn't?"

Benji shakes his head and hooks a thumb over his shoulder. "For official parish records like that, there's only one place to go."

My heart begins a slow, sinking descent to the floor. I know the exact place he's talking about, and it's literally the last place I want to go.

"What you need is to visit the church."

* * *

"So, basically, they're all torn between thinking I'm a murderer and thinking I made the body up in the first place," I say into my phone. "I can't decide which is worse. Being a murderer, obviously, but you know what I mean. How can an entire human being disappear like that?"

"Ellie."

My brother's warning tone is impossible to ignore, which is why I rush on. I have a pretty good idea of what comes next—his dire warnings and I-told-you-sos—and my desire to hear them is only slightly less than my desire to visit the local vicar. "And the worst part is that I don't have any of my equipment. Any footage that might have helped me solve this thing is gone, and it's not like they carry replacement parts at the local pub. Which, by the way, is the only thing besides a gas station and a vintage tea shop this place offers by way of entertainment."

"*Ellie.*"

His tone is even harder this time around, so I stop in front of the cute stonework cottage that lies about halfway between Castle Hartford and the village. Unlike the castle, everything about the cottage is neat and tidy and well cared for, with creeping vines artfully outlining each window and lingering crocuses showing off the last of their blooms in the side garden. An *actual* garden instead of just a mud pit.

It's not the village church. Despite Benji's helpful suggestion, I've made Thomas's cottage my destination instead. I tried to go to the church, I really did, and even asked for directions from a grizzled old man in a threadbare suit who made the sign of the cross when I walked to his side of the street. But religious institutions and I aren't the best of friends in the general order of things. Add the theft of important holy relics into the mix, and our friendship becomes downright terminal.

"If you're going to tell me that I'm in over my head, there's no need. I'm well aware of it. But I kind of have to solve the mystery now. I'm out ten thousand dollars with my broken equipment. If I walk away now, I have no chance of recovering it."

"Would you stop babbling for five seconds and listen?" Liam demands. "I don't care about your stupid job. I'm calling because of Winnie."

Winnie.

With that one word, my heart turns to molten lead in my chest, hot and heavy and robbing the breath from my lungs. Even though nothing around me changes, no breeze or flutter of wings, not even a cloud passing over the sun, I feel as though I'm racing through a tunnel.

"She's dead?" I ask, my voice wavering.

The pause that follows this remark doesn't bring either comfort or clarity—two things I could drastically use right now.

"Liam? Talk to me. What happened? And when? I don't believe you. She doesn't *feel* dead."

"That's because she isn't." He hesitates. "Yet."

"I think I need to sit down," I mutter, more to myself than Liam. My legs feel shaky and my arms weak. I cast my glance around, hoping to alight on a bench or a lawn chair or something to hold the suddenly catastrophic weight on my shoulders, but Thomas's lawn is too tidy.

Even though no welcoming lights fill the windows and no smoking chimney shows signs of life within, I try the front door. It snicks open to reveal an interior that's as cozy and welcoming as Castle Hartford is cavernous and crumbling. A cursory glance shows me that no one is home—a thing I'm far too preoccupied at the moment to worry too much about.

I sink to the floor, my back pressed against a wainscoted wall.

"Ellie?" Liam asks. "Are you still there?"

"I'm here," I say, my voice faint even to my own ears. "You can tell me now."

His sigh sounds a thousand years old.

"Like a Band-Aid," I instruct him. "Get it over with."

"There is no Band-Aid for this one," he mutters, but manages to find the words anyway. "I woke up to a message on my phone from Happy Acres. Apparently, Winnie slipped into a deeper coma yesterday. They have her on a breathing tube."

"A breathing tube?" Of all the horrors my sister has endured, being plugged in and wired was the one thing Liam and I both agreed we'd never force on her. It's too painful for all of us. "But we signed a DNR."

"I know. But that nurse you like, the one who usually takes care of her—"

"Peggy," I interrupt.

"Yeah, that's it. Peggy." Liam draws a deep breath. I wait, tracing the patterned outline of the wood planks with my forefinger. "She was with her at the time. She says Winnie woke up right before it happened."

My finger stops over a rough spot in the floor. "What? She woke up?"

And I wasn't there? I didn't get to say good-bye, hello, the thousands of things I still want to tell her?

"For just a second, yes. According to their report, she opened her eyes and started searching the room, looking for something. She stopped when she reached that nurse—Peggy—and said a few words." Liam's voice wavers. "She asked for you specifically. She said *tell Ellie* right before falling into a seizure."

The urge to smash up all of Thomas's lovely cottage takes overwhelming hold of me. I suddenly wish I was in the armory up at the castle. Although it's more of a hall than a room, it's filled with rusted bits of weaponry that would clatter and shatter in ways highly satisfactory to my current mood.

In the absence of mindless destruction, I jerk to my feet and start pacing the floor, brushing past a quaint sitting room into an even quainter kitchen, where a sleek black cat is curled up in front of an Aga stove. I barely register the picture they make before turning on my heel and stalking back the way I came.

"They thought it would be best to stabilize her and see if she woke up again," Liam adds as I start on my third revolution of Thomas's house. It's not large enough for *real* pacing. "But she hasn't, and the doctors don't sound very hopeful that she will. They, uh, want to know what we'd like to do."

"What we'd like to do?" I echo.

"Yeah. About the breathing tube. I told them not to touch anything until I had a chance to talk to you first. I figured you'd want to be there when . . ."

He doesn't finish. There's no need for him to. We both know enough about comas and semi-comas to understand the implication. They wouldn't have put Winnie on a ventilator unless she needs it in order to breathe. And if she needs it in order to breathe, then removing it will only mean we're sentencing her to death.

Our sister, the other part of us, our missing third.

"I don't understand," I say. And I don't understand—not any of it. Not why Nicholas hired me to come all this way only to block my investigation at every turn. Not where that pile of bones came from. Not why a mysteriously vanished body has no one fearing for their lives.

And I definitely don't understand why death—my friend, my companion, the entity I've relied on to make my living for years—is suddenly fighting back.

"You know what?" I ask in a purely rhetorical vein. "I'm done. I'm not playing this game anymore. If the police want to ask me any more questions, they're going to have to go through the embassy to do it."

"But—"

"No, don't try to change my mind. There's nothing keeping me here, not really, not if I don't need the money to pay for Happy Acres." In fact, the only thing I want right now is to hear Winnie's voice for myself, to listen to her call me *silly Ellie* in person—

"Wait a minute." I stop. "What time did all this happen?"

Liam sounds perplexed. "What do you mean?"

"The waking up, the seizure." The phrase that seems to be becoming a pattern as of late. "What time was it in New York when it happened?"

"I'm not sure . . . A little before noon, I think. Why?"

I do some quick mental arithmetic. Accounting for the time difference, that would have placed me in the early evening, right around the time I took a walk with Nicholas over his land.

And heard, from some faraway place I can't see or touch, a voice promising to come to my aid.

It can't be. I know the rules and limitations of our world, understand better than anyone that people will look for any kind of sign they can hinge their beliefs on. Hearing strange voices in a castle that I *know* is being manipulated by someone with an ulterior motive is no surprise; the only thing worth note is that I'm actually in danger of falling for it.

And yet . . .

"Don't unplug her," I say, shocked at the ferocity of my own voice. "Whatever they say or urge you to do, you can't let them. Not yet."

"I won't, of course, but—"

"She's *here*, Liam."

"Ellie."

"I know how it sounds, but I'm not kidding. I've heard her talking to me, teasing me. I didn't know who it was at first, but . . ." But there's no other rational explanation. For the voice or for any of this. "I think she might be trying to help me."

His tone of disbelief says it all. "Winnie is trying to help you find a fake ghost?"

No. She's trying to help me find a murderer. She's protecting me. I don't know what it is about Castle Hartford—if it's the age or the ambience, if it's a place where miracles really do happen—but she's been with me since the moment I first caught sight of it. It would explain why I feel so at home there, why even now, with so much danger hanging overhead, I'm eager to get back.

"Just trust me. I need a little more time, that's all. Whatever you do, don't let them take Winnie off that ventilator."

"I dunno. You're scaring me. If I didn't know any better, I'd say you sound like . . ."

I'm forced into a laugh. "Like someone who's losing her mind?"

"No," he counters. "Like someone who believes in the supernatural."

Last week, there would have been no stronger insult to launch at my head. To reopen the belief that Winnie is out there somewhere, just beyond my reach, is to reopen myself to everything I've spent the last decade struggling to overcome. Belief, hope, optimism, *love*.

Yet that's exactly what I'm doing, all common sense to the contrary. For the first time in my adult memory, I'm starting to think there might be a light at the end of the long, dark tunnel of my life. For the first time in my adult memory, I'm excited about what that light might hold.

"I'm sorry," I say, not the least bit sorry at all. "I'll call you later with more details. There are a few things I want to check out before I say more."

"But—"

"Just trust me, okay? I know things sound desperate, what with all the murders and bodies around here, but I'm not in any personal danger. I'm good."

There's another long pause, this one extending so long I suspect we lost our connection. My brother's voice eventually crackles over the line. "You aren't *good*. You've never been good. That's what worries me."

"I know," I admit with a laugh. "Which is why it's so fortunate I have you and Winnie to ground me."

There's nothing more for us to say, so I hang up and tuck the phone in my pocket, almost surprised to find that I'm still in-side Thomas's cottage. It's as eerily quiet and empty as before, as though no one has lived here for centuries, as if the man-of-all-work is, like the mustachioed man, nothing more than a fig-ment of my imagination.

In confirmation of my new belief in the paranormal, the black cat in front of the stove stretches and rises to its feet. Tra-dition has it that black cats are witches in disguise, the shape-shifting form of women just like me. But that would be taking things too far, even for someone who's suddenly decided that not everything in this world is exactly as it seems.

"Hello, pretty kitty." I reach down to the pet the animal. It holds itself back from my touch, watching me with a disdainful eye. "Where's your owner?"

The cat doesn't have an answer. Neither, it seems, does the house, because a cursory look around reveals nothing except that Thomas is an extraordinarily neat man with a well-stocked cupboard and one of the most enormous flat-screen TVs I've ever seen. The cat follows me from room to room, as though making sure I'm not about to steal anything.

There's no need. Unless I can find a way to cart the television out the front door, there doesn't appear to be much of value to take. Thomas is a simple man with simple pleasures, just as he appears on the outside. But where the devil is he?

The house doesn't appear to contain any answers, so I turn to the cat before I leave. "Do you have enough to eat?" I ask aloud.

I return to the kitchen to scout out the cat's food dish. I find it under the sink, which is partitioned off with a cheerful calico curtain. A few lingering bites of food remain in the dish, but the water bowl is empty. With a soft cry of protest, I hunt through the pantry until I find a plastic container of dry food and pour every last piece in the dish. I also grab the biggest mixing bowl I can find and fill it to the brim with water.

The cat begins immediately lapping at the liquid, so thirsty it remains still long enough for me to give it a cursory pat. I don't know where Thomas is staying on his "weekend off," but it's obviously not here. In fact, it looks almost as though he'd have let his pet die rather than risk coming home.

Because he witnessed a murder? I can't help thinking. *Or because he committed one?*

No answer is forthcoming, so I decide to head back before I leave too many more fingerprints lying around the place.

"I'll be back to check on you tomorrow," I say to the cat. "But if he gets home before then, you send him directly up to the castle, okay? I've got a few questions that need answering."

Predictably, the animal doesn't reply. It does, however, follow me to the door and watch my departure from the front window, its yellow-green eyes preternaturally bright.

I still have weeds to gather for my fake draught, and it's too late in the day to pay any more visits in the village, so I head in the direction of Castle Hartford. I have no idea what to expect when I get there, and not many more clues now than I did a few hours ago, but one thing is for sure: I'm not leaving here until I have answers.

To the murder, to the bones, to the ghost's secret identity.

And, most importantly, to my sister watching over it all.

Chapter 16

"Where is Thomas?" I ask, my voice low and crooning. When no immediate reply is forthcoming, I try again. "Where is the murdered man? And *who* is the murdered man?"

I strain to hear an answer—any answer. I don't move, don't breathe, don't even think, but all I get in response is the steady drip-drip of a faucet in need of repair and the sound of the refrigerator kicking on.

"Come on, Winnie. You have to help me out. Can you at least give me some sort of sign that you're listening?"

A gentle cough sounds to my right. Almost jumping up from where I sit cross-legged on the scrubbed wood kitchen table, I look up to find the exact opposite of my gentle, comatose sister reaching her spirit across time and space.

"What are you doing here?" I demand of Nicholas, who leans on the stairway door frame with the kind of ease that indicates he's been installed there for some minutes.

"I might ask the same of you," he says. "Didn't the police tell us to stay out of this room until they're finished gathering evidence?"

I cast a glance at the line of yellow police tape that is the only thing barring our entry—a line of yellow police tape that Nicholas, too, has seen fit to ignore, since he's standing on the opposite side of it. "I managed to break through their powerful force field," I say.

"So it would seem. Why?"

To attempt to communicate with a woman who's over three thousand miles away and deep in a coma, I think. Even though I'm under the impression that Nicholas was eavesdropping long enough to ascertain that for himself, it's not a sentence I'm ready to utter out loud just yet. So all I say is, "To gather my thoughts."

"Mind if I join you?"

I glance down at the kitchen table upon which I'm perched. "Um. Sure?"

He doesn't, as I halfway hope, climb up and adopt a Kumbaya pose with me. Ever elegant and composed, he pulls out one of the chairs and lowers himself to it instead. His eyes never leave mine as he crosses one leg over the other, his gray gaze disconcertingly direct. Fortunately for me, it's well into nighttime by now, and the kitchen lights are dim, so he can't see me blush.

Few things can embarrass a woman who's seen and done the things I have, but being caught trying to *genuinely* commune with the spirit world is one of them.

"I've always liked this room best of all the house," Nicholas says by way of breaking the silence. "It has good . . . energy."

I narrow my eyes. So he *did* overhear me.

"How is your sister, by the way?"

"Still a vegetable."

"I see. And, ah, was she able to answer any of your questions?" When I don't answer right away, he feels compelled to jolt my memory. "The location of Thomas, the murdered man . . ."

"Not directly," I say and turn a sweet smile on him. "But she did send me you. Do *you* know where Thomas or the murdered man are?"

"I understood it to be Thomas's long weekend" is his mild reply. "He only gets one of those a month, you know—he leaves late on Thursday and rarely reappears until Sunday night. My mother tells me he often goes fishing."

A reasonable explanation, of course, but I can't help thinking about the convenient timing of it all.

"It's strange that the police aren't more worried about his being gone, don't you think?" I ask.

"The police still believe we're dealing with nothing more than bones of ancient origin buried in a home of ancient origin," he replies. "Hardly the stuff of heady intrigue. By the by, what did our good inspector say about Rachel's drawing?"

I bite my lip. I don't know how Nicholas managed it, but he's turned things around so *I* feel like the guilty party. "Not much," I say with perfect honesty. "But I'm not too worried. I've got a few ideas of my own about his identity."

"Oh?" he asks politely.

"Yes. What I don't know, however, is where he could have possibly gone—or who took him there." I pause, hoping Nicholas will volunteer a few ideas of his own. When he doesn't, I decide that the only way I'm going to get anywhere is if I take a more direct route. Otherwise, Nicholas and I are going to continue dancing around the subject until one of us drops from exhaustion. "What can you tell me about the smuggling tunnels around here?"

He's betrayed into a laugh, a low, deep sound that carries a surprising amount of warmth. "Oh, dear. Has Thomas been feeding you those stories, or was it Fern?"

"Fern?" I echo.

His laugh dwindles into a chuckle. "You wouldn't think it to look at her now, but the three of us used to spend hours scampering over the countryside, trying to find the entrance to those tunnels. They've been a legend as long as there have been Hartfords on this land."

"Fern?" I say again. In the entire duration of my stay thus far, I've never seen her near a window, let alone in the great outdoors. At this point, I doubt whether her silky, wrinkle-free skin has ever seen the sun.

"Oh, yes. In fact, she's the one who instigated it. Once she heard the rumors of possible buried treasure, nothing would do but for her to bundle Thomas and me up to be her scouts. There wasn't a rabbit warren or molehill within a ten-mile radius that we didn't investigate to its source."

"Bundle you up?" I ask, slightly taken aback at his choice of words. "How old was Fern? How old were *you*?"

A conscious-stricken expression passes over his face, rendering him almost boyish. "Old enough to know we'd never find anything," he admits. "If no previous generation landed on a network of secret tunnels, there was little chance of our doing so. But we enjoyed ourselves. We used to have some grand adventures, once upon a time."

It's a strangely comforting picture to conjure up, a miniature authoritarian Nicholas, all starched up and forcing the two smaller children to do his bidding. "Did you often play with Thomas when you were kids? I was under the impression he's considerably younger than you."

"Only by a few years," he says with a casual air. Then, as if the thought just strikes him, "How old do you think I am?"

A psychic—fake or otherwise—knows better than to answer that question truthfully. "Late thirties?" I guess, knocking a good half decade off my real guess in the process.

He doesn't correct me or offer up his real age. All I get is a mild *harrumph* and an air of effrontery, which leads me to believe I may have overshot even that modest estimate.

"Why, Nicholas Hartford, did I hurt your feelings?" I can't help asking. "If it makes you feel any better, you look about twenty years younger when you smile. No, not that smile. That's a sneer. I'm talking about the *real* one."

"The real one?"

"Yeah. The one you save for Rachel and other people you don't continually look down on."

Even his half-hearted sneer drops after that. The look he casts me is so genuinely perplexed—so hurt—that I find it difficult not to take my words back.

"Is that what you think I do?" he asks, his voice quiet. "Look down on you?"

I'm not sure how to answer. In all honesty, I think Nicholas Hartford III looks down on everyone. He's rich and just close enough to handsome to get away with the epithet. He's the head of a family that's been established here for centuries. And although I wouldn't go so far as to call him charming, there's a magnetism to him that's impossible to ignore.

After all, I'm still here, aren't I? Drawn to this place? Drawn to *him*?

"I think you're used to getting things your own way," I admit. "I think you're so accustomed to having money and power, it doesn't occur to you that some people make do without them. I think you care about this house to the exclusion of everything else, and you use that to justify your actions to yourself."

"Anything else?" he asks, his voice low.

Yes, there is. I drop my own voice to match his. "I think you've never experienced the kind of pain and loss that make my profession necessary. And I think that can only be a good thing. No one deserves a life like mine. Not even me."

The kiss comes as if from out of nowhere. One moment, he's sitting next to me, all languid ease. The next, he's on his feet and looming overhead. My position on the table leaves me at a disadvantage, since there's nothing I can do and nowhere I can hide unless I intend to go limp and slide to the floor. Which, to be perfectly honest, isn't so far-fetched a reaction. In fact, one might argue that it's the *only* reaction when a man's arms become a wall of sorts, bracing either side of the table as his mouth comes crashing down.

It's not, despite my trapped condition, an unpleasant sensation. All of Nicholas's careful competence comes through as he lays an assault on my senses. *Controlling* is the only word I can think of to explain it, but I don't mean that in a bad way. Whatever drives this man to succeed—in business and in his private life—is so much a part of him that he can't lose hold of it, even in a passionate embrace like this one.

What he doesn't realize, however, is that my baser needs also derive from my personal experience. *He* might exude power and control with each movement of his lips over mine, but I'm driven by darker forces. Lust, mostly. Pride, gluttony, greed— you name it, I've tried it. If anything, I've learned to appreciate those rare moments of carnal simplicity more than most.

As soon as I begin to return his affections, however, which I do by winding my arms around his neck and deepening the kiss into something truly remarkable, he rears back as if bitten.

Actually, it would be more accurate to say he rears back *because* he's been bitten. Not hard, mind you, and not enough to draw blood, but if he thinks he can intimidate me with a kiss, he's far off the mark. I *will* kiss him back—and I'll do it better, too. Madame Eleanor doesn't leave much up to chance.

"You devil," he says, laughing as he presses the back of his hand to his mouth. "I should have known better."

"Yes," I agree. "You should have."

"Please accept my apologies for taking you by surprise like that. I . . ." He trails off, looking doubtful. His uncertainty is such a new experience—for the both of us, I suspect—that it takes him a moment to recover. "You're wrong about me, that's all. I don't look down on you."

I glance at him, still standing over the table, *literally* looking down, and lift a brow. "Is this where you tell me you aren't used to having things your own way either? Because I gotta be honest—you aren't making a very convincing case right now."

He laughs again and pushes himself up from the table. I feel the loss of his looming presence almost at once, but I'm not sure what shape that loss takes. Do I miss the warm solidity of his body pressing into mine? Or is this merely relief at having a potential threat back away?

"I'm not as old as you think I am, Eleanor," he says. "Nor am I as cold-blooded. I wouldn't have asked you to stay if that were the case."

I'm not sure what to make of that confession. Young, hot-headed men don't have any more need of fake mediums than old, cold ones. At least, not in my experience.

"I promised you I'd see this job through to the end, and I meant it," I say.

He looks pained again, but he doesn't reply. Nor does he make another move to kiss me. Whatever force compelled him to act in the first place has been fully quashed. He's a man who exercises power over his own demons.

As do I.

Nicholas Hartford III isn't the only person in this room who can push aside those squishy, human needs for the sake of something more. With no more than a fleeting regret that one nibble is all I'll get, I draw a deep breath and return to the task at hand. "Speaking of, does Thomas have any family in the area? Anyone who might know how to reach him, or who he might feel comfortable staying with for a few days?"

Nicholas's pained look doesn't lift, but he answers me levelly enough. "Not to my knowledge, no. His father died when he was young, his mother a few years after he reached adulthood. No siblings or, as far as I know, any kind of girlfriend or romantic attachment."

"So he's all alone?"

"He's not alone. He has us."

I bite back a sharp laugh. Somehow, I doubt a wealthy landowning employer can replace actual family. I don't care how long Thomas's people have served the Hartfords or how many hills they used to scamper over together as kids.

"And his cat," I say.

"Thomas has a cat?"

"Yes. You didn't know? I found it when I stopped by his cottage earlier this evening to take a look around."

He swivels his head to stare at me. "You did *what*?"

"It seemed prudent since no one else seems concerned that both a murdered man and your childhood friend have gone missing at the same time. I thought I might find him there. Or, at the very least, some sign of struggle or rapid flight." I pause. "I didn't, in case you're worried about him."

Nicholas's frown etches so deep it's a wonder he doesn't turn to stone. "Don't do that again."

At first, I'm not sure which act he's referring to—breaking into Thomas's home or trying to find him—but he soon clarifies it for me.

"You're already under suspicion for the bones under the stairs," he says. "We don't want Inspector Piper to start questioning the rest of your clandestine activities around here. Your presence is difficult enough to explain as it is."

In other words, Nicholas is less concerned about his childhood friend and more concerned about covering his own tracks.

"Ah, yes," I say, unable to keep the sarcasm out of my voice. "We wouldn't want anyone to find out you hired a fake psychic to con your own mother, would we? Forget Thomas. That would be something to *really* worry about."

The smile my words bring to Nicholas's face is his least authentic one yet. Cold and cruel, it twists his face into something almost unrecognizable.

It also unearths something almost unrecognizable within me: fear.

It's a strange sensation, and one I didn't think I was capable of anymore. Fear, like hope, is something I thought I dispensed with a long time ago. After all, the worst has already happened; I'm living my nightmare every day. No imaginable threat can touch the dark hole that cushions my heart.

But at the sight of that quick flash of Nicholas's malice, I feel the full weight of this situation settle on my shoulders. At least two people have died inside this house. At least one was left long enough to rot. And for reasons only I—and maybe Winnie—can understand, the key to it all rests in my hands.

When Nicholas finally speaks, however, his voice is as urbane as ever.

"Thomas is a grown man, fully capable of looking after himself," he says. "I'm sure he'll walk through the door tomorrow evening with a brace of trout in hand, and your concerns will have been revealed to be for nothing."

"You're sure of it?" I ask, unable to help myself. "In my line of work, I never make a promise like that unless I know I can back it up."

His mouth sets in a hard line as he turns to leave, all thoughts of kisses erased from sight. "Yes, Madame Eleanor. I'm sure."

Chapter 17

"What do you mean, you lost the key? I didn't even know there was a key." I stand in the hallway outside the yellow bedchamber, staring at the sealed wooden portal that stands between me and all my earthly belongings.

"I can't think how I came to do it." Vivian makes a show of searching her person. As this evening's outfit is a pair of purple athletic leggings and a black tunic top I'm ninety-nine percent sure is mine, it's a fruitless search. Unless the key is hidden in her shoe, there's no way she has it. There's nary a pocket to be seen. "I locked it after you went to gather herbs for your spell, of course, but I can't remember where I put the dratted key after that."

"Why *of course*?"

She drops all pretense of searching and blinks at me. "What's that?"

"You said *of course* you locked the door after I went herb gathering, but I don't understand. I didn't ask you to do that."

"Oh, the request didn't come from you, dear. I thought it was odd, but I make it a habit not to argue with Xavier. He's usually right about these things."

Xavier. He's back. It seems the police didn't scare him away, after all. And this time, the mischief he's caused is more than playful. I *need* access to that room.

"Where were you when Xavier made this request?" I ask.

"How can one tell these things?" she asks and then immediately contradicts herself by stating, "The foyer. That's where he usually comes to me when—"

She halts and looks conscious-stricken.

"Yes?" I urge. "That's where he comes to you when . . . ?"

Her conscious-stricken look transforms to one of bland innocence. "When he particularly wants my attention," she says in a way that's satisfactory to neither of us. "I expect he was feeling anxious about the yellow bedchamber, poor chap. I don't believe he likes it above half that you've taken it over. But don't worry. You can stay with Rachel for tonight."

"That's not—" I begin.

"Oh, it's no trouble, love. She won't mind. And I'm sure I'll remember where I put that key in the morning. With all the excitement these past few days, it's a wonder I remembered to put on a bra."

And with that, she saunters away, admiring the long, wispy sleeves of her—*my*—top as she goes. Watching her retreating form, I can't decide if I'm more angry or amused. What might, a few days ago, have been a mild annoyance is now a dangerous intervention. I'd been counting on the cover of night to perform another thorough check of that bedchamber, have been drinking coffee since dinner in hopes of staving off sleep in case my midnight marauder decides to stop by.

"It's no use getting upset with her," Rachel says from behind me. I whirl to find her leaning on the wall outside her room, a laugh lighting her eyes. "Uncle Nicholas is always trying to make her realize that she doesn't have to do everything Xavier says, just because he says it, but Grandmother prefers to go her own way. She's eccentric."

An eccentric matriarch, a delicate teenager, an autocratic son—this family loves to latch on to their labels, using them as an excuse to do exactly as they please.

"But I need to get in there," I protest. "Why would Xavier tell her to lock me out?"

Rachel shrugs, using the movement to push off from the wall. "Maybe he's mad at you. Maybe he feels like you're intruding on his space."

Yes, or maybe he wanted time to ransack my room at his own leisure. He could be inside there even now, pawing through my belongings, smashing everything of value I have left. *He better not be touching my wine.*

"You can have my bed," Rachel offers. "I'll sleep on the floor. I don't mind."

I smile and thank her. I doubt the ancient wooden slats will provide much in the way of comfort, but her manners are, as always, impeccable. "I wonder if your uncle knows about this," I muse aloud.

She shrugs again. "Probably. There's not much that goes on around here that Uncle Nicholas doesn't know about."

Given the circumstances, that statement strikes me as rather generous. "Except what Xavier wants," I say. "Or where all the dead bodies are coming from."

Rachel is forced into a laugh. "I suppose that's true. Did you get the dandelions you needed today?"

It takes me a moment to realize what she's talking about, but I recover before she has a chance to get suspicious. I pat the apothecary satchel hanging at my hip and nod. "Yes, thanks. Would you like to help me brew the summoning draught?"

"Can I really?" Rachel's eyes grow wide, pleasure filling them just as much as when Nicholas told her she could go on her art exchange. I don't know what Fern was thinking, keeping this poor child tied to this place, but it's obvious she hasn't had nearly as much fun in her lifetime as she deserves. The prospect of boiling weeds with a woman ten years her senior shouldn't bring that much joy to anyone.

"Of course," I reply. "Ideally, we'd have three women working together to strengthen the summons, but two should do the trick. We'll need to head down to the kitchen so we can use the stove, though—unless the fireplace in your room works?"

"None of the fireplaces on the second floor work except for Grandmother's," she says. "But I do have a hot plate, if that helps."

"A hot plate is just the thing," I reply before a thought occurs to me. I halt. "Wait a minute—were *you* the one cooking bacon the other morning?"

Rachel tries to hold her laughter back by pressing her hands to her mouth, but it's too late. At least one mystery around here has just been solved.

"You little wretch," I say as I sling an arm around her shoulders and direct her toward her room. "The next time you feel compelled to add to the intrigue around here, you can at least offer me a bite."

My recipe for summoning the dead requires a simmering time of at least two hours.

From a technical standpoint, I believe you're supposed to make the dandelion roots into a tonic, dry the mallow leaves and burn them, and wear the rowan twigs and berries like jewelry. If I had more time and a bigger audience, I might do all those things, but there's no real point now. I've convinced Rachel that tossing everything into a pot of water and letting it boil will bring the spirits to us, and that's good enough for me.

Besides, my coffee infusion is starting to wear off. I'm not emotionally prepared to chant and dance around with pieces of bark dangling around my neck until I get at least eight hours of sleep.

"So now we wait?" Rachel looks at the saucepan of bobbing

red berries with her nose wrinkled. The smell isn't quite as pleasant as I'd hoped it would be. "And he just . . . shows up?"

"We wait," I agree. "And he just shows up."

Which is how I find myself wearing a nightshirt of Rachel's, sitting cross-legged on her bed and braiding her hair while we wait for the spirit world to come to us. Or at least for the entire house to fall asleep so I can try to pry open my bedroom door without anyone noticing.

"Do that cute loopy thing you wore the first day," she commands as she leans her head against my knee. "Where'd you learn to do those fancy braids?"

YouTube tutorials doesn't have a very authentic ring to it, so I tell her the only other thing I can think of that also happens to be the truth.

"My sister." I gently position her head so it's tilted to one side and start weaving my fingers through her tawny strands. "Her hair is just as long and fine as mine, so I use her to practice on. She's a very patient model."

Rachel ruins my progress by twisting to peer up at me. "You have a sister? Oh, how lucky! I've always wanted one."

"Yes," I murmur as I set her head straight again. "I *am* lucky, especially since I have a brother, too. We're triplets."

"No, really? How exciting. Is it true what they say, that you can feel their pain and know when something is wrong, even if you're thousands of miles apart?"

"Yes," I say, and leave it at that. And not just because I'm getting to a tricky part of the first coil. It *is* the truth, even if I didn't believe it before I arrived here. I know now that there's a stronger connection between me and Winnie than I ever gave myself credit for. Maybe she's been trying to talk to me this whole time, and I just wasn't listening properly.

Rachel pauses for a moment. Fearful that I'm tugging too hard on her head—a thing I constantly worry about when I braid Winnie's hair, since she has no way to tell me whether I'm giving her a headache or not—I stop my progress.

"Am I hurting you?" I ask.

"It's awfully lonely, growing up in a place like this without anyone for company," she says by way of answer. "You have no idea how much."

"It does seem a rather harsh environment for a young girl," I reply. "But you have your family. You have friends. That boy who works at the village museum had an awful lot of nice things to say about you."

"Oh, please. That's just Benji. He doesn't count." She pauses. "Why? What did he say?"

"Nothing much," I reply in singsong. "Just that he lurrrves you."

Her head jerks upright. "He did not!"

"Rachel and Benji, sitting in a tree . . ."

"Madame Eleanor, stop! He never said any such thing!"

"I wish you'd call me Ellie," I say as I casually resume my braiding activities. The results are going to be lopsided, but I can hardly be blamed for my inexpert work. I'm not used to practicing on someone who moves and laughs, someone teeming with life. "So few people do anymore. It's what my sister used to call me."

Rachel is bright enough to pick up on the shift in my tone—not to mention that slight slip into the past tense. "Used to?"

"We were in a car accident when we were around your age," I say with commendable aplomb. "She's been in a kind of coma ever since. She hasn't called me anything in ten years."

Rachel's entire body stills, and there's a long pause before she speaks again. "I'm so sorry, Madame Elea—I mean, Ellie. That sounds terrible. Is that why . . . ? I mean, is that how . . . ?"

I continue with my work, grateful for the distraction her hair provides. "Is that why I'm a medium? Is that how I can commune with the dead?"

"Oh, no. I didn't . . ." She breaks off, confused.

"Yes, to both questions." I snap my fingers for her to hand up a rubber band. "But now it's my turn to ask a few. Rachel, why aren't you in school with normal kids? Don't feed me that line about being delicate—no one who's prone to illness could live in a place as cold as this one. Why does your mother keep you buried away out here?"

"I'm not *buried*," she says, her tone defensive.

"Sorry, bad word choice. I should have said sequestered."

I've finished with Rachel's hair, so I hand her a mirror and let her examine the results. Her quick smile indicates pleasure, but it's soon replaced with a worried look that makes her appear much older than her years. Then again, that could just be the ornate braid crowning her head. It's always worked wonders for me.

"What is it?" I ask, my voice gentle. "You can tell me, sweetie."

She hands me back the mirror. "Mum is . . ." She sighs and shakes her head. "I don't know how to explain it. She loves me, I think, but not the way other mothers love their children. She doesn't like me to go places, never takes me to London when she stays there. I'm a burden to her."

"I'm sure that's not true," I protest, but not very convincingly. Fern isn't exactly awash with maternal vibes. "And even if it was, you still have the rest of your family. Your mother might not be demonstrative, but your uncle certainly doesn't treat you like a burden."

At the mention of her uncle, Rachel loses some of her gloom. "Uncle Nicholas is a darling, isn't he? I checked the family bible once, hoping that he was my real father and everyone just pretended I belonged to mum, but it was written right there on the page, my name underneath hers."

Although a teenager's moment of parental crisis is hardly the right time to put the focus back on myself, I can't help but interrupt. "You've seen the page?"

She blinks. "Of course. Until Uncle Nicholas had everything

moved to the museum, it was kept in the library. Mum wanted him to throw it away, but he never would. He's weirdly keen on genealogy."

He seems weirdly keen on a lot of things, including fake mediums currently under his employ, but that's hardly the point. "Was there anything about the page that seemed off to you? Something that would make it worth throwing away?"

"I dunno. I mean, it's not an official record or anything, so the names were sort of jumbled about. But we were all there: Grandmother, Grandfather, Mum, Uncle Nicholas, Thomas, me."

"Thomas?" I ask, my voice sharp. "Thomas is related to you?"

"Well, no. Not really." She tilts her head, as if considering. "I think they added him when they were kids—as a joke, you know, because they spent so much time together. The penmanship was different. Scrawly-er. And I don't think he put in his real birthday, because that was never the day we celebrated. Why does your face look like that? Is it because of the smell?"

Until she spoke, I hadn't noticed anything amiss—either with my face or with the smell in the room—but the acrid tang of burning rowan berries and dandelion roots assails my nose.

"Ignis fatuus!" I cry, jumping to my feet and pulling the scalding pan off the heat source. There's just enough liquid in the bottom to slosh over the edge to the floor, the viscous red color not unlike blood.

"Ignis fatuus?" Rachel asks as we watch the mixture seep into the floorboards.

"It's the light over a swamp, a will o' the wisp," I explain. "It also makes for a good swear in a pinch. I'm afraid your room is going to smell like this for a long time. That isn't going to come out easily."

"Maybe we'll be more successful at drawing Xavier out this way," she suggests.

I eye the mess doubtfully. I don't know how good my burned summoning draught will be at bringing out the dead, but I can't regret the other thing it's produced: a confirmation that I'm on the right track. I have no idea what it is about that bible page that has everyone connected to this castle acting so suspiciously, but I'm more determined than ever to find out.

"Let's sleep on it and see." I suggest. Unlike Rachel's respected Uncle Nicholas, I'm not prepared to promise certainties where I have none. "After all, what's the worst that could happen overnight?"

Chapter 18

⟴

After a declaration like that, it's only natural that the worst is exactly what happens overnight.

"What time is it?" I ask, sitting up in Rachel's bed. The lingering scent of burned berries still taints the air, but it's much less powerful an elixir now. I glance around in hopes of finding the girl asleep on the floorboards, but she's nowhere to be seen.

Which, to be honest, is only to be expected. From the angle of the sun pouring through the window, I not only missed my chance to break into my room under cover of night, but I slept through breakfast—and possibly lunch, too.

Drat. I guess sleeping in a room that's neither haunted nor accessible via a stubbornly secret passageway turns out to be a great way to finally get some rest. I'd be delighted if it wasn't such terrible timing. Lolling about in bed is bad form for a medium trying to lay a ghost to rest; for a medium trying to solve a murder, it's catastrophic. There's no telling what kind of events have taken place or how many opportunities have passed while I caught up on my beauty rest.

Swinging my legs over the side of the bed, I prepare to face the day—or, rather, what's left of it. It's only then I remember that access to my room is limited and, with it, access to all my belongings. Clean clothes, underwear, even my toothbrush are out of reach until Vivian manages to unearth that key.

Either that or I need to find the secret passageway and get in that way.

"Well, Winnie," I say, "now would be a good time to stop by with a helpful clue. I'd even take a hint from Xavier at this point."

Not unsurprisingly, I receive no reply. I glance down at my spilled summoning draught with something akin to disgust. It's not as though I expected the darn thing to work, of course. It's a jumbled mix of half-authentic spells half-heartedly uttered. "But you could at least have given me *something*," I say.

Winnie remains stubbornly uncooperative, but Rachel proves to be worth her weight in gold. She's left me a pair of well-worn jeans and three sweaters with a note to take my pick, since my own clothes are locked up in the yellow bedchamber.

Woolly layers aren't exactly in keeping with my aesthetic, but I pull on two of the sweaters, making do by layering a hand-knit gray one on the top. I might not look the part of a medium about to make a murder breakthrough, but I have every intention of being one anyway.

I know exactly where I'm going to start, too. Grabbing a pair of Rachel's shoes and carrying them in one hand to reduce the chances of anyone overhearing me, I tiptoe out into the hallway and down the stairs.

"Hello, Madame Eleanor." Nicholas is lying in wait for me at the bottom. "I trust you passed a pleasant night?"

I barely stifle my scream in time. If I didn't know better, I'd say this man has cameras of his own installed around the castle, tracking my every movement so he can arrive where I least expect him, when I least expect it. But surely the police would have found evidence of that.

Wouldn't they?

"My night was perfect, thanks." I press a hand to my heart, which gives an erratic thump. For reasons I don't quite understand, I'm loath to admit that I fell asleep on the job—literally—so I follow up with, "I stayed up a bit late ghost-hunting, so it was nice to catch up on my sleep this morning."

"Ah, it seems there *is* the occasional rest for the wicked," he murmurs. "How comforting."

I open my mouth to defend myself, but he continues with a bland smile and an even blander "I'm glad I caught you in time. You aren't, by any chance, attending afternoon services, are you?"

My alarm at such a proposition must show on my face, because he chuckles and takes a predatory step forward. Standing my ground is difficult, but I do it, even when he reaches into his pocket with slow deliberation.

"Mother thought you might," he says as though we're two ordinary people having an ordinary conversation. Which, as it turns out, is exactly what we are. He dangles a key ring from one fingertip. "We're not church-going people ourselves, but she likes to offer her guests the use of the Land Rover if they want to attend."

"Land Rover?"

He gives the keys a shake. Their cheerful jingle fills the hallway and makes a mockery of my fears. "It's old and it's ugly, but it runs. And most of the village is used to my mother behind the wheel, so they'll steer a clear path when they see you."

"That's awfully nice of her," I say. What I'm thinking, however, is that it's awfully questionable of them both. Nothing about me indicates that I have traditional spiritual leanings or that I'd make a Sunday sojourn into the village to indulge them. Yet that was the precise location I had planned for the day.

"No, it's not," he says with a laugh. "She's always happy to do anything to get her visitors out the door."

"And you?" I can't help asking. "What's your motivation?"

"At the moment, nothing but the purest chivalry, I assure you. A few days' residence in this place is a surfeit even under the best of circumstances. Under *these* circumstances . . ."

It's not a very good answer. In fact, it sounds an awful lot as if he'd like to get rid of me for a few hours. *Or possibly forever.* I don't know much about old Land Rovers, but I imagine it's easier to cut the brakes on one of those than it would be to lure me up to the top of a staircase and give me a gentle shove.

"What time is the service?" I ask.

"One o'clock," he says. "We have a family pew near the front, but I don't recommend you sit there unless you'd like everyone to sprinkle salt in an arc around you. You'll most likely want to sneak in the back. And maybe wear something less . . ."

"It's not my fault," I say as I give the sweater a conspicuous tug. "Your mother lost the key to my room. Rachel was nice enough to loan me some of her clothes."

His lips twitch. "Ah, yes. I heard about that."

"It's not funny!" I cry, momentarily forgetting that this man has given me no reason to trust anything he says or does. "Everything I brought with me is in that room. Isn't there a locksmith or someone you could call?"

"Not on a Sunday, there's not. This is a very traditional village. We can't even buy bread."

"Yes, well. I can't lay a ghost to rest if my ghost-laying supplies are locked up." A thought occurs to me. "If Thomas were here, I bet he could find a way to break down the door."

"Possibly." Nicholas pauses, watching me. "But as we both know, he's currently enjoying his weekend away."

I'm rapidly beginning to lose my patience. "*Someone* pretended to be Xavier and told your mother to lock that door," I say. "And they did it either knowing she'd lose the key or with the intention of taking it from her at the first opportunity that afforded itself."

Nicholas surprises me with his answer. "I agree."

"And that doesn't bother you?"

"Not particularly, no. Of all the crimes under this roof, locking a door hardly seems like something to get worked up over."

True. Unless that locked door was designed to keep me from finding the passageway or reaching my personal effects, in much the same way my cameras were smashed. Even my bottles of Carlo Rossi are out of reach—and it's looking more and more like I'm going to need them, if only to dull the pain.

"But aren't you even a little curious about why?" I demand. "You've got someone sneaking around the house, hiding bones and moving bodies, pushing people down stairs and throwing birds out of chimneys. You've also got someone limiting my access to my investigative tools by using your mother as a dupe. At what point do you start to show alarm? At what point do you realize that everyone inside this house is in danger?"

I don't know the exact point in my speech when Nicholas crosses the floor, but I'm guessing it's about halfway through. By the time I get the last word out, he has me by the shoulders, though whether he's pushing me away or pulling me closer, I can't tell. All I know is that his grip is strong and his eyes are like steel as he scowls down at me.

"You think I don't know that? You think I'm not doing all that lies within my power to get to the bottom of this? Everything and everyone I care about is currently residing under this roof." His voice, which had been showing a tendency to rise in both volume and severity, lowers to a growl. "For crying out loud, Eleanor, I hired a con woman masquerading as a psychic to help me. I put my trust in a beautiful stranger who can manipulate people with wind machines and a smile. Believe me, it doesn't get any more desperate than that."

For a brief flash, I think he's going to kiss me again—another one of those hard embraces that will leave me feeling more confused than sated—but he doesn't. He just holds me there, staring down at me until I nod.

Nodding seems inadequate a response, but it's all I can do. Being called beautiful and manipulative in the same passionate breath will do that to a girl.

"Be careful in the village today," he says as he releases me. It's like being dropped from a pair of shackles, both literally and metaphorically. Gone are all signs of his anger and distress; he's back to his usual controlled self with no more than a blink. "I'll see what I can do about your room, but I can't make any promises."

It's not the response I'm looking for. What I'd *like* is for Nicholas to break his reserved façade, to kiss me or kill me or do whatever action he's nursing deep inside that chiseled bosom of his.

Unfortunately, all I get are the keys to the Land Rover and a polite, chilly smile. In other words, we're back to business as usual.

I don't, as Nicholas suggested, head directly to the village church. Nor do I take the Land Rover. There's somewhere I want to stop first, and I'd prefer not to advertise my destination to the entire neighborhood.

I'm wrapped up in a men's mackintosh that flaps around my knees and smells of the earth. Given its well-used condition and that alarmingly familiar scent, I'm guessing it belongs to Thomas. I grabbed it from the foyer closet as I made my way out the door, hit with yet another reminder that the man who owns it seems to have left in a mighty big hurry.

It's strange, wearing a coat that belongs to someone who may or may not be missing, but it was either this or a mottled fur that had equal chances of belonging to Fern or Vivian. Fern because no one else could make that monstrosity work, Vivian because she wouldn't care that it made her look like a half-ravaged wolf.

Unfortunately, the jacket ends up providing little protection against the biting November wind. By the time I cover no more than a mile of the rocky landscape and shivering scrubby bushes of the countryside, I'm halfway frozen and no closer to a solution than I was when I left the castle.

One of the hallmarks of both Occam's theories and my own is that the simplest solution to a haunting is the most likely one. Yes, it's possible that the ephemeral remnants of a long-dead human can wreak havoc on the material world; however, when compared with things like rats and faulty plumbing and people who can't be trusted to take you seriously when you show them a drawing of a dead man, that likelihood becomes very, very small.

And that's the problem. There is no simple solution to the Castle Hartford haunting. This is no teenage girl trying to get rid of her mother's lover. Rachel is no more capable of dragging bodies through thin air than I am. And this isn't a real estate developer trying to score a sweet deal on a piece of land, either. Even Cal would have figured out by now that no amount of bumps and moans in the night will convince Nicholas to sell.

No, this ghost is something else, something seriously disturbing. But I can't, for the life of me, put my finger on what that something is.

It doesn't take nearly as long as I expect to get to the Hartford cemetery. When we had driven by, those huddled lumps and weathered tombstones had seemed a long way out, but that's one of the deceptions about a place like this. The winding country lanes make all the landmarks seem much more distant than they really are. By foot—or by way of how the dove flies—almost everything around here is connected.

The cemetery is everything I expect from a family plot that's served multiple generations of highly esteemed Hartfords. There's enough ancient stone to erect a druid ruin, and it's in that quintessentially British condition where wild overgrowth and painstaking upkeep meet.

Unlike the files at the museum, however, there's no real order to the layout. The area in the center of the cemetery appears to be the oldest, with headstones so worn down by time and rain that it's difficult to make out the inscriptions. With the help of a piece of paper and a rubbing pencil, however, I do make them out. There are Charleses and Williams in abundance; Marthas and Abigails abound. But there's nary a Xavier to be seen.

Ah, well. It was a long shot to begin with. And I didn't really come out here with the expectation of finding anything related to the ghost.

Then why did you come, silly?

I whirl, even though I know by now that I won't find anyone behind me. I don't bother answering, either, since I'm fairly certain Winnie already knows.

I came because this place is important to Nicholas. I came because it's the one location where the dead are already at peace.

"Oh, dear." I blink at the sight of an incoming form in the distance, unsure if I'm seeing things. The weather is hardly conducive to creating a mirage, so I'm forced to conclude that fate is playing yet another cruel trick on me. "What's *he* doing here? Even a Land Rover with its brakes cut would be preferable to this."

"Well, well, well. Just the woman I've been hoping to see." Inspector Peter Piper doesn't pick up his pace as he approaches, the ubiquitous cigarette dangling from his fingertips as though he hasn't a care in the world. "Don't tell me. You sensed my plans to visit the cemetery today and came to meet me?"

"I'm afraid not," I reply with a tight smile. "No offense, but you're about as spiritually blocked as they come. You'd never be able to get a message across that way."

He takes a long drag, sucking down all that nicotine without so much as a blink. A neat series of smoke rings escape his lips, and he stands admiring them for a moment before speaking again. "Spiritually blocked, huh? That sounds like something my doctor would say."

I match my nonchalance to his. Since I don't have a terrible smoking habit to fall back on, I pretend to adjust the sleeves of my coat instead. "Actually, I think it would be more accurate to attribute that statement to your ex-wife. Although I imagine she interpreted it more as an emotional blockage than a spiritual one. Women often do. How long ago did she leave you?"

The tiny puffs of smoke stop leaving his lips.

"Don't look so surprised. I'm psychic, remember?"

He tosses his cigarette onto the grave of a venerable Hartford ancestor and crushes the butt under his heel. His lack of tidiness and respect for personal property leaves much to be desired, but I take pity on him anyway. Maybe it's because what I do isn't so far removed from the work of a detective. Perhaps it's because being on the good side of the law is something I should actively seek right now. It might even be that my sympathetic cords are struck at how forlorn he looks at the mention of an ex-wife. Whatever the reason, I let him in on my secret.

"You don't wear a wedding ring, but your thumb moves to your ring finger every time you bring the cigarette to your lips," I say. "It's as if you're trying to play with the band that used to be there, like you don't remember right away that it's gone."

Inspector Piper doesn't appear particularly surprised or pleased by my confession, but he is interested enough to ask, "How do you know she didn't die? Or that I wasn't the one who left her?"

"Because you have deplorable smoking habits. I don't just mean the smoking itself, but the way you fling the ashes everywhere. You're thoughtless with them, careless of where they land. A man who's emotionally available to his wife would have made *some* effort to curb the barbarism." I pause. "I bet it drove her crazy, didn't it?"

He makes a chuffing sound that isn't quite a laugh but is definitely on the spectrum. "Every bloody minute of every bloody day."

I splay my hands, a gesture common among street performers and magicians when they want to prove they have nothing more up their figurative sleeves. It means the same coming from me, though I doubt Inspector Piper is aware of it.

"Behold my powers," I say. "What was it you wanted to see me about?"

He doesn't look ready to give up talking about his ex-wife yet, but he clears his throat and allows his weasely gaze to land on mine. "I thought you might be interested to know that the bones under the stairs were placed there posthumously."

I blink, momentarily taken aback. The last thing I expect to find in Inspector Piper is an ally. The man obviously doesn't believe in the paranormal—or in me—and I doubt it's standard protocol to disclose the details of a case to the primary suspect. Call me paranoid, but I smell a trap.

"How interesting," I say in a neutral tone.

"Posthumously *and* recently."

Ah, yes. Now I'm starting to understand. "Really? How recently?"

"Based on the field kit results, we're looking at placement sometime within the last week." He glances sideways at me. "Probably around the time of your own arrival, in fact. There was no evidence of site decay, either under the stairs or anywhere else in the kitchen. For a dumping spot to be that clean, the body had to have been brought in from the outside."

"What does that have to do with me?" I ask, even though I already know the answer. Inspector Piper has already drawn his conclusions about who and what I am.

"Possibly nothing, but the timing is rather . . . convenient. Wouldn't you say?"

On the contrary, I'm starting to find the timing rather *in*convenient. "I don't plant old bones inside houses. Some mediums might not be opposed to such tactics, but it's not my style."

"And what is your style, if you don't mind my asking?"

"You've seen it." I look him squarely in the eyes, holding his gaze in hopes that it asserts my innocence rather than coming across as the calculated poise of a sociopath. "I read a room. I read people. I make educated guesses. The rest is magic."

He fumbles in his pocket until he extracts his pack of cigarettes. Tapping one out, he sticks it between his lips but doesn't light it. Like the constant reaching for his ring, it's a gesture that proves he's the sort of man who takes comfort in routines, in rules.

I'm half afraid those rules and routines are about to take over—all the way to the jailhouse door, in fact—but he only grunts and asks me a surprising question. "In your *magic* opinion, how did a body that's been rotting for fifty years get placed inside the Hartford kitchen without anyone knowing about it?"

"Fifty years? Is that how long the person's been dead?"

He grunts again. "Give or take a decade in either direction, yes."

"I have no idea," I say. "And you don't have to look so skeptical. I wouldn't even know where to find a body in that condition."

He casts a very obvious glance around us, his gaze skimming over the tops of gravestones until it finally comes to rest on me again. "No?"

Horror washes through me as I realize what he's saying. We're literally surrounded by corpses in various states of decay, but desecration of that kind goes beyond even my imagination. "You think someone dug up—? But which one—?"

Even though I've already done a fairly thorough investigation of the cemetery, I find myself scanning the sleepy graves and fog-dampened blades of grass, looking for any sign of a recent excavation. The soil is loose in places, such as might be caused by foot traffic or an animal scuffling in the underbrush, but I don't find anything to indicate one of the Hartford ancestors has been recently unearthed.

"We checked this cemetery already," Inspector Piper says with a calmness I'd like to strangle right out of him. He made me believe one of these bodies was dug up to gauge my reaction, purposefully filled me with disgust as an investigative ploy. "As well as several of the others in the area. Whoever this man is, he's not a local."

"How do you know he wasn't buried in someone's backyard?"

"Because he's been embalmed." Inspector Piper taps the side of his nose. "See, Ms. Wilde? I *do* know a thing or two about detective work. What do you make of that?"

"Of his having been embalmed, or of you doing your job?"

His only response to that is to stretch and scratch the back of his head. Since he gives every appearance of being willing to stand out here in the middle of a cemetery for the rest of the day if it means getting the better of me, I decide to answer the question for myself.

See, to Inspector Piper and the entire Hartford family, the bones are the real crux of the matter around here. Whether put there by human or spirit, they must have come from somewhere. From some*one*. And until they know who that someone is, they're not quite comfortable with their existence.

To me, however, the bones mean very little. They're a red herring, a side quest. Who cares about a person fifty years gone when there's someone else inside that house who's been more recently murdered? When there's someone inside that house who recently murdered?

"I think the bones are a distraction," I say, not mincing matters. "You're investigating the wrong death, Inspector. I know you don't believe me, but there was a man at the bottom of those stairs." When he opens his mouth to say the inevitable, I add, "A *dead* man. I know that as surely as I know you're alive and standing next to me."

"A pity your surveillance equipment didn't capture him," the inspector murmurs.

"A pity the murderer broke it all after he was done," I counter.

With that, we reach an inevitable impasse. I'm about to bid him farewell so I can get back to my *real* work when he surprises me with one last insight. "I did a little research into your profession. Fascinating stuff, spirit work."

The fact that he's calling it by its precise terminology does little to relieve my mind. I'd be among the first to say that much of the so-called spirit work out there is nothing more than a sham. "Oh?" I ask politely.

"Seems it's part of a booming industry for the sale of human remains. According to what I found, it's much easier for your kind to get a ghost talking if you're rattling around with his skeleton in your bag. Is that true?"

My horror at this fresh accusation is almost as high as when he'd implied that the bones under the stairs were from this cemetery. I know I'm no saint when it comes to this sort of thing, but if it weren't for Winnie, I like to think I'd be a nice, normal girl with a nice, normal job. A circus clown, perhaps. Or a chain-smoking detective.

"I don't sell human bones," I say, my teeth clamped tight. "I don't buy human bones. I don't dig up human bones. In fact, until I came to this godforsaken place, I can't say that I ever came into contact with any human bones except the ones inside my own skin."

I have a lot more to say on the subject, but I can recognize futility when it's staring at me with an unlit cigarette dangling from its lips. Without waiting for Inspector Piper to respond, I reach into my bag for the picture I've been carrying with me ever since Rachel drew the last whisker.

"Take it," I say. "It's the dead man. I don't know his name, but I do know he visited the village museum recently. Benji, the guy who works there, will confirm it for you."

He doesn't, as I expect, take the drawing. He looks at it for a long moment and then back at me.

I shake it. "I have reason to believe the man was snooping around the Hartford family files at the museum. He may have even removed some of them. No one I've talked to up at the castle admits to having seen him before, but I haven't confirmed yet with Thomas. I'm having a hard time getting in contact with him."

That gets the inspector to move, even if it's only to take the paper between two fingers and let it dangle. "Getting in contact with him . . . through the spirit world?"

"No." I stifle an indignant snort. And here I thought Inspector Piper and I were finally reaching an understanding. "He's not dead. At least, I don't think he is. But he's not at his house, and no one seems able to tell me where I can find him. You do know he's the only person at the castle not accounted for the night I stumbled on the body, right?"

Inspector Piper doesn't answer me, but something about the way his eyes narrow at the edges makes me think he's well aware of that fact—and as concerned about it as I am.

Huh. Maybe he's not as terrible a detective as I feared.

I indicate the picture with a nod. "So, are you going to talk to Benji and investigate that man's death or not? Because if you're just going to throw the sketch away, I'd rather hold onto it myself."

"I'll look into it," he says and pulls the picture out of my reach.

Sensing that my interrogation—for an interrogation it clearly was—is coming to an end, I add, "And you'll let me know once you identify who those bones belong to? That's how this works, right? I give you a lead, you give me one?"

In response to this, the inspector flattens me with a long look before finally moving to light his cigarette. I suspect he's going to laugh at my effrontery and tell me exactly what I can do with my meddlesome interference, but he eventually shrugs. "Why not? You be sure to keep me apprised of the facts as they become available, Ms. Wilde, and I'll see what I can do."

Chapter 19

❧

If it weren't for the obvious sacrilegious implications, I'd use institutions exactly like the village church for every séance, palm reading, and ghost-eliminating ceremony I hold. The square tower stands as a beacon for miles, tall and rocky and with a black crow perched ominously on top. The weathered stone exterior is pockmarked with moss. The doors are thrown open to reveal an interior that's dark and gloomy, with wood grain and musty-scented air at every angle.

It's perfect. Even Castle Hartford, with its rambling decrepitude, can't match the Anglicans when it comes to setting the mood.

By the time I arrive, the afternoon services have long since finished and the parishioners have disbursed, the timing of which is no accident. Flaunting tradition is something I enjoy as a general rule, but not when I've also been accused of being a witch and a murderer in the bargain. I was hoping to make this as understated a visit as possible.

I haven't spent so much time in churches that I know the protocol for hunting down a religious official, so I approach hesitantly. The echoing emptiness of the antechamber makes me think I may have missed my opportunity for a tête-à-tête with the local vicar, so I'm deeply appreciative when a round, pretty young woman with bobbing brown curls and a tasteful black suit comes around the corner to greet me.

"Hullo there," she says. "You look lost. Is there some way I can help you?"

"Actually, yes," I reply, instinctively drawn to that warm voice. "I'm looking for the vicar. Do you know where I can find him?"

The woman smiles and extends her hand. "No, but I know where you can find *her*. Lovely to meet you. I'm Annis. Annis Brown."

More out of habit than anything else, I take the hand being offered me and give it a perfunctory shake. It's only then that I note the woman's tasteful black suit bears a signature white notch at the throat.

"But you're so young," I say, unthinking.

"And female, too." She laughs. "The nerve."

"I didn't mean—" I begin, but I'm not sure how to finish. Mostly because I *did* mean it. In my head, the village vicar is a crabby, wizened old man shouting fire and brimstone down on everyone's head. This woman looks barely capable of lighting a match.

"Are you a tourist?" she asks, nothing but polite friendliness in her tone. She shifts from one well-heeled foot to the other. "If so, you'll want to see my curate, not me. I can discuss Ecclesiastes for hours, but I can't talk for more than two minutes on the history of this building. Crossbeams and keystones have never been my specialty."

"Um." I wince, finding myself at a loss. I'd been fully prepared for a confrontation with the crabby, wizened old man of my expectations—was almost looking forward to it, in fact.

This calm, smiling woman is something else entirely. "Actually, I'm here to see you."

"Oh?"

"To . . . apologize."

A flicker of understanding moves through her brown eyes, but she doesn't say anything. Emboldened by that soft look, I explain, "I, uh, may have inadvertently been the cause of your missing sacramental cup. I'm Eleanor. Madame Eleanor. From up at Castle Hartford."

"But you're so young," she says.

It takes me a few seconds to realize she's joking, her words an exact echo of my own. In fact, I'm still not a hundred percent convinced of it until a smile moves across her face, rendering her even more youthful and pretty than before.

She's not, it appears, going to run me out the door with a pitchfork. In fact, it's starting to look as though she might be the one person in this village who doesn't think I walk with the dead at night.

As if in proof of this, she adds, "I was hoping you'd pay me a visit. Though, to be honest, I was anticipating someone much more . . ."

"Sinister?" I offer.

"Let's say someone with a harder edge. You're awfully pretty for a psychic, aren't you?"

"I might say the same of you."

"It's a trial, isn't it? Such glamorous looks as ours?" Annis heaves a mock sigh. "It's a good thing we're such reasonable women, or it might go to our heads."

I can feel a grin tugging at my lips. "I don't think anyone has ever accused me of being reasonable before."

"Haven't they? I don't know what else one would label a calling like yours. What could be more reasonable than helping people be comfortable in their own homes?"

Her easy acceptance of my profession leaves me somewhat startled. For a moment, I fear that village gossip has misled her somehow, painted a portrait of me that's much more flattering than I deserve, but reality soon takes over. Annis called me a psychic—and a hard-edged one, at that. She also believes Mrs. Brennigan stole a sacramental cup at my instigation. Nothing dispels illusions faster than premeditated theft.

Like the perfect hostess Vivian has no desire to be, Annis gestures toward the nave, where rows upon rows of wooden pews lie in wait. "Would you care to sit down?" she asks. "We can have a much cozier chat that way."

Although it had been my intention to ask my questions and get out of here as quickly as possible, I find myself intrigued enough to follow her lead.

"I honestly didn't know Mrs. Brennigan was going to take your cup," I say as we slide into the closest pew to the back. The hard wood platform is as uncomfortable as it looks, but I find I don't mind as much as I might have, had Annis been literally anyone else. "I gave her a list of tasks to perform to help with my, um, spell. But none of them were meant to be harmful, I promise. It's just little stuff—fun stuff. I was only trying to help her regain some of her confidence."

"Were you? You'll have to let me know how it works. The poor dear could use some fun in her life. She's been rather mopish since her youngest went off to university." She smiles again. "Now. Tell me how I can assist you."

I glance around, half expecting one of the Hartfords to pop out of the woodwork. Either that or Inspector Piper with a tape recorder in one hand and a pair of handcuffs in the other. "Assist me?"

She folds her hands serenely in her lap. "Yes. You're not the only one with the power to see beyond the surface, you know. You're troubled by something."

I open my mouth and close it again. I'm troubled by many things, not the least of which is the fact that this woman seems to know an awful lot about me. Somehow, however, I doubt that's what she means.

"Is this your first encounter with death?" she prods.

"You mean the body I found?" I ask, startled. "God, no. I mean—Not God. Just regular no. *No*. Death and I have been friends for a long time."

"How terribly sad. You lost someone close to you?"

My pulse picks up as I decide how best to answer her. The situation calls for honesty, but discussing my relationship with the great beyond isn't something I care to do with a person's whose literal job is to bestow promises of eternity and rainbows.

"In a manner of speaking." I finger the frayed bottom of Thomas's jacket. "My sister isn't . . . well."

"She's ill?"

"In a coma." I speak with as much matter-of-factness, as much reasonableness, as I can muster. "Until a few days ago, she was able to breathe on her own, but she recently suffered a seizure. Now she's hooked up to machines, which is a thing I promised her I'd never do."

"I'm so sorry," she says simply. "That sounds terrible for you both."

"It is." I hesitate, wondering just how far I can push this woman on our first meeting. Feeling reckless, I decide to test my limits. "She communicates with me, you know. Up at the castle. I don't know what it is about that place, but I can hear her talking to me."

Annis's expression remains impassive. "Can you? What does she say?"

"She's helping me solve the murder."

That, at least, causes a twitch at her temple. Without losing eye contact, she asks, in a much gentler voice, "That would be the bones that were found?"

"No. That would be the dead body that *I* found. The dead body everyone thinks I made up." I root around in my bag and pull out my phone. I may have given Inspector Piper my only physical copy of Rachel's sketch, but I'm not so lost to common sense that I didn't snap a picture of it the second she finished drawing it. I hand the phone to Annis. Since she already seemed to know so much about *me* being here in the village, I can only assume she'd be equally acquainted with other visitors.

"This is him." I tap the screen. "Can you recall seeing him before? Maybe passing through town recently? Stopping by to admire the architecture?"

She takes the phone with a slightly lifted brow and gives it a brief perusal. "Sorry, he's not familiar. Like I said, my curate tends to handle the tourist trade. We have a guest book, though, if that might be of interest to you."

Since I don't know the man's name and I doubt he'd have so blatantly advertised his activities in the first place, the book is of little use. "No, thank you. But if it's not too much to ask, I would like to take a look at older church records."

"Older records?" she echoes.

"Yes. Benji—the boy who works at the village museum—said that if I wanted to search for a specific person in local history, that would be the best place to do it."

"Who are you looking for, if you don't mind my asking?"

"Anyone named Xavier."

"Xavier . . . ?"

"I don't know." I offer her a self-deprecating shrug. I didn't realize until I uttered my request aloud just how feeble it sounds. "I have no last names and no other identifying information. But I know the name doesn't appear anywhere in the Hartford files, so it must belong to some other family."

"And this will help you and your sister solve a murder?"

From the way Annis phrases the question, I can't decide if she's asking out of genuine curiosity or out of concern for my mental and spiritual well-being.

"It will help me make sense of what's been happening up at the castle," I hedge. "Which, to be fair, is exactly what I've been asked to do. If you're concerned about whether or not the Hartfords would approve, you can call Nicholas. He's the one who hired me."

"Oh, I never call Nicholas if I can avoid it," she says with a disarming grin.

When my only reply is to stare gape-mouthed at her, she adds, "Well, it's not the least use, is it? He never tells anyone what they want to hear, and then somehow turns every conversation around so he ends up getting his own way."

Although the portrait she paints is one hundred percent accurate, I'm having a hard time digesting the information. "You know Nicholas?" I manage.

"Of course. How do you think I'm so well-informed? He sought my advice before going to seek you out—you won't mind if I tell you that I had my reservations? But I can see now that you're exactly what was needed."

My head whirls with the implications of her forthright speech, but foremost in my mind is that I should have known something was up when Nicholas urged me to attend services today. It's the exact same thing he did with the dovecote— telling me what to investigate and when to investigate it, controlling my actions from afar.

Almost as though he's a puppeteer. Almost as though I'm his puppet.

"But how—?" I begin, more bewildered than I care to admit.

"You're not familiar with small English villages, are you?" She releases a kindly cluck. "We like to pretend we've adapted to modern times, but the reality is that we're just as married to our traditions now as we used to be. Nicholas helped me get my posting after I was ordained. I grew up here."

"Then you know Thomas, too?" I ask. "And Fern?"

"Oh, yes." She nods as though her intimacy with the family is the most natural thing in the world. "Nicholas and Thomas were a few years ahead of me, and the last thing they wanted was a grubby schoolgirl hanging on their every word, but I used to follow them around whenever they came into the village. I don't have to tell you that I fancied Thomas something terrible. He was bidding fair to become a dish, even back then."

For the first time in my life, I wish I had a better religious education. Annis is the first person I've encountered who might have answers to the unique family dynamics up at Castle Hartford, but I have no idea how to gauge her loyalties. She *seems* trustworthy, and I feel like there must be some kind of confessional rule in place to protect me, but everything is still so murky. How can I be sure that any questions I ask her won't find their way back to the castle? To Nicholas?

"Did you ever go with them on their quest to find the smuggling tunnels?" I ask, sensing this to be the most neutral territory.

She finds nothing odd in the question. That's how much a part of the local folklore those tunnels are. "Not directly, no. But you could often see them heading out for the day—ask anyone around these parts, and they'll tell you the same. Fern might have looked like the ringleader, marching those two little boys around, but no one ever doubted it was Nicholas who really wanted to find them. He's always had that masterful way about him."

I stop breathing; the picture that Annis's words conjure up is one I'm having a difficult time seeing clearly. Not because I don't believe her, but because I *do*. For the second time in as many days, I've been presented with an incongruous timeline of the Hartfords and Thomas in their youth. When Nicholas spoke of being bundled up by Fern, I'd assumed it was a figure of speech—one of those Britishisms that gets lost in translation. But Annis has just confirmed that my initial estimate of their respective ages was off.

Way off.

"Annis—Vicar Brown—Your honor—" I shake my head. "I'm sorry. I don't know what I'm supposed to call you."

She chuckles. "Annis is fine."

"Annis, can you tell me how old the Hartfords are?" I don't wait for her to answer. "Is Fern *older* than Nicholas?"

"Oh, yes. Well-preserved, isn't she? She always was accounted a beauty in her youth, but in my mind, she only improves with each passing year." Annis pauses and bites her lower lip, her eyes cast upward as if doing the mental math. "Let's see . . . the year she turned thirteen was about the time she stopped showing up in the village with the boys in tow. Thomas was nine, which would have made Nicholas around ten or eleven."

I shoot up out of the pew so fast it causes my head to spin. Annis isn't too far behind.

"Are you alright?" she asks. "What did I say?"

I don't answer her, too caught up in the implications of her revelation. All the pieces of the puzzle might not be falling into place yet, but I'm starting to get a clearer picture—and I'm not at all convinced that I like what I see. If Nicholas is younger than Fern, then he's not the heir to the estate. Fern is. *She's* the one who could decide to sell, the one who holds the fate of the Hartford lands in the palm of her hands.

All that talk of primogeniture and Vivian being sent to a home, of the possibility that Cal has been disguising himself as Xavier to drive down the property price—this whole time, it's been about Fern.

In other words, it's Fern who stands to inherit. It's Fern who has everything to gain. It's Fern who has everything to lose.

I don't realize how pale I've become until Annis touches my arm, forcing my attention back to my present surroundings. "Eleanor, perhaps you should sit down again. You look as though—well, to be perfectly frank, you look as though you've just seen a ghost. What is it?"

I shake my head, unable to answer her and therefore unwilling to try. I have no idea what I've stumbled on, but a deep sense of unease floods through me. Nothing Annis has just told me is revelatory in an extraordinary way—one look at the family's driver's licenses would have done just as well to apprise me of their respective ages. In fact, now that I think about it, the only person who told me with any certainty that Nicholas was the family heir was Rachel, who isn't the most trustworthy source of information. She could have easily misunderstood the details of the succession.

It's all those other things that alarm me: the death of a mystery man as interested in the Hartford family genealogy as I am; Thomas's disappearance; Cal slipping his dinner hostess a thousand pounds to secure an introduction to Fern . . .

"Cal," I gasp.

"Yes, Eleanor? What about him?"

Oh, nothing. Just that however little a fake ghost might compel *Nicholas* to sell his property, Fern would be much easier to sway. In fact, Fern has already voiced her willingness to pack up and leave the castle behind. One or two more torn dresses overnight, and she'll probably sign over the deed tomorrow.

Nicholas was right from the start. He is smarter than he looks, *our Cal*. He may have even been the one to plant the bones under the stairs in an effort to oust Fern faster. After all, he admitted to having access to bodies, didn't he? The very first night I met him, he told the tale of a cemetery attached to a recent property he'd sold, displayed an irreverence for the dead that not even I can match.

"Eleanor?" Annis prods.

I don't explain my sudden start. "Nothing," I say with a forced smile. "It's only a thought I had. Thank you so much for taking the time to talk to me, but I should probably head back to the castle. Besides, you must be very busy on a day like today."

"Nonsense. I always have time to help a friend."

"Is that what we are?" I ask, somewhat taken aback.

"Well, I meant Nicholas, but I do hope you and I can be friends, too." Her smile contains all of its earlier warmth as she takes my hand and presses it. "Especially if you'd like someone to talk to about your sister. I know it doesn't feel like it now, but you aren't alone. Not if you don't want to be."

I don't know how to take her words. They recall me to a sense of my current situation, to the fact that I'm burdened with a man who's dead and a sister who's not. Unfortunately, there's no time to unpack it all now. I have no idea how the dead man and the missing bible page fit in with everything yet, but I feel certain I'm just a fake spell or two away from figuring it out.

"I have to get back there," I say. "I have to get home."

"Home?" she echoes.

I blush as I realize what I've just said. "I mean that figuratively, of course. The place I'm staying, the castle. I should get back before anyone starts to worry."

I don't wait to see if my hasty explanation holds. I have no more of a right to that castle than, say, Nicholas Hartford III, but, like him, I'm finding it more and more difficult to cut myself off from it. And I don't even have the excuse of dozens of ancestors buried nearby.

I do, however, have a plan.

If Cal thinks he can use a ghost to spook Fern into selling a castle, then it's only fair that I use a ghost to spook Cal into admitting it. I know just how I'm going to do it, too. Not with bones and not with a Ouija board, but with the one thing that's never, in all my years of ghost hunting, let me down.

In other words, it's time for Madame Eleanor Wilde to hold a séance.

Chapter 20

"I need you to tell me everything you've discovered about Cal Whitkin." My phone is once again jammed under my chin as I attempt to multitask. "And I need you to tell me fast, because I have about five percent battery and no way to access my power cord."

"Hello to you, too," Liam promptly responds. "What happened to your power cord?"

"Four percent and counting. Here kitty, kitty. Nice kitty, kitty."

"That's it. I'm booking a seat on the next flight out there. You've finally cracked."

I sigh and draw the dish of tuna out of the cardboard box I've upended on its side. Even this demonstration of my innocence isn't enough to get the cat on the opposite side of Thomas's kitchen to look at me. She's been sitting above the sink, twitching her tail and disdainfully staring out the window, for at least half an hour now.

"I haven't cracked. I'm trying to abduct a cat, but she isn't being cooperative." I glare at the animal in question. I'd hoped the scent of the fish would draw her close enough that I could drop the box over her head, but she's no fool. I'm going to need to rethink my strategy. "The stupid thing would rather die than go with me. I'm no Dr. Doolittle, but I'm better than a slow and painful death by starvation."

"That's up for debate," Liam mutters. He's a much better sport than the cat, however, and starts rattling off what I need to know. "Cal Whitkin, forty-three years of age, college dropout, self-made man. Never married, no kids, net worth of around a hundred million, though that number varies depending on who you ask. Let's see, what else? He loves long walks on the beach and—"

"Three percent," I warn. "Stick to the facts, if you please."

"That is a fact!" Liam protests. "It says so on his dating profile."

Despite the fact that the cat has finally turned to face me, the twitch of her nose belying her disinterest, I allow myself to be momentarily diverted. "You dug up his dating profile?"

"I'm very thorough. Apparently, he loves both walking on the beach and flying kites."

"Aw. That's kind of sweet."

"Don't fall too much in love. He claims to only date women who are 'into fitness.'"

"Gross." I may not spend much time online, but even I know *into fitness* is code for unrealistic body expectations. "Okay, so he has an obscene amount of money and no class. I knew both those things already. What else?"

"Not much. Most of his money comes from real estate, though he kept himself buoyed during the housing bubble by buying up struggling tech companies."

"What kind of tech companies?" I ask.

"Software development? I dunno, Ellie, the guy is pretty straightforward. I mean, you can't get that rich without a little shady dealing, but nothing pops out. Maybe he just really loves that Fern lady."

I snort. "Sure."

"It happens, you know," he says, picking up on my disbelief in an instant. "Sometimes there aren't any ulterior motives. Sometimes people just do things because they care."

First of all, that's not true. People *always* have ulterior motives, whether it's money or sex or power or any combination thereof. Secondly, no one would stay in a castle to be cold, hungry, and beset by murderous ghosts without a very good reason.

I mean, *I'm* still here, obviously, but that doesn't count. My motives are nothing but ulterior. I'm attempting to kidnap a cat out of a missing man's house so I can use her in a séance, for crying out loud. If that doesn't smack of shady dealings, I don't know what does.

"Do you think a laser would do it?" I ask.

"Do what? And where would you even get a laser?"

"There has to be some kind of app," I reply, but I give up on the idea anyway. Thomas's cat doesn't strike me as the sort to go for playfully pouncing after electronic lights. "Not that I have the battery for it. Which reminds me . . . It might be a few days before I can call you again, but it's not a big deal, okay? No worrying and no flying out to rescue me. I'm really close to solving this thing. I know it. Save your energy for Winnie instead."

Liam's silence says almost everything: disbelief, disapproval, dismay. My phone's warning beep says the rest.

"She's holding on, right?" I ask. "She's stable?"

"Yeah, Ellie. She's holding on." He hesitates before adding, "The real question is, are *you*?"

I don't know whether to be relieved or disappointed that my phone chooses that moment to go dead. Maybe apprehensive is the best word for it. Although I've been alone in the cottage since I walked in, the solitary silence of it engulfs me all at once.

A cell phone might not be much protection against a murderer, but at least it was something—a helpline, an escape. With that last tie to my real life severed, I'm more adrift out here than I realized. It's almost like being stranded on a strange, foggy island.

Which, from a geographical standpoint, is exactly what this is.

"You'll save me, right?" I ask the cat. "You won't let me come to any harm?"

Giving up on the box trap entirely, I set the tuna on the counter, well within the animal's reach. Finally interested, she offers a tentative sniff.

"Oh, sure," I mutter. "*Now* you want to eat. I don't know how cats got such a mysterious reputation. You're more like a spoiled toddler than an underworld beast."

At the sound of the word *beast*, the cat's ears twitch.

"Do you know that word? Beast? Is that what Thomas calls you?"

The cat's ears twitch again. Although I wouldn't go so far as to say it's a sign, the name does seem to fit. It's not as if I can call her Cuddles.

"Okay, Beast." I prop my chin on my hands and stare at the animal, willing her to heed me. It's a stretch, I know, but I'm running out of options. "You obviously like it here, and I'm sure you have a secret food source I don't know about, but live up to those centuries of vilification and help a medium out. Come with me to the castle, and I'll make it worth your while."

Beast licks her paw.

"I don't need you to do much, just appear ominously in the background once or twice in the guise of a witch. Will you do it? Meow once for yes and twice for no."

Beast blinks.

"Honestly, I'd have a better chance trying to get assistance from Nicholas. I hope you're not just a figment of my imagination. I'm already close to losing all my credibility around here as it is."

Beast twitches a whisker.

Heaving a sigh, I give up. Communing with spirits is easy enough to fake, but animals are a much more unpredictable niche. "Fine. I'll do all the work on my own. As usual."

But something I either said or did seems finally to have gotten through to the animal. Beast steps close enough to the food to begin eating it—and in so doing, places herself well within my reach. Tentative at first, I extend a hand to give the sleek, glossy fur a pat. When Beast doesn't move away—or, as I halfway suspected, dig her teeth into my flesh—I grow bold enough to slip a hand under her belly, warm to the touch.

And that's it. I lift, and the cat is in my arms. Not purring, mind you, and not the least bit interested in a snuggling embrace, but with her head pulled back so she can stare at me with those uncanny yellow eyes.

Fine, human, those eyes seem to say. *We'll do this your way. But I don't like it.*

"Well, I don't like it either," I reply as I surreptitiously reach behind me for the cardboard box. It's not the most elegant method of transport, but I couldn't find a basket. "Sometimes, we have to do unpleasant tasks to get rid of unpleasant things."

With a laugh, I realize I may have just landed on a new business model.

Eleanor Wilde: spiritual medium, cat wrangler, doer of unpleasant tasks. Cleanses homes of ghosts and murderers. Sometimes in the same day.

And usually without getting herself arrested—or killed—in the bargain.

The task of sneaking a boxed cat into a castle isn't one I plan to repeat anytime soon. Or, if I have any say in the matter, ever again.

Fate smiles upon me for once, which means the only person I run into as I try to saunter nonchalantly through the front door with a screeching box clutched to my chest is Vivian. She takes one look at me, blinks, and says, "Is that Thomas's coat you're wearing?"

It takes me a moment to register her question, a task not helped along by the sudden thumping of Beast as she hurls herself at the walls of the box.

"Um, yes?" I say. A sharp claw digs through the cardboard and into my forearm, but I bite back my yelp of pain. My voice only slightly strangled, I add, "I borrowed it for my walk. It was hanging in the closet—I didn't think anyone would mind."

"How odd," Vivian murmurs. She returns her attention to a still life painting overhanging the fireplace, rapt in her contemplation of a bowl of grapes. "He never goes anywhere without that coat. It was his father's."

At this, a spike of alarm moves through me, but it's nothing compared to the spike of Beast's claw finding purchase in my flesh.

"I'll put it back when I'm done," I promise through a gasp. "Now, if you'll excuse me . . ."

Vivian waves, no more concerned with my box than she is with the fact that she's staring at what is quite possibly the ugliest painting I've ever seen. I assume she's lingering in the foyer in hopes that Xavier will whisper some more instructions to make my life difficult, but she could also be waiting to deter any more visitors laden with food. I don't put either task past her.

I'm not a monster, so I don't leave Beast in the box for long. I'm also not willing to risk exposure, so it's into the cleaning closet off the dining room she goes. Ideally, I'd prefer to keep her in the yellow bedchamber, where the chances of anyone else finding her are slim, but the door to that room remains obstinately shut.

"Now, I know this isn't ideal," I tell Beast as I tip her out of the box and onto the closet floor. The inside of the cardboard is riddled with the deep scratches of her discontent, but she does no more than settle into a stately position where she lands, her long tail curled around her body. "But I have yet to see anyone in this house so much as hold a mop, so you should be pretty safe in here. And it's not so bad, is it?"

I stand and look around, pleased with my choice. The closet is one of the three doors I tried when looking for the kitchen that first morning, a narrow, deep room lined with cupboards on both sides. I imagine it was used as a storeroom once upon a time, holding silver and linens and chafing dishes for food service. Now it's all crusted mops and cleaning products—not very charming, of course, but utilitarian enough for my purposes. There's plenty of room to lay out some food and a pan of loose soil for a litter box.

"It's practically palatial," I tell Beast, feeling guilty at the sight of the feline accepting her fate so calmly. "And it's only for one day. I'll check on you as soon as I can."

I'm not sure how I expect her to respond—a meow, a growl, another claw in my forearm—but all she does is begin a painstaking bathing ritual and turn her back on me, no longer interested in anything I have to say or do.

I close the door with a quiet click. Pausing only long enough to ensure no protests are immediately forthcoming, I leave the cat to her solitary and stately bath.

It's not as if I have any other choice. If I'm going to pull this thing off successfully, there's quite a bit of work still to be done.

Chapter 21

"With your permission, Mrs. Hartford, I'd like to hold a séance."

As I'd hoped, my announcement has the effect of rousing the Hartfords out of their various states of postprandial stupor. Well, *stupor* might be pushing things, since Nicholas is reading his invariable newspaper and Rachel is giggling as she texts something on her phone, but the casual indolence of the rest of those sitting around the parlor is palpable. Honestly, until I arrived, I have no idea how these people entertained themselves for twenty-four hours of every day.

"What's that, dear?" Vivian asks from where she stands over the sherry. She pours out a glass and hands it to me. "A séance? Delightful. I was wondering what was taking you so long."

I ignore the rebuke and continue my prepared speech. Unfortunately, I'm still in Rachel's clothes, and I now have a crystal glass in my hand, so it looks more like a friendly toast than a mysterious announcement.

"The timing isn't ideal, since the moon is in its waning cycle, but my summoning draught worked. Xavier's presence is stronger than ever before, and he has something he wishes to tell us—something that could shed some light on his origins and purpose here. If we don't give him a medium for providing a voice, it's likely that you'll begin to see irreparable damages throughout your home."

"But he does have a voice," Vivian points out. "He talked to me yesterday, remember?"

As I'm being forced to plan and conduct a séance entirely without my supplies, which remain behind the door he told her to lock, I remember just fine.

Nicholas clears his throat. "And one might, if one were particular, argue that human remains under the stairs already constitute irreparability. We'll never get that smell out."

I swivel to glare him into silence. My tolerance for this man's genteel irony has reached its nadir. Amusing at first, that irony is now nothing more than an obstruction.

If he'd only *told* me that the castle is set to be passed down to Fern, all of this might have been solved ages ago. All that strutting around, pretending like he owned the place, when in reality he's no more than a temporary caretaker like Thomas—what was the point? Pride? Arrogance?

Or, a niggling worry adds, *something darker*?

I shake off the worry. I can only accomplish so much in one day. First on my list is to get Cal to admit to being Xavier for the sake of getting his hands on Castle Hartford. The other lingering questions can wait.

"Are you alright?" Rachel asks when I don't speak right away. "Is he here now?"

"He's always here," I say with a level look at Cal. Lowering my voice so that he knows I mean business, I add, "I require that all of the family be in attendance at the séance, so please open up your schedules and your minds."

"Are you sure that includes me?" Cal asks, scratching his nose. "Seeing as how I'm not strictly family?"

"Yes. And Thomas, too."

Rachel glances at her grandmother. "Has he come back yet?"

Vivian shakes her head, a frown pulling at the edges of her brightly painted lips—pink this evening, a little rubbed off at the edges, but still plenty visible. Even though it's still technically Sunday and therefore Thomas's weekend off, his continued absence is starting to worry even her. "Not that I'm aware of. Nicholas—?"

Nicholas's calm exterior shows no sign of worry as he voices a similarly negative response. "I wish we'd stop raising a hue and cry over a man who is not, as of yet, the least bit missing. There's time enough for panic after Madame Eleanor swindles us all with this séance of hers."

Rachel bristles, opening her mouth to defend my honor—a thing I appreciate but in no way need. For the first time since I've arrived here, I'm fully in charge.

"Afraid of what will be revealed?" I ask.

He flattens me with a stare and a calm, "No. I'm afraid you're going to string a puppet on a wire and make a bad situation even worse."

A bad situation? That's all he thinks this is?

"Ten o'clock tomorrow night," I announce. "You must all be in attendance. Your very lives depend upon it."

"But what do we wear?" Fern asks.

I bite back an exasperated sigh. I'm pulling out all the stops over here, making ominous commands and taunting them with events to come. My past clients could attest to how rare it is for me to go full séance, but these Hartfords have yet to recognize even a hint of my genius.

"Black," I say, since it seems the most obvious choice. "Particularly items of sentimental value or that Xavier has interacted with in the past. Any emotional or spiritual energy will be useful in calling his spirit to us."

"But what about you, Madame Eleanor?" Nicholas asks—

taunts, I should say. "With all your belongings locked up, what will you wear?"

I know what he's really asking: How will I manage to pull off a séance if I don't have access to any of my usual supplies?

Too bad this man has no idea what I'm capable of, how many years I've spent scraping to get by. I basically live in a hearse. I spend my holidays in a long-term-care ward. Almost every penny I earn goes to my sister's maintenance or the job necessary to continue that maintenance.

Besides, there were mediums faking séances long before the invention of electricity. I'm not without options.

"Ten o'clock tomorrow night," I repeat with a tight smile. "I think you'll find the results to be very interesting, Mr. Hartford. I think you'll find them very interesting indeed."

Just as Nicholas predicted, Thomas saunters through the parlor door with mere minutes to go until midnight.

"Ah, Thomas. There you are." Nicholas looks up over the newspaper he's been rustling nonstop for the last half hour, almost like a man anxiously awaiting an arrival. "We've missed you."

We've missed you? A man is dead, and someone dug up a corpse and relocated it to the kitchen—and all Nicholas can think to say is that Thomas's absence was a slight emotional burden?

Thomas sets down the cooler in his hand and nudges it with his foot. "I tried to come in through the kitchen so I wouldn't disturb anyone, but the outer door was locked. This is for your mother. Flounder, mostly, and a bit of dab."

Nicholas casts a very obvious glance my way. "And how was the fishing this weekend?"

"Cold," Thomas says and laughs. As if just now noticing me sitting there, he turns and grins. "It always is this time of year. I hope there wasn't too much excitement while I was away. Any more birds come shooting out of the chimney?"

I have no idea how to begin the task of relaying the events of the past three days, so it's just as well that Rachel jumps in and does it for me. Despite the lateness of the hour, the three of us have remained awake and gathered in the parlor in a stalemate to see who would give up the Thomas vigil first. Vivian took herself off a few hours ago, tottering up the stairs with what was left of the sherry bottle, and Fern and Cal slipped out to enjoy their indecencies as soon as decency allowed.

"Oh, Thomas—you won't believe what's happened!" Rachel cries. "First Madame Eleanor got all her electronic voice phenomena equipment smashed, which was strange, because even *I* didn't know where she'd put half of it. Then she fell down the kitchen stairs because Xavier pulled that step up again, and then—"

"What?" Thomas's glance is sharp, his voice full of alarm. "That's not possible. I used the fifteen-centimeter nails. They should have been almost impossible to pull out. Eleanor, are you alright?"

As he's the first person to show any concern about my physical well-being, I'm inclined to forgive him for disappearing on us and causing so much trouble. But then I remember his cat's empty food dish and pause. Beast might be the least pleasant animal I've had the misfortune to come across, but that hasn't stopped me from sneaking into the cleaning closet three times since I locked her in there to make sure she's comfortable.

"I'm fine," I say with a tight smile. "I hurt my toe a little, but it's nothing to worry about."

"She didn't get hurt because she landed on a dead body," Rachel supplies before continuing to tell the rest of our grisly tale.

I watch Thomas's face as the story unfurls. Nicholas, I note, is doing the same to me—gauging my reaction, trying to read clues in the expressions I allow to cross my face. I imagine he's just as disappointed as I am by the end. Nothing Thomas says indicates anything but horror and disbelief.

"Is that why the kitchen door is locked?" he asks, looking between us in growing bewilderment. "Because it's a crime scene?"

"Well, no," Nicholas admits. "The police are interested in uncovering the origin of the bones, obviously, but Madame Eleanor's discovery isn't being actively investigated. I locked the door merely as a precaution."

"My discovery is perfectly active," I retort. "Even Inspector Piper seems inclined to believe me at this point."

"That's another thing," Nicholas says. "The inspector will want to interview you in the morning. You don't know anything about those bones, do you?"

"How could I?" Thomas asks in some confusion. "That area under the stairs hasn't been used for storage since we were kids. I can't remember the last time I was in there."

"And you were really fishing all weekend?" I ask, unable to help myself. "You took a boat out that late on a Thursday night?"

"Of course," he says, looking to Nicholas as if for confirmation. "I can't get my clipper out unless it's slack water. You know that, Nick. You can check with the harbormaster. He saw me go out. We chatted about lures."

"Oh, I know," Nicholas says with his imperturbable calm. "I called him the moment Rachel told me it was your weekend off. I gave the inspector a line, as well, so he shouldn't give you too much trouble."

It takes a moment for my shock to wear off and anger to take its place. "You *knew*?"

Startled by the vehemence of my outburst, Rachel's eyes grow wide. "Knew what?"

"That Thomas—That the boat—That I—" There's no way to finish any of those sentences in a way that paints me in a positive light, so I allow myself to sputter out.

Each of Nicholas's placid assurances, every time he promised me that Thomas was fine . . . It wasn't just lip service. He'd known from the start that Thomas's movements were both accounted for and easily explained away.

But not once did he actually tell me *how* he knew it. Not once did he mention a harbormaster I could call for confirmation.

"I didn't realize you were such an avid fisherman, that's all," I say in a manner that convinces no one. "But I'm glad you're back. I borrowed your coat, by the way."

Thomas blinks at me. "My coat?"

"Yes, from the front closet. My room is locked, and Vivian lost the key, so there's no way for me to get in there. I needed it to keep me warm."

Two thoughts suddenly occur to me. The first is a welcome one, and I nurse it against my bosom with an avidity that borders on the perverse. "Speaking of, if you could find a way to get me in there before you leave, I'd be eternally grateful," I say. "Apparently, Nicholas is physically incapable of breaking down a door, and I'm dying to get my hands on my phone charger."

"I'm sure Thomas is exhausted and wants to get home," Nicholas says with a slight choke.

"But—" I begin and immediately clamp down on my lip. I have to, because the second thought is causing me a serious pang.

Beast.

She's still in the cleaning closet. I don't know Thomas well enough to judge, but I'm guessing that if I admit to cat-napping, he's going to have a few questions as to why. Saying I panicked because he was gone for all of seventy-two hours makes me sound deranged, but not nearly as much as the fact that I plan to use his pet as a prop for a séance.

"I suppose tomorrow will work," I say, flushing slightly. "We'll talk then."

An amused look flickers across Nicholas's face, but he doesn't say anything. He does, however, rise elegantly to his feet and nod a dismissal at both me and Rachel. "I think it's best if you ladies call it a night. Thomas, I'll walk you down to put the fish in the freezer. They'll be a welcome addition to our bounty."

"Bounty?" he echoes.

Nicholas laughs and begins to regale him with tales of the influx of food from inquisitive neighbors. Other than holding the door as Rachel and I file out of the parlor, he dismisses us from his mind.

I only wish I could so easily dismiss him from mine. For whatever reason, Nicholas is determined to make me as ineffective at ghost hunting as possible. Withholding information, sending me on errands to dovecotes and churches, plying the suspicion on with a trowel—if I didn't know any better, I'd say he wants me to fail.

But at the rates he's paying me, that would be preposterous. *Right?*

Chapter 22

Setting up a séance using nothing but supplies casually borrowed from a centuries-old castle requires much more effort than it seems.

Now that Thomas is back, I toy with the idea of delaying the big event until he shows up and manages to break down my bedroom door, but I hate to be so obvious. A medium who can't conduct a séance without access to her luggage is a medium who's up to no good. If I'm going to make this a convincing show, then I need to get results in a way that will mystify all.

"Well, Madame Eleanor, we meet again."

I smell Inspector Piper's cigarette before I hear his voice. I'm currently perched on top of a stool as I tack a length of black fabric to the ceiling of the parlor, so it's not the most ideal time for a rendezvous. But then, a worn sheet I had to dye using rusty nails soaked in a bathtub overnight isn't an ideal decoration. Sometimes, you just have to wing it.

"Can you do me a favor and hold the other end of this?" I indicate the drooping strip with a tilt of my chin. "I'm trying to ensure the room is as soundproof and dark as possible for the séance tonight, and I could use an extra hand."

He hesitates but eventually scrapes a chair across the floor. With slow, deliberate movements, he climbs on top and lifts the sheet. It hasn't fully dried from its overnight soak, so his fingers are probably going to turn black to match, but they're already stained by nicotine, so who's he to complain?

"Are you here to interview Thomas?" I ask in what I hope is a conversational tone.

"No."

"Spread the edges out a little more, please." I wait only until he complies before thumbing a few tacks in place and leaning back to admire my handiwork. "You aren't going to question him at all? That seems like shoddy police work."

He examines the damp pads of black dye on his fingers and grunts. "This seems like shoddy medium work, but you don't hear me complaining. He came by the office this morning."

"Oh."

I wait, hoping he'll tell me something to indicate whether he finds that whole the-harbormaster-gave-me-an-alibi thing suspicious, but all he does is glance around the transformation in the parlor with an inscrutable look in his eyes. Shoddy work the dyed sheet might be on its own, but as part of the whole picture, I'm quite pleased with the result. What the decaying grandeur of the parlor hasn't supplied on its own, I've made up for with wispy shawls and scarves borrowed from the ladies of the house tossed over light fixtures and on top of every painting and mirror. With the lights off and a few tapers strategically located near the draftiest spots, the result will be decidedly funereal. Especially since the shawls provide the additional advantage of hiding a few small upgrades I've added to the room for the night.

"Was there something you wanted?" I ask. "I hate to be

rude, but I've got quite a bit of work left to do before the séance tonight."

"What kind of work?"

I cast an obvious look at his cigarette. "Well, for one, I'm going to have to smudge the room with lavender to get rid of that smell."

"Smudge?"

"Burn aromatics to purify the air and call the spirits."

To my surprise, he puts the cigarette out, though he does it in a bowl that looks to be made of Waterford crystal. "And that works?"

I'm not sure how comfortable I am lying to him, so I hedge with "It doesn't hurt. Lavender can be very soothing to the soul. They used it inside Egyptian mummies all the time."

"Funny you should mention the Egyptians." Inspector Piper coughs. "Thomas seemed rather concerned about a cat of his that's gone missing. They had cats, too, didn't they?"

"Um."

"Strange thing, cats. My wife kept two nasty little brutes, always bringing dead mice and birds into the house. I told him they have a way of returning home on their own most of the time. I'm sure that's what will happen here." Inspector Piper's steely look is nothing short of a command.

"Yes," I agree with a gulp, "I'm sure it will."

Apparently satisfied with my response, the inspector begins a cursory examination of the parlor. His hands are clasped behind his back, and he does no more than peer closely at a few of my fixtures with a low *hmm* on his lips, but I can feel a cold sweat breaking out on my upper lip. In the bright light of daytime, and with the knowledge that Beast is shut up in the cleaning cupboard a few doors down, I'm feeling none too confident in my position. But he does nothing more than wander back to where I'm standing, his lips spread thin.

"By the way, Ms. Wilde, we identified your body."

Surprise prevents me from speaking right away, but I'm coming to learn that the good inspector relies on theatrical pauses as much as a fake medium. He stands and watches me, unblinking, until I gather my scattered wits.

"The bones?" I gasp. "Who are they?"

He gives a slight shake of his head. "Not that body. The other one. The, er, *fresh one.*"

His parroting use of my own words does little to abate the sudden thump-thump of my heart. "Holy hypnosis. You actually found it?"

"Not quite. We identified the man based on your sketch. Walter Powell, a trade compliance officer reported missing from his London home two days ago."

"I knew it!" I cry, much more triumphant than is seemly for a man who's been killed—and under this roof, no less. Tempering my excitement, I add, "Who is he?"

"Walter Powell, a trade compliance officer reported missing from his London home two days ago."

"Yes, I understood the first time. I mean *who* is he? His personality, his hopes and dreams, his reason for being inside this house in the first place . . . ?"

"If I knew all of that, I wouldn't need a psychic, would I?"

If I'm surprised to hear that the police have identified the dead body, it's nothing compared to my feelings at hearing the words *need* and *psychic* coming from those thin lips—however disdainfully that second one dangles.

"I'm sorry?" I ask, somewhat dazed.

He fingers a wisp of scarf. "I want a bloody cigarette," he mutters but doesn't reach for one. With a deep breath, he raises his eyes to mine with a directness that's disconcerting in the extreme. "I haven't told anyone outside the force about my findings just yet. If—and I want you to know how much this pains me—*if* you were to mention the name during your little séance tonight, I might find it in me to overlook your other crimes."

"But I haven't committed any crimes," I protest before remembering Mrs. Brennigan and the cat. Also possibly the fact that I've been using Thomas's house as a Liam calling center all weekend.

"The man's family is desperate for answers," Inspector Piper continues as though I haven't spoken. "They can't tell me what he was doing in Sussex or why he'd be mixed up with a family like the Hartfords."

"You could always ask them," I suggest.

"True. But in my experience, murderers tend to lie when asked direct questions like that. I can't imagine why." His sarcasm is so dry it sucks all the moisture out of the room. "Please, Ms. Wilde. You'd be doing me a big favor."

"Just dropping the name, all casual-like?"

He stares at me as though my IQ has sloughed off like a snake's skin. "Someone in this house knows more than they're letting on. Perhaps your . . . manipulations will rouse one of them to action."

"Oh." Awareness dawns, and with it, a burgeoning respect for Inspector Piper. I'm starting to realize he's a man after my own heart. "It's like arsonists watching a house burn after the firemen arrive. You want me to scare the murderer into checking on the body."

He tilts his head in a gesture that's half acceptance, half doubt. "That would be a best-case scenario, but yes. At this point, I'll settle for someone in the room blinking too many times. You'll do it?"

Well, yes. Naturally. A cat looking ominous in the background and warnings uttered under the guise of eternal damnation are good, but they're not *that* good. The name of the dead man is just the piece this puzzle has been missing.

"Wait—does this mean you're going to want to be present at this séance?" I ask. It's going to be bad enough having Nicholas watching my every move; I hardly need a detective added into the mix. "No offense, but no one is going to believe you're suddenly interested in the occult."

"My men and I will be stationed at various points around the grounds," he says, speaking down as if to a child. "In the event that your séance works."

Oh, it'll work. I have yet to perform a séance that didn't leave at least one person in hysterics. "Okay, but you're going to have to get a nicotine patch or something before you start your stakeout. If you leave piles of cigarette butts around, you're sure to give your location away."

He laughs, a dry, papery sound that's brittle from misuse. "You do your job, Ms. Wilde," he says, that brittle sound cracking open, "and I'll do mine."

There's no sign of Beast when I return to the cleaning closet.

Her food dish looks as though it hasn't been touched. The water dish bobs with clean provisions. Even the litter box appears not to have been used. In fact, if those items weren't still installed in the closet, I might have assumed I dreamed the whole thing.

But I didn't. I haven't dreamed any of this past week. All of it, from the gothic castle to the pile of bones to the team of cops waiting outside for me to set my trap, has been eerily, uneasily real.

"Beast?" I hiss, afraid to speak too loud for fear of being overheard. "Kitty, kitty?"

Nothing. Like the murdered man at the bottom of the stairs, the cat seems to have vanished into thin air.

"Come on, Beast," I hiss again, louder this time. "This isn't funny. The séance starts in a few hours. I need to hide you inside the game cupboard."

"Madame Eleanor? Hello? Madame Eleanor?" Cal's loud, officious voice sounds from somewhere in the dining room.

I contemplate the wisdom of crouching in the back of the

closet until he takes himself off again before deciding against it. For one, I still have quite a few last touches to put on my séance, and there's no telling how long Cal could spend snacking in the next room. For another, he notices the open door and pokes his vibrant head in before I land on a good hiding spot. The dumbwaiter is rusted shut, and I'm not sure I can fit my whole body inside one of those cupboards.

"I thought I heard you slip in here," he says, squeezing his large frame through the door and shutting it behind him. "Good thinking. I can never get over how many strange little rooms these old homes have. Just think—there were Hartfords living here all the way back when our ancestors across the pond were enjoying a little thing they like to call the Revolution."

The Hartford home is an interesting topic in light of recent revelations, but I don't like the fact that he's blocking my only exit. Cal Whitkin is a large man, no question. He's also my top Xavier suspect. I don't *think* he'll hurt me with so many people milling around the house right now, but I'm no clairvoyant. The future is a thing I can neither predict nor control.

I can, however, control conversations. As long as I'm trapped, I might as well make good use of my time.

"Yes, Nicholas was telling me a little bit about the place a few days ago," I say, casting my mind back on our walk along the rocky bluffs. "Apparently, it's very costly to maintain in this day and age. A money pit, I believe, was his exact term."

"Undoubtedly, undoubtedly. I know a little something of the profit margins around these parts myself."

My heartbeat picks up. "Oh?"

"Real estate, Madame Eleanor," he booms. "Real estate and tech. There's money to be made in this world, but only if you know where to look."

I'm unaccountably disappointed by this utterance, which is almost a verbatim replica of what Rachel already told me. Cal's Machiavellian tendencies are showing again. If he's going to be the villain of my piece, I'd like him to show at least a *little* more finesse.

A strange silence settles over us as I contemplate my next move. Cal seems strangely loath to leave me, but not in an intimidating way. By the time he opens and closes his mouth three times in succession without any words issuing forth, I realize there's something on his mind.

"You didn't come here to chat about real estate," I say and wait. When he still doesn't speak, I add, "There's something else that's troubling you."

It's eerily close to what Annis said to me yesterday—*you're troubled by something*—and a twinge of guilt fills me at having borrowed her phrase. She meant only to ease my burden; I'm trying to trick Cal into revealing more of his secrets. Though, in a way, I guess that's exactly what a vicar does: manipulates people into opening up, convinces them to share parts of themselves that are so deeply private they're closed even to God.

"It's the boy," Cal says after one more mouth-opening-and-closing attempt. No boys rise immediately to memory, and my expression says as much. To clarify, he adds, "The one who went missing."

The boy who went missing? "You mean Thomas?"

Cal casts a furtive look behind him, but the door to the closet remains firmly shut. As it's an interior room and there are no windows, he safely—and accurately—accepts that we're alone. "Something isn't right there," he says.

It's a sentiment I share, but I'm not yet sure what Cal's angle is, so I don't say anything.

"I've been staying here at the castle for eight weeks already. Can you believe it? Me, Cal Whitkin, rusticating in a dump like this for a woman."

"Love is a powerful thing," I say with a vague air. More realistically, I'd say that a warm body in your bed is a powerful thing, but that lacks a certain savoir faire.

"Between you and me," Cal adds with a conspiratorial air, "I normally stay somewhere with Wi-Fi and, well . . ."

"Room service?" I suggest.

He guffaws, the sound bouncing from the close walls, but it's a short-lived merriment. With a seriousness that's almost alarming, coming, as it does, from so ridiculous a man, he says, "From what I've seen, that Thomas kid gets every Wednesday off as well as his one long weekend a month."

"Tedious hours for a tedious job," I murmur.

"Sure is," he agrees. "But what I find strange is that he had his weekend off not too long before you arrived. Made a big show of it, too—came back with a bucket full of smelt. Nasty little buggers, smelt. I had to stock up on supplies. I figured it'd be just like old Viv to serve them for dinner all week."

I stare at him for a full ten seconds, his words taking that long to penetrate.

"He already had his weekend off this month?" I echo.

Cal nods and, as if afraid I didn't catch the rest of the story, adds, "Smelt fishing."

"But his whereabouts have been confirmed. By Nicholas and Rachel and—" I'm thinking of Inspector Piper and the harbor-master, but Cal's not supposed to know that I've spoken with the detective.

In the end, it doesn't matter, because Cal understands me just fine.

"This whole family is hiding something, to my way of thinking." His brows lower just enough to hint at the hard-edged businessman behind his massive fortune. "Excepting Fern, of course. That lamb couldn't tell you what month we're in, let alone what day. She's timeless."

Fern is neither timeless nor ageless, as we both well know.

"She'd never admit to it, but she's the oldest in the family. Did you know that?"

I stop, unsure if I heard him correctly. "Um. What?"

He winks. "You didn't hear it from me, but she's three years older than her brother. Of course, I'm not supposed to know it, but Cal Whitkin's no fool. She and the old lady signed this crumbling heap over to Rachel rather than admit her age publicly. Kept the kid out of school, too, which seems a little hard, but beautiful women are always difficult. Worth it, most of the time. Well, Fern is, anyway."

"I don't understand," I say, even though I understand the concept just fine. In fact, it explains quite a few things. A teenage daughter ages a woman in ways nothing else can. In order to hide her own advancing years, Fern would have to hide Rachel's—maybe even going so far as to keep her out of school and tucked away where the world can't see her.

But what I don't understand is why Cal is telling me this. And now, of all times.

"I'm just saying the family keeps things close, that's all. Rachel's uncle holds the place in trust for her, and does a good job of it, if you ask me, but what with Xavier and those bones . . ." He gives a rueful shake of his head. "I'd look into it myself, but I can't. Not without Fern knowing I'm on to her real age, so to speak. Got to keep the waters calm."

"So you don't want this property?" I ask. "You aren't trying to buy it from Fern?"

At this, Cal's eyes, never his most attractive feature, practically goggle out of his head. "What for? A man can't develop a National Heritage site like this one—not with the regulations this blasted country has in place. You've never seen people so in love with old rocks."

My head fairly spins with the information being hurtled my way. All the mysteries I thought I'd unraveled, the idea that Cal was behind everything, are now tied up even tighter than before.

"I'm sure there's a logical explanation for it all," Cal says in a tone that sounds falsely hearty, even for him. "Could be I'm blowing smoke before there's a fire, but I thought you'd want to know. Seeing as how that body just up and walked away from you around the same time that boy went fishing . . ."

"You believe me, don't you?" I ask, unable to stop myself. I don't normally suffer from such low self-esteem that I need to seek out reassurances from men like Cal, but I can't help it. Yes, I've started hearing my sister's voice, and yes, I'm halfway starting to believe the dead *can* walk around here, but I'm still the most rational person under this roof. That's one of the few things I do know for sure. "About finding the man at the bottom of the stairs?"

He seems slightly taken aback. "Well, of course I do. Why wouldn't I?" He leans closer even though his voice doesn't lower any. "In fact, that's the only reason I mentioned it at all. From some of the things Fern has told me . . ."

Once again, I'm back to carefully calculated silence. I'd love to hear some of the things Fern has told him, but I don't necessarily want *him* to know that.

He straightens again. "He'd do anything for the family, that boy. He's loyal. Well, stands to reason he'd have to be—he was born and bred here."

"They were good friends growing up, weren't they?" I ask. "Nicholas and Thomas?"

Cal looks pleased at my having filled in the blanks of his somewhat obscure speech. "Like brothers," he agrees.

I think of my own brother, Liam, so angry at the world, so angry at me for making what I can of it. I think of my sister, too, who hasn't felt an emotion of any kind—at least, not the kind I'm capable of understanding—in over a decade. As complicated as my relationships with them are, there's not a whole lot I wouldn't do for either of them.

Even murder?

This time, I can't tell if the voice is Winnie's or if it comes from somewhere deep inside me. The answer, however, is one hundred percent my own.

Yes. Even murder.

Enlightening though the realization is, it doesn't bring much in the way of clarity. Family loyalty is a strange thing and, as my instincts prove, a powerful one. But who is loyal to whom here? Is Nicholas preserving the house for Rachel's sake, or his own? Is Thomas so attached to the Hartfords that he'd resort to killing a man to protect them, or is he just another in a long line of victims to their villainy? And where does Rachel fit in their schemes?

The continued seriousness of the conversation seems to be palling on Cal, as though being anything but congenial is a physical trial. I'm feeling rather wearied myself, which is only natural when all of my suspicions have been turned on their head.

"Thank you, Cal," I say as I extend my hand in a gesture of goodwill. "I appreciate you taking the time to warn me. You have a high level of extrasensory sensitivity for a man of your age."

His grin spreads as he pumps my hand. "Do I?"

"Not everyone would be able to tap into the castle's emotional vibrations the way you have. You're aware of undercurrents even the Hartfords seem to have missed, despite their long tenure here."

"I am, aren't I?"

Cal hasn't yet let go of my hand, still moving it up and down in a hearty grip that's likely to leave me feeling sore for days. Which is why it's such a surprise when the movements stop, his palm clasping mine with sudden force. "Madame Wilde, if you want to leave this place, I can make it happen."

"What?" I ask, taken aback. I try to extract my hand from his grip, but I'm caught in its crushing power. "What do you mean?"

"I know the inspector asked you to stay until they find out who belongs to those bones, but I know people. I have friends." He pauses. "I can get you safely out of the country, no questions asked."

It's a strangely generous offer, especially coming from a man I was planning on publicly accusing in just a few short hours, and I can't help being affected by it. Like my first evening here, when he surprised me with snack foods, Cal's kindness is both unexpected and comforting.

"But what about Xavier?" I ask, even though the ghost is the least of my worries right now. "I can't just leave the Hartfords at his mercy."

He finally relinquishes his hold on my hand, dropping it with one last squeeze. "No, of course not."

"Besides, I'm a woman who sees things through to the end," I add, though I suspect I'm not convincing Cal so much as I am myself. "There are too many unanswered questions for me to feel comfortable leaving now."

It's nothing more than the truth. Unanswered questions seem to be all I have anymore.

"A woman with a work ethic," Cal says with a nod of approval. "Can't argue against that."

I think that's the end of it, our interview closed and a chance for me to investigate this room more thoroughly for séance purposes, but Cal allows himself one more serious moment first.

"If you change your mind, Madame Wilde, all you have to do is say the word. I can have a chopper here within the hour."

Chapter 23

By the time the entire Hartford family enters the parlor, the gothic wonderland effect has taken hold. What my decorations haven't supplied, atmosphere has; there's nothing like poor lighting and drafty breezes to make even the most cheerful house seem haunted.

And this house, shadowed with death and shrouded in mystery, is hardly what one would call cheerful in the first place.

"Please, come in," I say, inviting Cal, the four Hartfords, and Thomas across the threshold as if welcoming them to my home rather than their own. Of course, they quickly quash any feelings of superiority I might be feeling with their invariable comments on the changes I've wrought.

"Did she add *more* cobwebs to this room?" Fern asks with a shudder. "Just when I thought this place couldn't get any worse . . ."

Rachel leaps to my defense. "I think it's gorgeous—like a haunted bordello. I can't believe you did all this in one day, Eleanor."

"I only hope she didn't permanently remove the Gainsborough," Vivian mutters to no one in particular.

Cal is the last to offer his insight. "Well, look at that," he says in a voice that booms off the walls despite my addition of various scarves and sheets. "I barely recognize the place."

As if to reassure himself that I haven't, in fact, magically exchanged one centuries-old room for another, he yanks at the corner of a scarf, pulling down a strip of fabric and all five of the thumbtacks holding it in as he does. "Hard to see with all this fluff dancing around, though, if you don't mind my saying."

As a matter of fact, I do mind, but I paste a bland look on my face and invite him to sit at the table in the center of the room instead. In true séance form, I've arranged the furnishings around the outside of the room so they're out of the way. All that remains in the center is a round table covered in a blood-red velvet damask cloth I discovered in the linen cupboard. I even managed to weight the edges at various intervals with fishing sinkers from the garden shed. They have a handy way of tickling knees and causing my audience to take sudden fright.

"Why are there eight chairs around the table?" Rachel asks after counting the seats under her breath. "There are only seven of us. Is someone else coming?"

"I imagine it's reserved for Xavier," Nicholas murmurs. "How predictable."

He's right, of course, but I don't appreciate the way the family's running commentary is ruining the mood. "He is the guest of honor, after all," I say with some severity.

Rachel gives a delighted gasp and drops to the chair closest to her. "Can we please leave this one next to me open? I want to be the one he sits next to."

Fortunately for me, she's chosen the chair I intended to keep empty for our mythical final guest. I try not to do too much in the way of seating arrangements and making decrees when planning a séance like this, since they tend to alert the crowd to a pre-arranged agenda. One way to accomplish this is to use the most uncomfortable-looking seat for the ghost and to set it up as far away from the door as possible.

It worked, of course. It almost always does.

"I'll ask everyone to place their cell phones and other electronic devices in here," I say and pass around a wicker basket to hold their various pieces of tech. "We want as pure an environment as possible."

Everyone complies as the basket is moved around. Only Cal seems strangely loath to part with his phone.

"I'm expecting a call," he explains, casting a lingering look at his screen. "Business, you know. It doesn't stop, even for the dead. I've been saying so all week."

"Oh, are you planning on leaving us soon, Cal?" Vivian perks up at this, all pretense of talking in whispers and setting the mood now laid to waste. "What a pity. We'll miss you."

"He's not going anywhere, Mother." Fern winds her arm through Cal's and draws him to the nearest chair. "He's just making a joke."

Cal rubs the side of his nose and flashes a guilty look at his beloved. They, like most of the people in the room, have dressed as I requested, wearing formal wear that would work equally well at a wake or a wedding. Only Thomas has opted to stick to his usual attire, his jeans and plaid now a familiar sight.

"Now, love. You know I'm going to have to get back to New York eventually." Cal's guilty look transfers to me. "No offense, but this isn't the kind of house party I'm used to. Ghosts and bones, you know."

Nicholas's eyebrows lift. "Believe me, Cal, when I say this is new territory for all of us."

Determined to take hold of this séance before it gets any further out of control, I snuff the tapered candles I have located around the room's perimeter. In order to keep all eyes where I want them—namely, on me—it's important to cloak the rest of the room as much as possible. A single table lamp is the only light in the room. I place it behind me so that it silhouettes my figure, which is shrouded in a black lace tablecloth I've cut down into a makeshift mantilla. The effect is only slightly marred by the fact that it smells like mothballs.

Without waiting for anyone to comment on that, too, I sit opposite the empty chair. Next to me, Fern lowers herself to her own seat, sniffing at the theatrics that cast her so firmly in a supporting role. "This had better work," she says. "I'm getting mightily tired of playing Xavier's games."

Since I assume she's using Xavier as a euphemism for Madame Eleanor, I don't answer. Especially not when Nicholas takes the seat on my other side.

"Please bow your heads and take the hands of those seated next to you. It's important that the chain remains unbroken." I keep my voice low as two palms are slipped into my own. Fern's hand is soft and cool; Nicholas's is strong. He also shifts so that the entire length of his leg presses against mine, his foot brushing against my toes.

I think for a moment that he's flirting with me—using my temporary distraction to lay an amorous assault on my nether limbs—but his low chuckle corrects that assumption. He's just checking to see if there are any levers or bells I plan to hit with my feet, the jerk. He's loving this.

Well, two can play that game.

"I'd also like you to link feet at this time," I add. "Cross your ankle with your partner's and leave your feet flat on the floor. This will strengthen the chain and also ensure that no one is doing anything to disrupt the spirits."

"Touché," Nicholas says under his breath as he follows my command.

It's not the most comfortable way to sit, all of us tangled up like a game of Twister, but it's a fairly common trick I employ when facing a restless, cynical crowd. Table thumping and lifting with the knees are no longer used by any medium worth her salt, but those tend to be the main two things people look for.

"Now, I'm going to ask all of you to channel your thoughts toward the other world. Not to Xavier, specifically, but to the ethereal realm he inhabits. We're not trying to make contact with him so much as with the afterlife in general. He's one small part of a vast network. We must first access the network before we can access him."

"Like dial-up," Vivian says knowledgeably.

Across the table, Rachel snickers.

"Bow your heads and clear your minds," I command.

The bowing of heads is how I plan to get things started. I can make the moment last for as short or as long as I'd like, and according to my best guess, I have about a minute before the cold air is going to move through the room.

My usual methods are similar to what I did at the Levitt's house, with an air conditioner on a timer, but Thomas never stopped by to unlock my door, so I'm sadly air conditioner-less. I had to make do by copying the methods used by our bird bandit.

There was no evidence of a pigeon's nest inside the parlor chimney, but there is a damper on the flue. Anyone who wanted to propel pigeons into the room could have easily put the birds in the chimney ahead of time and attached a string to the damper. One quick, discreet tug, and the flue would have been opened at just the right moment.

At least, that's how I would have done it. The fact that there was a broken bit of twine underneath an unused log at the back of the fireplace only helped convince me. Someone in this room has a deep creative streak.

I can't tug a piece of twine without giving myself away, but I did open the flue and then shove a piece of wadding in there, precarious enough that it shouldn't stay up for long. As soon as it falls out, the cold from outside should pull all the air out of the parlor, which is warmer than usual thanks to my hard work heating it with a toaster oven I borrowed from the kitchen.

Before the cold fully hits, a low hum fills the room. It begins at the doorway and echoes back toward our table, courtesy of a little voice-throwing trick it took me about two years and a lot of YouTube videos to perfect. The result is that a cold air creeps from one direction, the voice from another. They meet in the middle of a table, causing a shiver to move down more than one spine in the room.

"It's happening!" Rachel cries in a soft voice. Someone— Vivian, I think—shushes her.

I allow a tremor to move through my body, the same kind of jerky spasm that happens right before a person falls asleep. Without allowing the low hum to stop, I slump in my chair. Depending on how alarmist you are, you might either think I've fallen asleep . . . or that I've died.

There's no stopping the outbursts after that.

"What happened to Madame Eleanor?"

"Is she—?"

"Has she reached Xavier?"

Jerking upright once again, I crunch down on the pill I've been holding under my tongue. It contains about a quarter of a teaspoon of the liquid from inside the glow stick Nicholas and I found in the kitchen catch-all, piped into a vitamin capsule from Vivian's medicine cabinet. It's not the most delicious substance in the world, but the bitter tang results in a convincing glow inside my mouth and over my teeth.

And that's it, really. With a wide-eyed look of wonder, I greet the table with a serene smile and an air of innocence.

"Hello."

"Xavier?" Vivian leans forward and squints. "Is that you?"

I release a bark of laughter that's bitter around the edges. "Who's Xavier?" I ask with a slight British lilt. A week in England, and I can feel the upper-crust tones taking over already. "The name is Powell. Walter Powell."

I can feel a ripple of confusion move through the circle. It's evident in jerking hands and low murmurs, in the way disbelief wars with excitement. Sitting patiently, I wait for the excitement to win. It usually does.

"Walter?" Fern eventually asks. As expected, she doesn't sound pleased at yet another manifestation appearing to steal the spotlight. "Who's that supposed to be?"

"*Another* ghost?" Cal grunts. "I hope you're not as bad as that other one."

"How did you die?" Rachel asks. "Was it murder? Are you the bones?"

I don't want to give too much of the story away, so I recite the message from the note left in my floorboards. I don't have it with me anymore, since it, like most of my belongings, is still trapped in my room, but the gist of it isn't hard to paraphrase.

"The dead walk at night. The spirits ever fight." I allow a strong shudder to shake my frame. "Those who betray will step into the light."

Beside me, Nicholas grows perfectly still. My eyes are busy doing this freakish rolling thing that always gets people's screams going, so I can't gauge his reaction. With one last jerk of my head, I release a preternatural howl and drop the hands of both Nicholas and Fern.

"Someone is trying to push me away," I cry in the voice of Walter Powell. "Someone else is here."

"Xavier!" Rachel gasps.

I bring my hands to my head as though in intense pain. In reality, there's one last deception for me to bring into play. I hadn't been kidding when I told Nicholas that I was a tricks of the light and wind power sort of girl. Nor was I bluffing when I assured him I could pull off a séance even without my bag of tricks.

The sole lamp, so efficient in the way it's casting light around the room, isn't just there for effect. I replaced the bulb so that it's supporting a much higher wattage than the voltage allows— a dangerous wattage, in fact. It's either going to fizzle out or, assuming the electricity around this place has been updated from the knob-and-tube wiring of the 1930s, cause a breaker to trip. Either way, I get a nice burst of darkness.

It takes a little longer than I'd have liked, but the breaker trips after another ninety seconds or so, plunging the room into darkness. With the heavily covered windows and door closed tight, it's the kind of darkness that nightmares are made of. Since I don't want to get caught in the fray of people running around and tripping over furniture, I stay exactly where I am, slightly slumped so that I'll look plenty exhausted by the time I'm roused back to awareness.

Which is why it comes as such a surprise to find myself yanked up and out of my seat within seconds of the curtain coming down. Even more surprising is the fact that I'm being yanked by a tight bolt of fabric around my throat.

I think, at first, that it's a side effect of the natural mayhem; until someone gets to a window or flings open the door, there's bound to be a little thumping and bumping taking place. But my airways don't open as I'm pulled out of the chair and dragged toward the back of the room by my mantilla. I realize, too late, that either end has been crossed over my throat and is acting as a noose being pulled from behind. My heels kick ineffectively at the floor, and I grab at the fabric, trying to loosen its grip.

It's fruitless. There's too much dark and too much noise, the sound of the ocean rushing through my brain.

I guess I'm going to be stuck in this castle forever, I think as a flash of light fills my eyes. Since the room is still plunged into darkness, I can only assume the light is coming from the end of the tunnel, so to speak. Where it will just be me and Xavier and Walter Powell. Together. For all eternity.

Don't be so dramatic, Ellie.

Maybe it's because I've lost almost all oxygen to my brain, but the voice sounds clearer this time, almost as though a pair of lips are pressed against my ear.

You never were happy unless you had a crowd.

I want to tell Winnie that it isn't true—that fame and fortune and attention would mean nothing if only she'd wake up again—but there isn't a chance. It's too late.

I can't see. I can't move. I can't breathe. The light at the end of the tunnel turns off with a snap.

And for good or for bad, there's nothing waiting for me on the other side.

Chapter 24

The afterlife proves itself to be a profound disappointment.

I'd always assumed it wouldn't smell like anything—or, if it had to carry a scent at all, it would be daisies or brimstone, depending on where I end up. In reality, it smells mostly like burned feathers.

It's also wetter than I thought it would be. Nowhere in the heavy religious tomes I mine for useful mythologies does it say anything about cascading sprays of water hitting you in the face. But that's exactly what I get.

I sputter, choking on a mouthful of water that tastes like rotting vegetation, wondering how I could have gotten my wires so crossed.

"I think she's coming to," an anxious voice says from somewhere above my head.

"Empty the other vase over her head just in case," commands another voice. "And tell Fern to stop burning those feathers. It smells like we're roasting pigeons in here. I'll never be able to get that smell out of the drapes."

"It's alright," a third voice says. It's not very anxious, either, the deep, masculine tones both ironic and familiar. "You weren't badly hurt."

"Yes, I was," I croak. The rasp of my own voice against my throat is painful and raw. I think about opening my eyes, but the task seems too wearisome to attempt. Making it halfway to death's door before returning back again is a lot more grueling a task than it seems. "I almost died."

"I imagine it takes more than a scarf snagged on a chair to kill you," the voice chides. Despite the lack of sympathy in his voice, Nicholas's large, cool hand drops to my neck, his touch gentle as it traces a line across my throat. It's only then that I realize I'm lying on the ground, semi-cradled in his pristine lap. "Do you think you can drink some of this brandy?"

He doesn't wait for me to answer as a glass is placed against my lips and a scorching dollop of hard liquor poured down my gullet. Nicholas lifts my head just enough for gravity to take over most of the work of swallowing, which is a good thing, since I don't feel equal to the task on my own.

As the alcohol begins to take effect, I become aware of my surroundings. As expected, I'm in the decimated remains of a typical Madame Eleanor séance. Chairs are upended, the table is knocked onto one side, and black scarves lie scattered around like a raging wake took place only moments before. Even more to the point, a bewildered and slightly shaken party stands in a semicircle around me.

Of course, they're usually shaken and bewildered because of the horrors of the great beyond, not because I was almost murdered in their midst.

Nicholas lifts the brandy glass again, but I shake my head, causing my tablecloth mantilla to slide from my neck and flutter to the ground. He seems inclined to force the drink on me, but I struggle into a sitting position. It's enough to convince him that my death isn't imminent, though I notice he keeps one arm bracing my back in the event that I fall into another swoon.

His other arm goes immediately to the scrap of tablecloth, which he tucks into his pocket before anyone has a chance to take a good look at it. From the brief glimpse I get, however, I can see that there's a large rent along one side, the delicate lace crushed at either end.

The ends used to strangle me.

"Is that what happened, Uncle Nicholas?" Rachel asks, her eyes wide. She looks as though she's been crying. "She caught her lace on a chair?"

"Decidedly so," Nicholas says before I have a chance to suggest otherwise. Now that I'm sitting up, my head swims and my throat burns even more, making it difficult to release the torrent of abuse I'd like to bring down upon his head. "She got the wind knocked out of her, that's all."

I open my mouth to argue, but Nicholas begins issuing curt orders to the room at large. In order to be heard over him, I'd have to shout, which is far beyond my means right now. Leaning against his arm and wishing I could rest my head on his strong, capable shoulder is all I seem able to manage.

I won't do it, of course. I might be half dead and well on my way to drunk, but I'm no fool. Therein lies desire, dependency, *madness*.

"Cal, please get the furniture back in an upright position. It would be nice if we could make it look a little less like a tropical storm moved through here. Yes, Fern, that is a very striking pose, but perhaps you could take your daughter down to the kitchen and make us all some coffee. Yes, *that* kitchen. I'm sorry, but it's the only one we have."

At this point, I'd like to remind him that breaking the group up into parts isn't the wisest idea, seeing as how one of them just tried to murder me, but I can't. Sensing that I'm fast regaining my strength and intend to use it, Nicholas tightens his hold on me, squeezing my rib cage so much that it's all I can do to keep breathing.

"Mother, I believe you have some liniment in your room that might work for this slight, ah, laceration on Eleanor's throat."

"Of course, dear," Vivian assures him, her voice low. "Whatever you say. She's alright? After that Walter fellow took her body over, and—"

"She's fine," Nicholas states firmly.

"I'm fine," I croak in agreement. It's a bald-faced lie, and playing into this man's arrogant handling of this situation rubs me in a very irritating manner, but I say it anyway. Vivian looks one strong wind away from toppling over altogether. Considering how happy she'd been before this whole séance started, as excited as if someone had just given her a pony for her birthday, her subdued air now feels almost oppressive.

"See? She's fine. Ah, Thomas. There you are. If you and Cal could clear the room a little now that it's back in a semblance of order? Yes, just those chairs there—and maybe that big table. Take them to the armory for now. That will get them out of the way."

I realize, with a start, that *getting them out of the way* is precisely what he's doing. As soon as Cal and Thomas hoist the table between them and cart it out the doorway, I'm left with Nicholas.

Alone. In the room where someone lately tried to kill me. Where someone seated nearby—say, in the seat directly next to me—tried to kill me.

The maidenly swoon that's been threatening to overtake me disappears at once. I scurry out of his arms and jump to my feet, ignoring the sudden loss of blood to my head and its accompanying dizziness.

There are still a few chairs standing around the room, so I find one and arrange myself behind it. It's not much—I'd have better luck holding back a lion with it—but I feel a little better once there's an object between us.

Nicholas just laughs in that cool, mocking way of his. "If I wanted you dead, Eleanor, you'd be dead. Have no fears on that score."

"Is that supposed to make me feel better?"

"Yes." With no more explanation than that, he whisks the lace tablecloth from his pocket and examines it. "It's fortunate this thing is so flimsy. A stouter fabric might have done you in. Do you have any idea who it was?"

I stare at him, agog, my mouth open.

"When we managed to get the lights back up, the entire room was in disarray, and there was no way to determine who'd attacked you. You were passed out in front of the fireplace. Did you notice anything in particular about the hands, smell or feel anything?"

"Did I feel anything?" I echo. Is he kidding? I felt a band around my neck, the air leaving my lungs, my soul leaving my body. Wasn't that enough?

He wraps the cloth around his forearm and crosses one end over the other in an approximation of what it must have looked like around my neck. Holding his arm in my direction, he asks in a mild tone, "Would you mind?"

I can only stare at him.

"For the sake of research, if you will. I'm curious about the amount of strength required."

His curiosity is contagious enough that I take a tentative step around the chair. Nicholas wants to know the likelihood of a woman—young, old, or anywhere in between—being the one to pull the scarf around my neck. In other words, he wants to know if his niece, his mother, or his sister was the one who had tried to kill me.

It's a difficult concept for me to wrap my head around. I always knew, on some level, that someone in this house—no matter how much I might like them—is capable of evil.

But to actually try to kill me? Vivian? Fern? *Rachel?*

There's nothing to do after that but comply with Nicholas's

request. Only slightly nervous at drawing close while my ability to scream is still so compromised, I take either end of the
lace and yank as hard as I can—a murderous yank, designed to
choke the life out of Nicholas's forearm. He doesn't wince or
cry out or anything like that, but from the way he gently tells
me to stop and a worried pleat lowers on his brow, I know the
experiment has been a success.

If success you can call it.

"It could have been any one of us," he says as he hands me
back the mantilla. "I'm sorry."

I want to ask him why he's sorry—for being the one to bring
me out here to die? for his inability to narrow the pool of suspects?—but the room fills with various Hartfords and their
satellites before I have the opportunity. The scent of Rachel and
Fern's coffee mixes with the mentholated jar of salve that Vivian carries in her hand. Cal's boisterous voice proclaims his
delight at seeing me standing. Only Thomas remains unobtru-
sive, posted at the door with a hard expression on his face. He
looks up and sees me watching him, the hard expression deepening.

If I didn't know any better, I'd almost say he looks angry.
At *me*.

"Put some of this on," Vivian says as she hands over the
salve. I try to reach for it myself, but Nicholas beats her to it.

There's something incredibly disconcerting about receiving
first aid in front of a crowd of curious onlookers. Even though
Nicholas is nothing but coolly polite as he commands me to lift
the strands of hair that have come loose from my knot, there's
no mistaking the intimacy of his fingers as they move over my
throat—careful, gentle. I've always been susceptible to a man's
hands running up and down my neck, lived for the moment
when he buries those same hands in my hair, tugging at my complicated knots and whirls. In fact, I almost fear that Nicholas is
going to do just that while his mother and sister look on, but he

stops almost as quickly as he began. He also shoves the jar into my hand.

"Apply it every six hours or so. I know it smells odd, but my mother is surprisingly adept at making these concoctions."

"I was a hippie for a good ten years," Vivian confesses. She also winks. "Let me know if there are any other . . . medicinal recipes you'd like to get your hands on."

"I hope her medicinal recipes aren't anything like her culinary ones," Cal says in a voice that's supposed to be an undertone but falls about ten decibels short of its goal.

Vivian, ever a lady, feigns deafness. "Well, that was an interesting experience, Madame Eleanor. Do you often get injured during these things?"

I'm not sure how to respond. Half of me wants to warn Vivian—warn all of them—that there's something deeply sinister going on inside this house. The other half has every intention of holding her peace. To admit to the murderer that I'm afraid would only invite them to try again.

In the end, I decide to use the moment to my advantage.

"Unfortunately, yes. I do. Connecting with the spirit world is a physical, emotional, and spiritual hazard, but it's often the only way to gather concrete evidence." I feign a thoughtful pause, allowing my gaze to wander from face to face. With the exception of Thomas over by the door, everyone looks much the same as they always do. If one of them tried to kill me, they don't seem too disappointed by the fact that I'm alive. "Without the séance, we might have never met Walter."

I hold perfectly still, hoping one of them will show a glimmer of recognition at the name. Either they're exceptional actors or the murderer didn't know the identity of the dead man, because no one shows so much as a hint of alarm. In fact, the only person to react is Fern, who groans in a highly theatrical way.

"Not this again," she moans, a hand pressed to her forehead. "If these séances and summonings are only going to keep adding ghosts, I, for one, vote we stop having them."

"That is the first sensible thing I've heard you say all week," Nicholas says. "Come along, Madame Eleanor. It's high time you were in bed."

I think of Inspector Piper lying in wait outside and balk. "But I'm not tired."

"Too bad. *I* am. I don't know how much more of this I'm willing to swallow." He takes me by the arm with a grip so firm, I suspect it will leave a bruise behind. One more mauling added onto the heap isn't something to cavil at this point, and I find myself being led away before I have a chance to fully voice my protest.

Besides, to be perfectly frank, bed isn't the worst idea I've heard today. The brandy is causing my head to whirl in lop-sided revolutions, and I'm so shaky from nerves and adrenaline I can barely walk. I just need some time to compose myself, a few minutes of reflection, and then I can slip outside to tell the inspector what happened. I think he'll find this new turn of events quite interesting.

I know I do.

"Nick, wait—" Thomas says in a harsh undertone as I'm pulled past him.

"Not now, Thomas."

"But—"

Nicholas turns on him with a wrath I never knew he was capable of. The heavy lines of his face are sealed into an angry mask, his brows knit tight. "Not now," he repeats, his words almost a curse. "I think you've already done enough, haven't you?"

My interest, roused by the unprecedented show of passion displayed by Nicholas, reaches its zenith. Thomas wasn't seated close enough to easily strangle me, but he's young and has shown himself to be suitably athletic to pull it off.

Then again, if the strength of Nicholas's fingers pressing into my forearm are any indication, so is he.

"I think perhaps I should stay downstairs," I suggest as we

move out of the parlor and into the relative isolation of the hall-way. "Where the witnesses are."

Nicholas is betrayed into a sharp laugh that causes him to loosen his grip. "Sorry. I didn't mean to hurt you." He takes my hand and lifts it, gently pushing up the sleeve of my bor-rowed sweater to examine his damages. There's something sen-sual in the way he does it, this act of undressing, the movement of his fingers as he exposes the gently beating pulse of my radial artery.

As if he, too, is aware of how delicate the life flowing through my veins is, Nicholas lifts my wrist and drops a gentle kiss. He holds it there a moment, his lips pressed against my skin, causing my heartbeat to leap erratically under his touch. For a moment, I think we're going to stay like that forever, but he finally releases me and steps back.

"What was that for?" I ask in a tight voice.

"Don't do that again, alright? I won't allow it."

I blink, unsure which of my many nefarious deeds he's refer-ring to.

His expression gentles just enough to cause my heart to flut-ter again. "I've grown rather fond of you, Madame Eleanor. There will be no dying until I've had a chance to figure out why. Now. Up to bed with you."

I'm so dazed by that confession—and by the way he utters it—that I allow myself to be led up the stairs. Past the artichoke wallpaper where my camera used to be. Beyond the door to the yellow bedchamber, which I'm starting to think I'll never see again. Through to Rachel's bedroom, where the rowan-berry-stained floor reminds me where I am and what I came here to do.

"Rest," Nicholas commands. Like my episode with Cal in the cleaning closet earlier, he stands in the doorway, blocking my exit. I don't have time to be alarmed by it, however, since he adds, smiling down at me, "I'll send Rachel up so you have a witness."

There are several questions I'd like to put to him, but he precludes these by asking, "How did you know, by the way? About our childhood rhyme?"

It takes me a moment to process the question. By the time I pinpoint the rhyme he's referring to as the note I quoted during the séance, he shakes his head. "I should know better than to ask by now, shouldn't I? You know everything. You'll be safe enough in here with Rachel. There's something I need to check on before we talk."

"Nicholas," I call, extending a hand. I'm not sure what I'm hoping to do with it—keep him close so I can kiss him? keep him closer so I can question him?—so I end up dropping it again. "Be careful, okay? Someone doesn't like how close we're getting."

His laugh is short and doesn't ring true. "Who are you kidding? Someone doesn't like how close we already are."

I only get a few moments to myself before Rachel joins me, entering the room quietly and shutting the door behind her.

"Ellie?" she asks, her voice small and her eyes large. The juxtaposition of the two extremes renders her absurdly youthful. "How are you feeling?"

Her eyes, I note, are fixed on my throat, where the marks of my near-strangulation linger. Thanks to Vivian's salve, they glisten, too. I can hardly blame the girl for being unable to look away.

I pat the bed where I've laid myself out, reposing in rapt contemplation of the ceiling as I try to figure out what my next steps are. In the short time it's taken Rachel to head my way, the only real plan I've come up with is to join Inspector Piper's vigil outside as soon as possible. He'd been correct in thinking the dead man's name would get a reaction out of someone: my neck can attest to that. Instead of going after the existing dead body, however, they tried making a new one.

"I'm fine, sweetie," I promise and pat again until she crosses the room to join me. "I always forget how drained I get after a séance. A good night's sleep, and I'll be back to my cheerful ghost-hunting self."

She lowers herself to the bed and sinks into the mattress next to me, but her pose isn't one of rest. She sits tense and rigid, her legs dangling and her hands twisted in her lap.

My heart wrings for the poor girl. Granted, she does own this castle, and if Nicholas holds it in trust for her, I'm assuming there will be funds enough to maintain it in perpetuity, but that doesn't change the fact that she's spent most of her life hidden away where the world can't see—or age—her.

"Just like Sleeping Beauty," I murmur, running my hand through her hair.

"What's that?" she asks, turning her violet eyes toward me. She doesn't wait for an answer. "Ellie, I need to confess something. Something terrible."

I sit up in the bed, heedless of how the quick movement sets my senses reeling again. "What do you mean? It's been a difficult evening, I know, and I'm sorry if the séance was too much for you, but nothing that happened was your fault."

She shakes her head, her eyes brimming with tears. Dashing a quick hand across her face, she holds them in abeyance. "It wasn't too much for *me*, but you can't go through that again. I won't let you. Not when—"

"Not when what?" I prod.

She forces a deep breath, steeling herself as if for war. "I did it. It was me. I'm Xavier."

My response is automatic. "Don't be silly. Of course you're not."

She doesn't say anything right away, her silence stiff and unyielding.

"Rachel? What are you talking about? How can you be Xavier? He's—" I halt, trying to think of the best way to finish that sentence. Dangerous? Evil? Intent on finishing what he started?

I finally settle on "—a ghost."

"Not always."

The certainty in her voice is alarming, but not nearly as much as my reaction to it. Part of me buoys up in triumph at her confession, since I've always felt as though Xavier bore the hallmarks of a cooped-up, angry teenage girl. Another part—the part that should balk in fear—feels only relief.

Well, relief and the absolute certainty that whatever this girl did, whoever she hurt, I can't let her uncle know.

It will break Nicholas's heart.

I take her icy hands in mine and give them a reassuring squeeze. "It's alright, Rachel. I promise. We can make this okay. You just have to tell me what you did."

She sniffles loudly, but she doesn't pull away. "I didn't mean to hurt anyone, and I didn't know things would go this far. It was only meant to be a prank."

"Of course it was," I say soothingly.

"It's so boring—being stuck in this village, going nowhere, seeing no one." She blinks rapidly, causing a lone tear to loosen and fall down her cheek. She leaves it there, a testament to her penitence. "Uncle Nicholas already talked to Mum about Italy, and I think he might even convince her to let me go, but I can't. Not now. Not with what I've done."

"What exactly have you done?" I ask, starting to feel really alarmed now. Flitting through my head is a vision of everyone nestled in their beds while Rachel single-handedly drags a dead man into a hiding place known only to her. Even with an imagination like mine, I'm having a hard time making it fit.

"So many things," she says and hangs her head. "The torn dresses, the lie about the tray flying through the air and almost hitting me, whispering to Grandmother sometimes in an empty corridor."

I wait, assuming her careful pause is a precursor for more. I'm not disappointed.

"And those noises and lights in your room the first night." She glances up, her lower lip caught between her teeth. "I'm sorry about that, Ellie. I didn't mean to scare you. I was afraid that if Xavier didn't do anything, you might not find any evidence of a ghost and leave."

I wait again, wondering how long it will take her to build up to the real crimes taking place under this roof, but she closes her mouth and watches me with an expectant air.

"Is there anything else?" I prod. "The birds? The bones? The pulled-up stair?" I can't bring myself to mention the dead man or all my broken equipment, so I leave things there.

Rachel shakes her head. "No, of course not. I'd never hurt anyone or anything, I promise. I only wanted to get rid of Cal, so I made Xavier do things."

At the mention of Cal, Rachel's chin lifts in a mulish angle, all the personal agony of her confession flying out the window. She looks defiant and proud and so much like Nicholas, I almost laugh.

I don't, though. Not even when she adds "He doesn't even want to be here, you know. I heard them arguing once. Cal wants to leave, but Mum told him that she can't go or Uncle Nicholas will take over the castle for good. It's the primogeniture. I told you."

On the contrary, what Rachel told me about the primogeniture is what caused so many problems in the first place. The girl obviously has no idea that it's her mother and not Nicholas who is the eldest of the family. She also doesn't know that the castle has already been signed over to her.

Given Fern's fixation on youth and beauty, I can understand why. I don't approve of it, but I understand it. She kept her age and the inheritance a secret from her daughter for all these years to avoid publicly admitting her age.

Everything is starting to make sense. She refused to send

Rachel to school. She wouldn't take Rachel with her on her regular trips to London. The girl really *is* like Sleeping Beauty. Any moment, she's going to wake up and find that this entire kingdom is hers.

What I can't understand, however, is why Nicholas would agree to go along with it. If he cares about Rachel—truly cares about her—then he should have done something to help her years ago.

Unless, of course, he has another motive in place.

Another realization strikes, then, this one much easier to put into words. "Hang on. If you've been whispering to your grandmother, does that mean you're the one who told her to lock my room?"

"No, that wasn't me." Her chin comes down a fraction. "Not all of it is me. I only help sometimes, when it feels like Xavier hasn't made an appearance in a while. Most of what he does is totally real."

Most of what he does is a real pain in my neck, but I know better than to try to argue that point. "You screamed in my room in the middle of the night?" I ask.

Rachel nods.

"You used flash paper to try to blind me?"

Her mouth falls open. "You could tell that was flash paper?"

"Wait a minute—does that mean you know another way into that room?" I'm on my feet in a matter of seconds. "Rachel, if you have access to a secret passageway anywhere in this house, you have to tell me. Even if you're not supposed to. Even if it means betraying someone you love."

"But there isn't a secret passageway," she insists. "There isn't a secret anything, Ellie, I swear. I came in through the door while you were asleep like a normal person."

"Then how did you escape without running into your uncle? He was there within seconds. He would have seen you in the hallway."

She seems confused. "Uncle Nicholas wasn't in the hallway."

"What? That's not possible."

"I slammed a book against the floor a few times and made all those noises and then I ran," she insists. "I knew it would only be a few minutes before the entire house came to investigate, so I hid on the top stair. It's so deep that if I lie perfectly flat, no one can see me from the hallway. And, of course, no one thought to look for Xavier there. They were all too busy in your room. Once everyone was distracted, I slipped down to the kitchen and pretended to have a glass of milk, but no one came to look for me, so it didn't matter."

"You saw everyone heading into my room?"

She nods.

"And your uncle wasn't one of them?"

She shakes her head.

"Tell me, Rachel. Tell me exactly who came and in what order."

She seems puzzled by my command—and the urgent way in which I voice it—but she complies. "Grandmother came first, and she was so excited, she practically skipped the whole way. She's going to be so disappointed if you manage to get rid of Xavier. She loves being the only one of her friends to have a ghost."

At my look of impatience, Rachel quickly rattles off the rest.

"Then my mum, of course, and she slammed the door to her room so hard she woke up Cal. I don't think he would've bothered coming otherwise—he's a very heavy sleeper, you know."

"No, I don't know," I say. "Although I'm not surprised you do."

She has the decency to blush. "Yes, well. I tried once to scare him with a sheet hung at the end of the bed, but he wouldn't wake up, even when I pinched his toes. He snores loud enough to wake the dead."

"You hung a sheet at the end of the bed?" I ask, incredulous.

"It wasn't a *nice* sheet or anything. It's one of the ones Grandmother saves for guests, so it's all worn through, and there's this huge brown stain on one end. I hung it on a string and waggled it about."

At that particular confession, I'm almost ready to forgive her for everything, but my brain is much too busy putting the final pieces together. And my brain, poor thing, is none too happy with the way the facts are aligning.

If Nicholas never entered my room through the door on that first night, it means he must have entered through the secret passageway—the secret passageway no one is willing to admit exists. And his motives for doing so can't be good. Either he wanted to pretend to be Xavier himself, or his presence was somehow related to the note that was planted the next night.

The childhood rhyme. The childhood rhyme that somehow ties him and Thomas—those most loyal of bosom bows—together.

Nicholas is also rich and, if Liam is to be believed, terribly so. Money will buy a lot of things in this world, but I doubt it could get him this place. Not in name, anyway. Vivian and Fern already saw to that by signing it over to Rachel. All Nicholas gets is the responsibility of maintaining it—a money pit, in his own words, and the most important thing in his life.

Of course, there are ways around the Vivian and Fern issues. Vivian he's already threatened to send to a home for believing in ghosts. Fern might be more difficult to dislodge—as her determination to stay put despite Cal's wish to leave proves—but it's not impossible. With Rachel sent off to art school and a bona fide psychic medium on his side, he can easily clear a path to ownership, especially if there are dead bodies turning up in abundance.

And the bodies. Oh, the bodies. I don't know what that Walter guy was doing here or what he found in that bible to interest him, but there was only one person in this house who was unaccounted for when Walter was moved from the bottom of the stairs: Thomas.

Thomas, who didn't really have a weekend off.

Thomas, who used to search for tunnels with Nicholas when they were kids.

Thomas, whose secretive actions compelled even Cal to offer me a warning and a way out of here.

"Rachel, I think you should come outside with me," I say. I strive to keep the panic out of my voice, but the words come out thin.

"Outside?" she echoes. "Why?"

Because there are policemen down there, I think but don't say. Out loud, I answer, "For air. It's awfully stuffy in here."

It's not the least bit stuffy in here—in fact, it's practically glacial—but Rachel takes one look at my white face and trembling hands and accedes. She must think I'm still rattled from the séance, which is true to an extent. I *am* rattled from the séance. I don't know whether it was Thomas or Nicholas who tried to strangle me in the dark, but I do know one thing for certain: they're not getting a second chance.

But . . . "It's locked," Rachel says as she rattles the handle.

"What? It can't be." I rush to the door and try for myself, but she wasn't mistaken. No matter how hard I twist or shake, there's no budging it. I kick and pound for a full minute, even adding a few shouts for good measure, but no one comes to our aid.

I wish I could say I'm surprised, but I'm not. Nicholas lured us up here on purpose. He wanted us out of the way, trapped where he could keep us until he was ready. And I, dazzled by his reverent kiss on my wrist, fell for it.

Idiot. Fool. Silly, silly Ellie.

"Was it . . . Xavier?" Rachel asks, her voice trembling. "Like what happened with the stairs?"

I don't answer her. Mostly because the answer—a definite yes—will only cause her to panic. "Do you have your phone?" I ask instead. "We can call for help."

She shakes her head. "You made us put them in the basket, remember?"

I do remember, and I could curse myself for being so short-sighted. An attempt to force open one of the lead-paned windows along the outer wall proves equally fruitless. They don't appear to have been opened since the nineteenth century, if ever. Setting aside the fire hazards of such a setup, how the devil are we supposed to get out of here?

"Ellie, what's going on?" Rachel asks. "Why did Xavier lock us in here?"

"I don't know," I say. "But I'm not going to sit around and wait to find out."

Closing my eyes, I summon every bit of belief I've ever held in magic, miracles, and myself. It's a long shot, I know, but it's all I have. Just me and Winnie. Just that tenuous connection that no amount of life—or death—can sever.

"Winnie, my love, I need you. I know I say that a lot, but I mean it this time. Get off whatever unicorn you're riding through the clouds and help me. Help *us*."

"Ellie?"

I shush the girl without opening my eyes. "Just a second, Rachel. I'm almost there. Seriously, Winnie. It's now or never. Otherwise, there's a good chance I'm going to end up reaching the afterlife before you. How's that for irony?"

"Um, Ellie?"

"Not now. She's close. I can feel it."

Rachel puts her hands on my shoulders and gives me a turn. "No, she's not close. I think she's already here."

Winnie. My eyes fly open, my heart in my throat. Without quite knowing why, my gaze moves to the spilled rowan berry mixture on the floorboards. I fully expect to see my sister sitting there—in the flesh, her beaming smile reassuring me that everything will be okay again—but of course she's not. That would defy everything I know to be true.

Fortunately, she's sent an emissary instead.

"Beast!" I cry, falling to my knees in front of the cat, sleek and black and conjured as if out of thin air. "You little monster. How did you get here?"

When I twist to look up at Rachel, she's watching me with an expression of rapt wonder, her finger pointing toward the head of her enormous Elizabethan bed. "He appeared from out of nowhere. One second, there was nothing but an empty bed. I looked away for four, maybe five, seconds. When I turned back, there he was, sitting on the pillow like it was no big deal. Ellie, is it—? Can it be—?"

I scoop up the cat, cradling her against my chest as she writhes and scratches and wriggles to be free.

"The secret passageway," I say, releasing a sound that's equal parts laughter and hysteria. "It's about time someone found it."

Chapter 25

❧

The huge Elizabethan beds in both my and Rachel's room aren't, as I first suspected, pushed against the wall. They're literally part of it—the giant wood-paneled headboards are inseparable from the plaster above and around them.

Making this discovery requires Rachel and me to use our full strength as we try to dislodge the headboard even a fraction of an inch.

"No wonder I could never get the bed to move," I pant after our third failed attempt. Trying to jam any kind of tool behind the headboard is equally fruitless, since the seam between wall and wood is permanently affixed.

From there, the conclusion is a natural one—that the two beds share this wall and, with it, access to the passageway. I run my finger along the outer edge of the headboard, the ornate scrollwork bumpy under my touch. "It's not just heavy. It's built in. But how—?"

My answer comes as my finger snags on a particularly knobby piece of scrollwork. With one firm press, the furthest headboard panel unlatches at the outer edge. Because the headboard hangs over either side of the mattress by a good foot, it's possible to slide the panel into a pocket door built into the wall—and to do it without disturbing anyone who happens to be in the bed at the time.

Including me.

"I don't believe it," I breathe, pushing the door in and out, watching the ease with which the portal comes and goes.

It helps that the track appears to have been oiled recently, much like the doors Nicholas asked Thomas to attend to when I first arrived. All it takes is one quick and effortless push, and I've created a hole big enough for anyone—cat or human—to slip through.

"Beast, you perfect genius!" I call. The cat has distanced herself from us to avoid another one of those affectionate scoops, so I have to content myself with blowing her a kiss. "She must have found the inside latch and slipped through when you weren't paying attention. This explains everything."

"I can't believe this has been here my whole life and I never knew," Rachel breathes, eyes rapt. "I wonder if anyone else knows about it?"

Nicholas does, that's for sure. He must have snuck in while I was sleeping, then used my distraction as I searched for him to slip back through again.

"Wait—what are you doing?" Rachel asks as I lift a leg and prepare to enter the troublesome hole. "You can't go in there. You don't know where it leads."

On the contrary, I have a pretty good notion that it will let me out in the cleaning closet downstairs. All those built-in cupboards are ideal for hiding another panel like this one. "Rachel, we can't stay up here. I know it seems exciting, being locked in by a ghost, but it's not. As long as we stay where he wants us, we're completely at his mercy."

For once, I'm not talking about the ghost, but Rachel doesn't know that—especially since I've never been more earnest in my life. The color drains from her face. "You think he wants to kills us?"

I have no idea *what* he wants, but I do know that I'm not about to sit around and wait to find out. "I think getting you to safety is the most important thing," I say. "And I think the passage is the only way to do it. Winnie wouldn't have shown it to me otherwise."

Light steps from the hallway propel me into action. My sister may have proven herself more than helpful in getting us out of here, but even she's not going to be able to stop a fully grown man from exacting vengeance if we're trapped like sitting ducks. Without waiting for the girl to protest, I grab Rachel by the arm and yank her forward.

"*Now*, Rachel," I say. "I'm sorry, but it's the only way."

Her eyes fly open wide as I shove her into the bed panel. "But whoever that is can let us out now."

True. Whoever that is can also murder us where we stand. I'm not so confident in my physical prowess that I'm willing to fight off Nicholas or Thomas, especially in my current condition.

"*Go*, Rachel. I'm right behind you."

The urgency in my voice compels her to comply. "The cat—?" she asks as she slips into the hole. I take a last look around the room, but Beast is nowhere to be seen. As much as I hate to abandon the animal to her fate, I have a strong suspicion that of all of us, she's the most likely to make it out of here intact.

"We'll come back for her," I promise and follow Rachel into the panel.

I have no way of knowing who is at the door to her bedroom or how much time we have to spare. As soon as we make it past the headboard, I close the panel and plunge us into a darkness so profound, it's unlike anything I've experienced before. It seems impossible, but it's colder in here, too, as though the cause of the house's extreme temperature is this icy barrier between it and the rest of the world.

"Ellie?" Rachel squeaks as she reaches for my hand.

"I'm here," I promise. I'd like to use both hands to feel around me, but I have to make do with the one she leaves free. From my cursory exploration, it seems as though we're in a small tunnel, just high enough for me to stand without hitting my head on the ceiling, although a taller person would have to stoop. The walls are made of stone and are slick with moisture, the ground underfoot made of dirt and rubble that seems to have fallen away from the walls over the years. "We'll take it very slowly, okay? One step at a time."

"But I don't understand," she says, fear trembling her voice. "What are we running from?"

"Xavier," I lie, unwilling to name her uncle for fear it will cause a breakdown before I can get her outside and to safety. To reassure her, I give her hand a squeeze as we start moving forward. I use my outstretched arm to fumble along the passageway, trying to gauge distance and direction without sight. I'm not sure about anything until my foot hits a rough step and I find myself moving down. This must be where the hollow space between the yellow bedchamber and Rachel's room hits the outer wall. There's some kind of secret stair that will take us down to the main floor and to the cleaning closet.

More confident now that I've got my bearings, I take the next two steps quickly. I regret it almost immediately.

"Oh, God." Behind me, Rachel wretches. "What's that smell?"

Death, is my best guess—and fresh death at that. The same cloying decay from the bones under the stairs is evident here, but in a much larger concentration. My eyes water as I realize it's only getting stronger the farther down we go.

"I think it's the mustachioed man," I say, choking on a gag of my own. I press my hand to my mouth. "I'm sorry, but it's going to get worse before it gets better."

"I can't." She tries to yank away from me, but I have her held firm. "Ellie, I can't."

"We have to. Just breathe through your mouth and focus on each step forward."

Now, more than ever, the need to keep going is strong. There's no longer any denying it: Thomas and Nicholas were working together, which means one of them killed Walter Powell and stashed his body in this tunnel. It's only a matter of time before they figure out we've escaped this way and come after us.

"It's only one dead body. It'll be okay."

I don't know if it's the confined space that causes it, but the smell becomes more noxious with each step we take. Based on how cold it is in this passageway, hovering near freezing, I'd have thought Walter Powell's decaying process would be slower.

That's when I hear the crunch.

Rachel screams. I whirl and clamp my hand over her mouth, but the sound echoes long enough that I'm sure we'll be overheard. It also echoes long enough that I'm starting to have serious concerns about where this tunnel ends. Surely, we should have reached the cleaning closet by now?

"What was that?" Rachel asks, her voice wavering.

"I don't know." Nor do I particularly want to find out, but when I take another step, I not only hear the crunch, I feel it.

"Ellie?"

Since I doubt I'll get her to move unless I have some kind of answer, I squat down and grasp my hand around in the dark until it comes into contact with the source of that sound.

I jolt upright almost immediately.

"Keep walking."

"But—"

"Don't ask questions, Rachel, and don't pay any attention to what you're stepping on. We have to get out of here."

I don't know how many steps it takes before she realizes what's underfoot. We've leveled out by now but have descended so many steps I think we might have bypassed the first floor and gone straight to the kitchen in the basement. In fact, I wouldn't be at all surprised if we've stumbled onto the infamous smuggling tunnels, since the rocky walls have become replaced by dirt.

The only question is, how far do they go? And, more importantly, how are we supposed to find our way out of them without a light?

"Oh, my God," Rachel says, her voice hollow. "They're bones. We're walking on bones. We're walking on dead people."

As if in confirmation, she steps on one. It must be a femur or something, because it rolls and she slides forward. Only by making a frantic grab for her am I able to keep us both standing. We're shaking, our bodies rocked by spasms as we hold one another. I can't tell if the shaking is caused by the cold or because we both realize that escape from this place might not be as simple as I'd hoped.

"How many?" she demands.

"I don't know," I say. When she remains silent, demanding an answer, I add, "Too many."

"Who put them here?"

"I don't know that either," I say.

But I do. Suddenly, I know it all.

"Educational materials," I breathe.

"What?"

Educational materials. That day in the Hartford family cemetery, Inspector Piper implied that spirit workers have cornered the market on the sale of human remains, but it isn't true. Yes, there are mediums and spiritual practitioners who will pay a pretty penny for a bone or two, but there are plenty of other organizations out there who would pay to get their hands on fully intact skeletons—and who aren't always willing to wait for someone to donate their body to science to do it.

Colleges and universities, private schools and research centers, even black-market pharmaceuticals—they all create a strong demand.

Of course, getting your hands on illegal human remains isn't easy. You need a source, a method of transport, and a way to conduct your business outside of prying eyes. In other words, you need a man who buys up old English properties with the cemeteries attached. You need a smuggling tunnel that leads directly to the ocean where a fishing vessel lies in wait. You also need to be paying off someone who works in the trade compliance offices.

You need the combined efforts of Cal, Thomas, and Nicholas to make it work. And you need to be able to kill anyone who threatens to get in the way.

"Rachel, we're going to keep running along this tunnel, okay? The end of it should be somewhere near the ocean. It's going to be a long trip, and it's going to be dark and scary and full of bones, but you have to keep going. And if we get separated for whatever reason—"

"No!"

"If we get separated for whatever reason," I repeat, more firmly this time, "you have to find Inspector Piper and tell him what we found."

It's a good thing I manage to get my instructions out in time, because we're hit with a brilliant flash of light as a doorway from somewhere back at the house is opened. The light is strong enough to illuminate the bodies in the passageway, which I can see now are piled in rows along the edges, shrouded as though ready for transport. It's only our frantic movements that have dislodged them and caused bits and pieces to fall away.

Having my suspicion confirmed in such a way does little to reassure me, especially when a voice—gruff and frantic—calls out from the direction of the light.

"Eleanor!" It's Nicholas. "Eleanor, you're safe. You can come out now."

"Uncle Ni—" Rachel begins, but I push her gently in the opposite direction.

"Don't, Rachel."

There's just enough light for me to see the way her eyes widen with understanding, the quick nod and short intake of breath as she realizes that if her uncle knows about this passage, then he has to know about the bodies contained within it. Without waiting for more, she turns on her heel and scuttles off in the opposite direction.

I'm not one for prayer, as anyone who's ever met me can attest, and sending whatever positive energies I have out into the world doesn't feel like enough to keep her out of harm's way. The only thing I can do for certain is keep Nicholas distracted long enough for her to make good her escape.

"I don't know how much time we have," Nicholas calls again. He steps farther into the tunnel. "Come on. We've got to get you out of here. Is Rachel with you?"

I'm debating between telling him the truth and lying to protect her when my world goes black for the second time today. Since I'm not wearing a lace tablecloth and the sickening thud of what I fear is a human bone against my skull precedes my loss of consciousness, I can only assume the attack comes from behind.

Oh, dear, I think before my body slumps to the ground to join the others. *I really was hoping not to die here today.*

Chapter 26

❧

I awaken, groggy and gagged, in the middle of the ocean.

Well, I assume it's the middle of the ocean, but only because I have a tendency toward seasickness and I can't account for the interminable nausea any other way.

"Oh, good. She's awake. I didn't think she was ever going to come around."

I blink, my gaze swimming as the world comes into focus around me. The boat we're on isn't a large one, which would explain why I'm being tossed about like a tree in a windstorm, but there seem to be plenty of people in the fish-scented cabin. Nicholas, of course, looking like a shiny penny without a hair out of place or a wrinkle in his crisp white shirt. Thomas, clad in a parka and soaking wet, having just come in from the howling outside. And Fern, still in her séance blacks, holding a leveled gun at my head. I recognize it as one of the rusted showpieces from the armory, its pearl handles yellowed with age. By the look of it, it hasn't been shot since the eighteenth century, but that doesn't make me feel much better about having it directed my way.

"Fern?" I ask somewhat thickly, the words difficult to force out through the cloth shoved in my mouth. "What are you doing here?"

No one can make any sense of what I'm saying, which is probably for the best, since the answer is provided for me a few seconds later.

"Would you please let me shoot her and toss her overboard?" Fern asks, annoyed. "I don't know why you didn't let me do it in the passageway. I'm sure we're far enough from the castle by now. Thomas's clipper gets excellent speed."

Nicholas releases a gentle cough—that sound of his that captures so many of his qualities. His genteel irony. His polite disinterest.

His downright villainy.

"A few more kilometers should do it," he says. "We want to be sure she won't wash up on shore. Everyone in the village knows she was staying with us, so we have to make sure she's totally unidentifiable. Thomas? You have us on course?"

Thomas sighs and pushes his plastered hair back from his forehead. Unlike Fern and Nicholas, he looks exhausted. I can only imagine it's because he's had to do all of the work piloting his clipper in a rainstorm. Even now, with the three childhood friends banding together for murder, he's the one carrying most of the weight.

"Yes, we're good." He casts me an anxious look. "Are we sure—?"

"We're sure," Nicholas says with the kind of commanding formality I doubt many have withstood. "Fern, why don't you give me the gun? I don't know how reliable that piece is. We might be better off strangling her."

Fern doesn't relinquish her hold on the weapon. "I tried that already. She's much more difficult to kill than you'd think, looking at her."

"Perhaps you aren't strong enough," Nicholas suggests with another of those slight coughs.

Fern turns her glare on him instead. "I was strong enough to push Walter down the stairs, wasn't I? Thomas, be a darling and stop the boat here. We've gone far enough. I want to get back before Mother and Cal start to ask questions."

I watch the three interact with a kind of wary detachment, almost as though I'm floating above my body rather than inside it—my first out-of-body experience. I've heard enough of the stories of their youth that I can picture them as children just as easily as I see them now. Fern in charge, ordering the two younger boys to do her bidding, excitement over a smuggling tunnel and buried treasure causing them to band together against the world.

Too bad the buried treasure is human remains. Too bad they're murders and scavengers, not children.

Thomas doesn't appear happy to go back outside, where rain spatters the windows and the dark, howling wind has turned the sea into a creature from my nightmares, but he departs when Nicholas nods his agreement.

"What are you going to do about Rachel?" Nicholas asks as soon as the door shuts behind him. "You know she's going to ask questions."

"I can handle my baby," Fern says.

"I don't know if you've noticed, but she's not a baby anymore."

Fern whirls on him, her eyes flashing. "I'll thank you not to concern yourself with my affairs. I don't know why you came out here in the first place. This isn't your scheme. This isn't your money. You did enough damage bringing this psycho out here in the first place."

"Psy*chic*," Nicholas corrects her.

"What?"

"She's a psychic, not a psycho. And all I wanted to do was figure out who was trying to drive Mother mad with all those ghost antics. What *was* the purpose of Xavier, by the by?"

By this time, my head is feeling less foggy, the train-wreck sensation abated and replaced with a dull ache that matches the nausea roiling through my gut. This conversation, however, is starting to make me believe the damage is lasting. Shouldn't Nicholas know the answer to that question already?

"Who can say?" Fern shrugs. "Perhaps he's a real ghost."

"Now, Fern. You know as well as I do that there's no such thing as ghosts."

For reasons I can neither name nor understand, that mocking rebuke galls me more than the rest. How dare he continue to disparage my profession? The least he could do if he's going to have Fern hit me over the head with bones and tie me to chairs is show my work the respect it deserves.

"There is too," I say around my gag.

"What's that?" Fern asks, leaning closer.

"Ghosts *are* real," I say, striving for clarity.

Nicholas sighs. "I fear you're going to have to remove her gag if you want her to make any sense. For all we know, she's putting a curse on us. I don't know about that ghost nonsense, but the spells could be authentic. She came very highly recommended."

Fern casts a sharp, suspicious look at me and eyes the handle of her gun, as if debating the merits of knocking me out with it again. I find it strange to think of such a lithe, delicate woman resorting to physical violence, but there's more determination to her than I first realized.

That was my biggest mistake. Her beauty lulled me into thinking she was frail, shallow. I should have known that any woman who would treat her own child like a mirror that must be hidden away is capable of anything.

"Do you think she's already cursed us?" Fern asks.

"It's possible." Nicholas shoves his hands deep in his pockets. "She found the secret passageway after less than a week at the castle. Not even I managed that, and I've lived there my whole life. If I hadn't forced Thomas to show me how those wine racks in the kitchen cubby opened up, I doubt I ever would have. How did she do it, if not through magic?"

A look of anxiety crosses Fern's face. It's the first time I've seen any real expression there, and it makes her look uncommonly like her brother. "Maybe Walter showed it to her. I told you he found the coordinates Thomas was stupid enough to inscribe on that bible page."

The bible page. Of course. What was it Rachel had said? That the date was written in an unmatched hand that didn't coincide with his actual birth? Thomas and Fern must have found that passage as children, recorded the location for posterity.

Like an adventure, like it was fun.

Unfortunately, I don't think it's very fun anymore. At least, it's not for me.

Nicholas shakes his head. "There wasn't time. He found that page before she arrived." He pauses and looks first at Fern and then at me. The glance at Fern I understand; the one at me much less so. He doesn't seem at all like a man who's bent on my death. I feel as though he wants me to do something, say something. But what? I'm tied to a chair, my arms behind my back, my mouth stuffed closed. Other than blinking rapidly, I've got nothing.

"Was it really necessary to kill him over it, my dear?" he adds.

"Don't talk to me like that," Fern snaps. She waves the gun until he takes a step back from my chair. "I did what I had to do. He was already asking too many questions. Once he knew where the tunnels were, he was going to demand a bigger cut."

"You could have given it to him."

"Don't you dare." She turns to her brother, the gun now much closer to his head than to mine. "You have no idea how hard I had to work to get everything set up and running smoothly. How hard it was to convince Thomas to help run the bones on his weekends off, how many nights I've spent in that man's bed so my supply of cemeteries doesn't run low. He'll buy any property I tell him to, but it comes at a price." Her mouth puckers, as if the taste of Cal's kisses linger. "Oh, it comes at a price."

Poor Cal. Despite my precarious position at the mercy of this sorry lot, I can't help feeling a pang for the guy. He was always so nice, offering me biscuits and—

I tilt my head, unsure if I'm hearing things and unwilling to indulge optimism that far. But then I receive another one of Nicholas's hard looks, and optimism starts to demand attention. Either the rain is picking up in earnest or something is happening outside.

"What is that?" Fern asks, sending her brother a wild look. "What's that sound?"

"It's the witch," he says and points at me. "She's summoning something."

Oh, it's the witch, alright. And she's not just summoning something. She's fighting back. As long as Fern holds the gun, there's nothing that either of the men—Nicholas or Thomas—can do to save me.

But I can save myself. I can wield the one weapon that has always served me well.

I begin with my favorite rotation of "rhubarb carrots and peas." With the gag in my mouth, it's not as though I can form an actual curse, and the mutterings are ominous enough to do the trick. I also roll my eyes back in my head and start thumping and banging the chair all over the boat's cabin. I don't love the idea of taking my gaze away from Fern and that unstable-looking pistol, but I realize by now that Nicholas is planning something. He knows full well that I'm no witch . . . and that the only thing I can summon is a headache.

"What's she doing?" Fern cries out. Her words are barely audible over the roaring sound picking up outside. "What's coming?"

"Fern, give me the gun," Nicholas says. In contrast to her increasingly shrill panic, his own voice is hard, cold. "We have to turn the boat around. There's no telling what she'll do otherwise."

"You just want to stop me. You always want to have things your way."

The cabin door slams open, eerily like that first night at Castle Hartford, when Thomas announced that it was time for dinner. Because I'm thinking of that evening—and of all that's happened since then—I'm not surprised to see him step through the doorway, rain-slicked but otherwise exactly the same.

Fern, however, gasps and whirls. Already shaken so far out of her comfort zone, the appearance of a dark form causes her hand to lift and the gun to line up with his body. Nicholas dives to stop her, but it's no use. He can no more prevent a bullet from leaving that gun than I can save my sister from a lifetime of inertia.

We're both just ordinary human beings. And we're both too late.

Thomas crumples to the ground in a solid heap. He makes no noise other than a grunt and a moan before descending into silence, a dark pool of blood forming under his body and mixing with the water to create rivulets that drain into the cabin.

The moment Fern realizes what she's done, she lets out a scream and drops the gun, falling to her knees in front of Thomas. It says a lot about her state of mind that she doesn't seem to notice or care about the mess that her silk pantsuit has become. She does, however, have enough presence of mind to start building a defense against herself, her voice keening as she cries, "She made me do it! Look what she made me do!"

"Stand aside, Fern." Nicholas crouches next to her and pockets the gun. He also begins assessing his friend's injuries, his movements neat and assured. To look at him, you'd think he was accustomed to heroic measures and makeshift first aid, but that's only until you catch a glimpse of his face, bleak with determination—and something more.

He is capable of real emotion, of real pain. But only when he kisses me. Only when he's struggling to save his childhood friend.

I want so much to reach out to him—to help in some way—but I'm still bound to the chair and unable to move. Nicholas can't attend to Thomas and to me at the same time, especially not while Fern remains keening on the floor.

It seems as good a time as any to call on Winnie again. After all, what's the point of having a powerful supernatural connection unless you can use it when you need it most?

"Get us out of this, sister dear," I mutter into my gag. "I promise I'll make it up to you."

Almost immediately, a bright light from above hits the boat, casting our horrific tableau into brilliant illumination. The effect is surreal, and despite my better instincts, I make a note of it. I can use that—maybe not from a helicopter coming to aid a boat in distress, but a spotlight in a dark room, a moment of clarity amidst all the confusion.

Yes, that could be very effective, indeed . . .

"What is that?" Fern cries. She bolts to her feet again and makes as if to plunge through the door. Nicholas jumps up and stops her, his arms holding her tightly around the shoulders. I can't tell if it's an embrace or a restraint, but I suspect it's a little of both. "Nicholas, she's called something! I heard her do it. Something is coming to get us!"

"Yes, yes, she has," Nicholas says in a low, soothing voice. "She's called Cal. He's coming to get us out of here."

"But she's tied up. She's gagged. How—?"

Nicholas looks over Fern's shoulder at me, his eyes difficult to read. Underneath all the pain, there's something else, something warm. "I don't know, Fern. But I'm coming to learn that when it comes to the things Madame Eleanor is capable of, it's usually best not to ask."

Chapter 27

"Miss—Ma'am—Madame."

"Oh, for crying out loud, just call me Eleanor," I tell the inspector. "I think we've gone past formalities by now, don't you?"

He flips through his notebook, which now bears what looks like a picture of a peacock instead of a donkey. "Eleanor," he says, my name rolling on his tongue as though it tastes unpleasant. "You're asking me to believe that your comatose sister on the other side of the world showed you where the tunnel was?"

"Yes," I say.

"Which she did through the guise of a cat?"

"Yes."

"A cat that you stole from Thomas's home with the intent of using it as part of a fake séance designed to extract his confession?"

"Um." When he puts it that way, it does sound rather farfetched. "It's been a strange week."

He clucks his tongue and shakes his head, but the notebook snaps closed, so I count it as a good sign. "Lucky for you, we were able to talk with Thomas as soon as he awoke from surgery.

Both he and the other witness reports corroborate your tale. I doubt even this family could invent something that outlandish."

Inspector Piper rises to his feet, his hand beating an impatient tattoo on his leg. For the first time since I've met him, his fingers don't appear to have nicotine stains.

"How's the quitting going?" I ask as I, too, get to my feet. We're holding this interview in the parlor at Castle Hartford, which seems like a fitting end to an ill-fitting story. "Have you started to climb the walls yet?"

He casts me a shrewd look but accepts my clairvoyance with a shrug. "A little. It's only been a few hours."

"Hmm. As soon as the new moon hits, I'd be happy to say a little chant to help you along. All I need is some mint, an amethyst—"

He steps back, hands up and his mouth twisted in a panicked grimace. "I'll stick to the old-fashioned method, thank you. You've done more than enough around here as it is."

He's not wrong. I think of the crew called to the castle, ready to pull bodies out of the tunnel so they can be identified and returned to their families, and wince. I also think of Thomas, handcuffed to a hospital bed, and Fern, handcuffed to her prison cell. No one's life is going to be the same after this—least of all mine.

"Does this mean I'm finally free to leave the country?" I ask.

"Yes, Madame Eleanor. I'm happy to say that England has officially seen enough of you—and your spells."

At the mention of my spells, my eyes fly open, and I cast a hurried glance at the clock on the wall. I have yet to go to bed after the events of the previous night, but I doubt I'll be able to sleep for a while. Besides, I'm not even sure if anyone has found the key to the yellow bedchamber. I *could* slip in through Rachel's headboard, but I'm feeling understandably wary of that particular entry point.

"What is it?" Inspector Piper asks.

"The sun is almost touching the top of the evergreens," I say. And at his look of perplexity, I add, "Eleven o'clock. Mrs. Brennigan."

He opens his mouth and closes it again. Since I'm not keen on directly defying police orders, I don't wait for him to issue the command. Turning on my heel, I fly out of the room and prepare for one last trip through the cow fields toward the village.

"Mind if I join you?" a cool voice asks as I reach the foyer. I skid to a halt and turn to find Nicholas leaning against the wall, Winnie's cream-colored shawl in hand.

Without waiting for me to answer, he draws forward and wraps the shawl around my shoulders. His hands linger where they land, his touch warm and heavy, which is my excuse for why it takes a moment to understand the implication.

"The key," I gasp, whirling on him. "It was you. You told your mother to lock me out and then stole the key."

His hands remain on my shoulders, holding me in place before him. The long night shows on his face but not in his bearing, which remains as erect as always. "I'm sorry," he says. "I hated to deceive you, but I couldn't let you sleep in there. Not while I was still uncertain how Xavier was getting in."

"But—"

For the first time since the night's proceedings, a slight smile moves across his face. Even though it doesn't last, I can tell it's the real one—the heart-wrenching one. "It was the least I could do after I forced you to stay," he says.

"Oh, please. You didn't force me."

"Persuaded you."

"You didn't persuade me, either."

He tilts his head, his examining eyes intense. "Why did you remain here, then?"

"To recoup my losses on all that broken equipment, of course," I reply primly. "I wasn't about to leave before I could charge you at least twenty grand for my services."

My reward for that is to have Nicholas pounce on me with a kiss so severe it takes me a good thirty seconds to get over the shock of it. As before, his lips move with careful intensity, each expert flick of his tongue designed to break me down and open me up. As before, I retaliate with my own version of a good snog—arms wrapped around his neck, my hands buried in his hair, a leg hitched so he's forced to grab me or we'll risk toppling over into the suit of armor watching over our embrace.

"No biting this time," he murmurs against my mouth, his breath mingling with mine.

"Don't tell me what to do," I reply and tug his lower lip between my teeth.

From the way he reacts, by sweeping me into his arms and doing a fair bit of nibbling of his own, I'm guessing not many women have stood up to him like that before.

"See how much more fun that is when you actually let yourself go?" I ask a good two minutes later, my breath short and my borrowed sweater decidedly askew. Even Nicholas looks less than his pristine self, his hair standing on end and a dazed look in his eyes. "I know a spell or two for that, in case you're interested."

"Oh, I'm interested, Eleanor. I've been interested since the moment I met you."

As he punctuates these words by straightening the shawl on my shoulders and offering me his arm, I'm not able to swoon properly. I do, however, draw comfort from his strength as he leads me out the front door and in the direction of the shortcut to the village. I'd been too afraid to appreciate that strength properly before, but I'm starting to realize how nice the feeling is.

It's been a long time since I've been able to lean on anyone.

We wait until we're out of sight of the castle before we start talking, bound by an unspoken need to be free of that place's overwhelming influence before we begin to unpack the night's events. As soon as the top of the tallest turret disappears from view, I withdraw my arm from his and slow my steps.

"How's Rachel holding up?" I ask.

If he's displeased with my primary point of interest, it doesn't show. He mostly sounds relieved. "As well as can be expected, given the circumstances. She's never been . . . close to Fern, so it's less of a shock than it could have been. When I left her, she was getting ready to go to bed in my mother's room."

"Good. Sleep will help."

"You gave her something?"

I wave a hand. "It was basically diluted chamomile and lavender. The effects were more placebo than anything else."

He nods. "Thank you."

"She deserves better, poor thing."

"I don't mean thank you for Rachel. I mean thank you for helping me. Thank you for solving this thing."

I halt my steps, uncomfortable with the role he's assigning me in all this. Until I woke up on Thomas's boat to find Fern holding a gun on me, I'd solved nothing. In fact, if I'd have run into Inspector Piper at any point after I'd left the room with Rachel, I would have gladly handed Nicholas over to him with a demand that he be locked up for the rest of his life.

"I only spoke with Inspector Piper briefly, but it sounds as though the Xavier activities Rachel isn't claiming were done by Thomas. Apparently, he'd started having doubts a few months back. The scheme was supposed to stay small, confined to minor pranks, but it started getting out of hand. He was trying to scare Fern into giving it up."

I nod, easily able to accept this version of events. "The pulled-up stair, banging around the yellow bedchamber, the pigeons . . . They would have been easy enough for him to do, since he could come and go without anyone questioning him."

"Moving Walter Powell's body, too."

I look up, startled, but am instantly soothed by the reassuring glance Nicholas casts down on me.

"Fern admitted to killing him, I know, but she's never been great at cleaning up after herself. Thomas came across him lying there and assumed it was his stair that caused it. Hiding the body was the only thing he *could* do—though he wasn't able to finish the job before we arrived."

"That makes sense," I agree, thinking of those first displaced bones under the stair. They must have been dislodged as Thomas struggled to get Walter Powell safely inside the tunnel. "He would have been coming downstairs from smashing the equipment."

"No, that was Fern."

"What? How do you know? Did she confess?"

He extracts a frayed cord from his pocket. I recognize it as the one he confiscated from the kitchen catch-all. "There's fingernail polish scraped off along this side." He extends it for me to see. "Red fingernail polish."

"So? Lots of people have red fingernail polish." I hold out my own hand, where the deep red of my trade is shellacked and shining. "Including me."

"I know. That's why I didn't say anything."

"You villain!" I shout, half laughing. "You thought I smashed my own equipment?"

"I wasn't sure what to think."

"*You* were the one hiding in my room that first night. Rachel admitted it."

"For your protection, merely. I snuck in and sat on the chair in the corner for hours. I couldn't let you be attacked after I brought you all this way."

"You also kept sending me on fruitless errands to the garden and the church."

"Annis asked me to. She wanted to meet you." He casts me a level stare. "And perhaps you should dismount from that particular horse before you fall off, my dear. You thought I was part of Thomas's and Fern's schemes."

I flush guiltily, unable to meet his eye. I *did* think it, and for much longer than I've been willing to admit, even to myself.

"To be fair, I thought Cal was part of it, too," I mumble.

His crack of laughter does much to bring forgiveness. He takes me by the arm again, and we begin our stately progress across Hartford lands—a cool, crisp gentleman who just discovered his sister is a murderer, and the fraud of a psychic who helped him do it.

"If Thomas wasn't smashing my equipment that night, then he was probably leaving the note in my room," I say, mostly to myself. "The one with your childhood rhyme."

Nicholas nods. "He might not have been able to scare Fern off with pigeons and stairs, but that message had the power to spook her. It was a game we used to play, a blood pact we made. If one of us found the tunnel and didn't tell the others, that was the price we'd pay. Well, it *did* spook her. I don't know how much attention you were paying during the séance, but that rhyme caused a much bigger reaction than Walter Powell's name. That was a risky move, Eleanor."

I swivel my head to stare up at him. "You think she would have killed me?"

"Yes," he says, his mouth grim as he looks off in the distance. I'm not sure what he's seeing, but I imagine it's the ghosts of their childhood selves. "It was all she could do. She was backed into a corner. *I* backed her into a corner."

I don't ask him to clarify, aware that the full story is coming. For the first time, I'm not sure I'm comfortable with my role as confessor. My job is done; there's no need for him to tell me more.

Unless he wants to. Unless he genuinely cares what I think.

"Once Fern recruited Thomas's help in moving those bodies, it was all over for her. She'll do anything for money—I knew that. I *know* that." He sighs and runs a hand along the back of his neck. "She only signed the castle over to Rachel because I made her. I knew she'd sell it otherwise, passing it off to the highest bidder as soon as my mother dies. Mother knew it, too. That's why she agreed to give it over—to Rachel in deed and me in trust."

I nod, easily able to swallow the tale thus far. Vivian wouldn't care about any of it so long as she's allowed to remain comfortable.

"In exchange for keeping the estate in the family, I promised to pay for everything. Fern's lifestyle, the castle's upkeep, Rachel's education insofar as she'd allow it. But she wanted more. She always wanted more."

I'm hit with a pang of understanding—and of heartrending pain. Placing my hand on his forearm, I ask, "So, when you said you liked Cal for this, you meant Cal *and* Fern, didn't you? You thought she was trying to find a way to get the estate back."

His expression turns bleak. "I didn't want it to be her. She's my *sister*, Eleanor."

I choke back a sob. I don't know for sure what Nicholas is feeling right now—losing his trust in a childhood friend and his sister in one fell swoop—but I do know that nothing in this world or the next can replace the bond that exists between siblings.

I tuck my hand in his and give it a squeeze, content to leave things there. He seems content, too, his grip strong and unrelenting as we continue our walk in companionable silence. We don't stop until we reach the outer edges of the village, where the tea shop sits in picturesque welcome. Mrs. Brennigan is waiting out behind the garbage bins, looking furtive as she clutches a parcel in her hands.

With an apologetic wince, I extract my hand from Nicholas's. "You'll have to stay here," I say. As much as he could use the entertainment value of watching me convince a lonely, middle-aged woman that burning her husband's hair and dancing naked under the moonlight will restore their marriage to its pre-child passions, I'm not that cruel.

"You go do what you do best, Eleanor. Help that woman, make her believe in the impossible. Don't worry. I'll wait for you."

There's something in his voice, heavy and warm like honey. I glance up, unsure what I'll find there—if that mocking smile will be back—but I only see a tender softening of his eyes. My breath catches as he lifts my hand to his lips and presses a kiss on the palm. I understand, without quite knowing how, that we're not talking about murder and ghosts anymore. We're talking about something else entirely.

"I'll wait as long as you need."

Epilogue

"Ashes to ashes, dust to dust." I stand over Winnie's grave, the newly turned earth filling the air with its loamy scent, and try to think of all the other platitudes I've heard—and uttered—in my lifetime. "To everything there is a season. Death is but the next great adventure. Um, rub a dub dub, thanks for the grub?"

Liam sighs and crouches, setting a bundle of flowers next to the headstone. They look unnaturally bright and cheerful next to that cold slab of stone, but he insisted on bringing them.

"Are you saying your good-byes or inviting her to dinner?" he asks, a slight tinge of exasperation in his voice.

"Both," I reply, unwilling to let that exasperation get to me. "Besides, a prayer's a prayer. I don't think what you say matters nearly as much as the sentiment."

"Oh? Are you the expert now?"

"I've always been the expert, Liam. You just refused to acknowledge it." I offer a serene smile from across the grave. "She's okay, you know. She's happy."

His glance is sharp. "How do you know? Did she say—?"

I shake my head, wishing I could give him more. I've been

home for several weeks now, ever since Nicholas flew me back on his private jet, but nothing I say or do seems to reach her. Ever since I stepped foot off Thomas's boat, she's been inaccessible.

Gone.

Which is fine, really. It seems I was right when I said Winnie was there to help me solve the murder and nothing more. I don't know how or why it happened, or why Castle Hartford was a conduit for our communication, but I don't mind. I don't need to know. Some things in this world aren't meant to be explained away by science or reason.

I guess that means I believe in the miraculous again. Or maybe it means I never really stopped in the first place.

"Then how can you be so sure she's happy?" Liam demands.

I don't have an answer for him—and for the first time in my life, I don't pretend otherwise. I don't know anything more about the afterworld than he does. All I have to go on is faith.

"I like it here, don't you?" I ask instead. It's a strange thing, visiting the grave of a loved one who's been gone—really gone—as long as Winnie has, but I find I don't mind it as much as I thought I would. I've been around so many dead people lately—new ones and old ones, strangers and people I know— that being here with her is almost commonplace. *Just another day with the Wilde sisters.* "It's so green and peaceful. It reminds me of Sussex."

Liam mutters something about needing a strong drink, but I just breathe deep and take in the ambience. To be honest, it's not all that different from those times I stopped by Happy Acres. I might not be able to physically reach out and touch Winnie anymore, but that physical connection was never really what those visits were about, anyway.

"Are you coming with me?" Liam asks. He places a hand on her headstone before quickly lifting it away. "Or did you want to stick around a little longer?"

"I'm going to stay and chat for a while," I say. "But you should go. You've been through enough lately."

He doesn't argue. He *has* been through enough, the poor guy. With one sister dying on him and the other plunging into murderous international ghost hunts, he's had more than enough to worry him.

I wait only until he lifts a hand in farewell before settling myself cross-legged on the ground, my back pressed against the cold, damp headstone. And then I do what I've always done best—I talk to my sister.

"I chatted on the phone with the Hartfords for a bit this morning," I tell her. "You'd be so proud of how far Rachel's come in just a few short weeks. Weirdly enough, she's starting to really bond with Cal. He felt bad, just leaving the family in the lurch after everything that happened, so he flew in some five-star chef to cook all the meals and shows every sign of staying until they're all back on their feet again. Vivian is livid."

A gentle breeze whispers through the cemetery, lifting leaves and twirling them around me in a show of color and light. Now that Liam is gone, I don't see anyone else around, but I don't mind. It's nice to be alone for a change.

"And Nicholas promised to look after Beast, too, so that's good. I wanted to bring her home with me, but Liam's allergic and I doubt she'd take kindly to living in the back of my hearse. I miss her, though. In fact, I might go back to England for a visit soon. A long one—maybe even permanently. You don't mind if I leave the States, do you?"

If Winnie has any opinion on my plans, she doesn't share them.

"Nicholas needs me," I explain. "It's my spiritual guidance and comfort—at least, that's what Annis thinks. She says I have a restful, healing way about me. How ridiculous is that? I didn't have the heart to tell her that I'm worse than an escaped prisoner on the run. You know the only reason I've ever stayed in one place is because I had you to anchor me."

Good thing you still have me, then.

I sit upright, the headstone leaving a cold impression on my back that extends all over my body. Nothing about the cemetery has changed, but the air feels suddenly freezing.

I suspect that I'm overwrought, that the emotions of letting go are taking over and transforming me into a neurotic, blubbering mess, but that voice sounds again, so loud and clear this time it's almost as though Winnie is talking directly to me.

Silly Ellie, she says, and I could swear her laughter shakes the ground. *I'm not going anywhere. You didn't think it was going to be that easy to get rid of me, did you?*

Stay tuned for more adventures with

Ellie Wilde

Coming soon from

Tamara Berry

and

Kensington Books